~~to~~

this is actually the very first "corrected" book. (still not perfect, but as good as it's gonna get) LOL

I don't even have one like this yet.

Enjoy the ramblings of a wayward Man.

Cay Suffer

a novel

CARY STEFFENS

THE VOYAGE OF WILLIE B. LOVD

THE VOYAGE OF WILLIE B. LOUD

© 2022, CARY STEFFENS. All rights reserved.

This book or any portion thereof may not be reproduced or used in any manner whatsoever without the express written permission of the publisher except for the use of brief quotations in a book review.

THIS BOOK IS ENTIRELY A WORK OF FICTION. ANY SIMILARITIES DRAWN TO ACTUAL PEOPLE, PLACES OR THINGS ARE UNINTENTIONAL AND PURELY COINCIDENTAL.

Print ISBN: 978-1-66785-565-3
eBook ISBN: 978-1-66785-566-0

**COVER DESIGN
By Savanna Hope Steffens
sedonahopedesign.com**

WILLIE ONCE SAID THERE WAS LITTLE IN ONE'S life that a person could actually control. Autism had afflicted Devlin to the point that there was even less that he could control. There was one thing he could control and that was Willie, so Willie no longer needed to worry about not being in control. He was in Devlin's hands now. While Willie pleaded with Hope to savor the marvels of nature and the world around her, Devlin didn't need to be told that. He never missed seeing the moon.

ACKNOWLEDGEMENTS

THE CHARACTER IN THE VOYAGE OF WILLIE B. LOVD, that I can best relate to is Anson, the bar patron in Australia. I too still believe and somedays hope that the computer is a passing fad. OK, just shot, shute,sho, shoot me. You get the picture? I can't type and couldn't find home row with a road map. I take consolation in the fact that I'm pretty sure Herman Melville, didn't peck out *MOBY-DICK*, on a Pentium Word Processor, either. Of course, someone had to suffer because of my short coming.

Gayle Lewin miraculously was able to transpose the entirety of my hand-written scribbling to type. That was no small feat. Let's just say my handwriting would make a doctor's cursive look like fine print.

"Gayle, continue to have your eye doctor bill me for your visits. I hear the issues caused by the strain will go away soon." In all seriousness, Gayle, I can't thank you enuf, enough, enotbh, oh, the hell with it. You know what I mean.

PROLOGUE

It's been said there are no longer any original thoughts. Being inspired by others, may be all we have left. To that end, I am indebted to the thoughts of two of my favorite authors.

> **The human heart in conflict with itself is the source of all great writing.**
>
> WILLIAM FAULKNER

> **Write Drunk. Edit sober.**
>
> ERNEST HEMINGWAY

This book is dedicated to my own micro-subset among the billions of people who inhabit earth.

Dylan Reed   Jesse Renee   Donovan Luke   Savanna Hope

Whether this book makes you laugh, cry or quit your day job I hope you enjoy..…..

THE VOYAGE OF WILLIE B. LOVD

a novel
CARY STEFFENS

CHAPTER ONE

WILLIE PARKED IN THE FARTHEST MOST REMOTE space in the lot as always. Hopefully it was far enough away from the door bangers. He got out and walked toward the complex, never being able to resist turning back and taking a glance at today's car of choice. Just one of the many sicknesses he had, he liked to joke. He would learn of a new one today. Beautiful day, beautiful car.

Presenting himself at the reception counter he waited for the glass partition to slide open. "Why Linda you are looking exceptionally bodacious today."

"I supposed that is a compliment, right Willie?"

"Well, it used to be," said Willie".

"Okay I'll take your word for it then. Anything changed since your last visit?"

"Well, I've gotten a little older."

"That's better than the alternative. Do you still have the same insurance?"

"Yeah, for what it is worth.""

"Hear that all the time, no points for originality there...are you allergic to anything?"

"Just pain."

"Good one, have a seat Dr. Lillenberg's assistant will call you up shortly."

"Dr. Lillenberg? Sounds serious. I was looking forward to just seeing Mike."

"Call him what you want, you're the patient. Have a seat and catch up on the social scene in Hollywood. I need to warn you though, some of those people have died since we put those issues out there.

"Like whom, Humphrey Bogart, laughed Willie. Willie grabbed the latest People magazine, at least the latest one there. He quickly scanned the pages and commented to the attractive middle-aged lady next to him,

"Who are all these people anyway? If it wasn't for the CarCrashians, I would never have heard of any of them."

The lady laughed "it's Kardashians by the way."

"Really? What are they famous for anyway?"

"Well, I guess their famous for being famous."

"That seems like a great paying gig if you can get it. At least I escaped the annual issue of the ten worst dressed people again."

"Is that a big concern of yours," the lady asked.

"You can never be too careful," replied Willie with a laugh.

"Mr. Lovd, you're up," the assistant called.

"With a name like that, you should be in an issue," the lady commented.

"It's just my stage name, but you can use it if you like. He got up and followed the assistant down the corridor to the awaiting scale.

"A few pounds lighter, not that you needed to lose any weight. What's the secret?"

"I cheated. Willie replied, I picked lighter weight clothes, clipped my nails, shaved and just between you and me I'm going commando today."

"TMI, Willie, TMI, laughed the assistant. You can wait in Doctor Lillenberg's office." Willie took a seat behind Mike's desk.

They had known each other since college and had always stayed close. Often even outside of the medical arena. Mike had done well with his medical practice and enjoyed the lifestyle it provided for himself and his family. Although he often complained about the cost of insurance, bureaucracy and the paperwork involved, he still truly liked the profession he had chosen and had earned a reputation as a respectable physician in the area. Everyone liked Dr. Mike. His wall of fame was covered with the usual medical proclamations typical of every doctor's office and a desk adorned with family photos. Family members Willie also knew personally. Willie took tennis lessons from Mike's son Darren. Darren was a tennis prodigy starting at age 3, continuing on to become a successful college team player.

The door opened. Mike walk behind his desk and took his seat. Mike asked, "can I get you a coffee, water, shot of Jack maybe."

Willie reply "No I'm good". They both laughed as they occasionally had drinks together.

"It took a little longer to get all the results back than I thought it might, but I like to be sure about these kind of things" Mike stated.

"That's why they pay you the big bucks, what's the word"?

"Ok Willie, I have good news and bad news. Which would you like to hear first?"

"Mike, you know how I hate when you do that. Let's go with the good news first this time."

"Alright then, how was your Christmas?"

"It was good. I got together with the kids. Reed came in from California and Hope took a day off work for the holiday."

"That's good to hear. I'm glad you had a good Christmas Willie, because it was your last one" A silence fell over the room. Mike knew it was best not to speak for a bit. He knew he just delivered a life shattering bombshell. He watched Willie for a reaction, but Willie's face was a stone, with eyes unblinking. Damn, how he hated this part of his job. News he never liked delivering, especially now to a lifelong friend.

Willie's brain was in overdrive, one half was trying to process the information while the other half was trying to deny having even heard it. Yes, this was a possible result, but it was predicted to be a very remote one. Maybe the diagnosis is wrong, yet maybe it's right? The room seemed absolutely silent, yet his mind was screaming.

"Are you ok Willie? I know it's a wallop."

"I'm fine, I'm just taking a moment to prepare myself for what the bad news is," laughed Willie.

"Ok, here it comes. I'm going to have to find a new patient so I can continue to keep making my Porsche payments. Mike would never have joked like this with anyone other than Willie during times like this, but he knew how Willie was wired, and he knew it was best to maintain the lifelong status quo between the two.

"I do have to say, I guess you were absent in Med school when they had the class on bedside manners."

"Med school, joked Mike? Oh, you mean that three-month ordeal in Havana. Yeah, between the senoritas and the margaritas there wasn't much time for that. Oh yeah and occasionally one of Hemingway's mojitos of course. Seriously though Willie, I dreaded telling you this as much as I'm sure you dreaded hearing it."

"This is one time I'm going to have to disagree with you Mike"

"I wish I knew a better way to tell someone they are going to die. I Wish I could ask them how they would like me to tell them the news. It kills me every time. It's especially rough when the patient is relatively young and seemingly healthy like yourself. That also makes it harder for the patient to accept. Hell, I can't be dying, I feel fine, they think. You're the typical male, you're active and healthy and won't go to doctor unless something is hanging from you. Then this creeps up on you and it's too late. I bet Cherise told you a dozen times to see a doctor while you were married about a dozen different things. You were probably 50 before you even came to see me professionally and then it was just because your insurance company insisted you finally get a physical."

"Not sure a lecture is going to do me much good now, but you're right I always follow my grandfather's advice who outlived two of his doctors. Never go to a hospital, more people die there than anywhere."

"That kind of talk is not going to keep me in a Porsche, laughed Mike."

"Let's assume I think your diagnosis is right. So, what's in store for me?"

"Willie, I know denial is a natural part of this but, I'm not going to blow sunshine up your skirt. I'm sure the diagnosis is right. Sorry. You will have months when you almost convince yourself I'm wrong because you will feel normal. After a while and it's hard to say how soon, because you're in good physical shape, your body will start to deteriorate. At that time, I'll work with you to ease some pain and do what I can to keep you functioning as best as possible. If you're going to ask about some treatment program maybe there is one, but they are Not usually very successful and often causes some loss of quality of life that you may still be able to experience if you just let life run its course. The choice is yours. A treatment program may allow you to see next

Christmas, but I don't think that it would get you to next New Year's Eve party, again sorry."

"Mike, I've changed my mind."

"About what?"

"I'll take that shot of Jack after all".

"I'll say this, you have one attribute that's going to help you get through this the best way possible."

"Yeah, what's that?"

"A sense of humor."

"I would have never made it this far without one."

"That makes two of us buddy."

"I have one favor to ask, Mike?"

"Anything, almost, laughed Mike."

"Let's keep this between the two of us until I have a chance to figure out how I'm going to pass this information on to Cherise and the kids since the divorce."

"Of course. You've kept pretty close to Cherise since the divorce. More than most couples do. That may turn out to be a good thing too."

"Luckily Mike, your marriage is solid and hopefully you will never experience divorce but let me tell you, "That till death do you part" line doesn't refer to your marriage it refers to the divorce. A person may not be married to the same person their whole life, but they will be divorced to that person until they die. Especially so, if there are kids involved. You can't cut and run. My thoughts always were whatever I do to help her, helps the kids."

"Maybe it's your attitude about life in addition to your sense of humor that will calm your journey. You were dealt a tough hand, but you did well with it all. Especially the kids, and don't let anyone ever tell you different, not even the kids."

"Now I've got a favor to ask you, Willie."

"After what you told me today you want a favor? Maybe I'll just get "Here Lies a Sucker" chiseled on my tombstone," laughed Willie.

"Ok, what is it?"

"I was just wondering what you are going to do with all of them."

"I don't really know. Reed's not really into them. I'm not sure he can drive a stick. I had tried to teach him once and it costs me a clutch!"

"Well in that case, I would be honored to have the GTO. Of course, I would subtract it from your medical bills.

"That's big of you, again after what you've told me, how about one of those rear end collision exploding Pintos," joked Willie.

"Yeah right, like you have a Pinto in your collection?"

"Ok, you got work to do, let me get out of here."

"Again Willie, I can't tell you how much this tears me up. I want to make some time together with you outside the office just for grins."

"Sounds good to me. you're welcome to make me all the time you can. "See you around, Dr. Lillenberg"

"Don't ever call me that."

Willie rose to leave on somewhat shaky legs, then headed out the office. "Fuck, I'm going to die."

Once outside, Willie spotted a person standing next to his car. "Oh great, the car paparazzi." Willie usually enjoyed talking with the people his cars attracted. There were always questions about the cars and stories about how they themselves or a relative or a friend of theirs had one just like it once. Willie heard that one so often it seemed to exceed the production number of the particular cars they were talking about. Willie appreciated their appreciation, and most people respected his type of cars. He was never the Porsche type. He once asked Doctor Mike if he knew the difference between a porcupine and a Porsche.

Mike said no, and bit at the joke. "Well, it's easy a porcupine has the pricks on the outside. Sorry Mike, you picked the car."

Willie was going to make this quick. Today he really wasn't in a mood to get into a lengthy historical discussion about the car.

"Is it a 66?" the guy seemed nice enough, as he asked.

"No, it's a 67. They are a lot alike", Willie wasn't about to get into a drawn-out story about all the actual differences between the two model years.

"Do you drive it a lot?"

"As often as I can, weather permitting. The more you drive them the better they seem to act, yet these old cars can still pick the damnedest time to act their age". Both laughed at that.

"That's why they make cell phones and tow trucks," Willie offered up. Though rarely did that ever have to happen.

"Thanks for talking to me about it, she's a beauty."

"No problem" said Willie as he fished the keys from his pocket and got in".

The car started with a twist of the key. The sound of the exhaust from the factory original side pipes as it resonated through the small interior compartment always put a smile on Willie's face. It was music to his ears. He rarely listened to the radio in his cars, especially in this Corvette. The sound that an engine like this makes could no longer be bought. Why not listen to it, he thought? He put the car in gear and headed out of the parking lot.

CHAPTER TWO

IT WAS EARLY AFTERNOON, PAST THE LUNCH crowd. The bar was light. Willie decided he needed a little self-medication after today's news. Fuck, I'm going to die. He found his seat at the end of the bar, took out his cell and called his secretary. Ashley answered after a few rings.

"Hey Ashley, it's Willie, is Vera available?"

"Sure, I'll connect you."

"Thanks" Vera answered promptly, as she always did.

"Hey Vera," it's Willie, you've probably figured out by now that I'm not coming in today. Is everything good there?"

"Sure, everything is fine; Same old thing, they come, and they go."

"How did it go with your doctor appointment?"

"Oh, it's all good," Willie lied. Which he rarely did with Vera.

Vera was his godsend. She was an excellent manager. Her competence allowed Willie all the free time he enjoyed. She had been with him since he opened his first assisted living center and stayed through the opening of two more. She was there for him during the struggle with his divorce and all the hardship that brought on. At the time, she did more than her share to keep things running smoothly while he became mired in personal problems. He appreciated her deeply and she knew it. He never failed to let her know how indispensable she was. She was as tough as she needed to be, something her and Willie both had in common.

"I'll be in, in the morning to catch up."

"OK, see you then, all's well here."

"Thanks Vera"

"Malley's, who names an Irish pub Malley's?"

Willie always wondered if all the O's had been taken. He liked it here though. The mood was right and unpretentious. He could be comfortable in a five-star restaurant but preferred something more down to earth. He used to joke; a good tavern was one with a hook on the restroom door. The better tavern had the hook missing and the best tavern had the door missing. He also had a good rapport with Lisa, the main bartender. He remembered his first time here was also her first day here. So, they joked they were the originals.

"You still have time to order, but the kitchen closes at two until the evening shift. So, make it quick if you want something." Lisa suggested.

"Sure, I'll have the lunch size Cobb salad, no dressing."

"Boring. Are you still on a health kick, questioned Lisa, or you planning on living forever?"

"You know what, screw that, I'll have a cheeseburger and fries."

"Now you're talking. You know all the things people say are bad for us are the only things that make life worth living in the first place."

"You're right. I'll do the Jack and coke again too"

"And make it hurt, right?"

"May as well, it's been that kind of day."

"Willie, I'm led to believe your worst day would be a fantasy for me in my life. "

Willie thought, and I'm led to believe you've been led astray if you would like to trade today with me. If she only knew.

Admittedly though, Lisa had it hard, but that was probably a more common situation than many people chose to know or care about. He knew she had a daughter by her first marriage who she treasured more than life itself. She managed to get out of her second marriage without another child or without anything else either. She was approaching 30 rapidly and often felt her options were running out. Willie disagreed with her. She was still young and attractive. Her problem seemed to be in her selective process of partners. Willie openly gave her a hard time, not meaning to be critical of her, for he truly cared for her well-being and considered her a friend. He thought she sold herself short too easily, and she had inherited a boatload of drama because of it. She was a good-looking, intelligent girl, but lacked a certain amount of self-esteem that kept her from pursuing a better lifestyle that she deserved for herself and her daughter. She did possess one attribute. She was a survivor, thankfully, in addition to having a sense of humor and an easy smile.

Willie watched her as she plied her trade among the few afternoon bar customers. She could sell herself well. She should stick to that instead of giving herself away. Lisa probably did well with the bar tips but supporting herself and her daughter on her own didn't come cheap. Not much does.

She brought Willie his meal and let him go at that uninterrupted. She knew he preferred that. Once he asked her why she thought only waitresses and dentists waited to ask a question until people had their mouths full.

After a bit, she came back and asked, "how was it?"

Willie replied "well I was hungry before I ate it and now, I'm not. You can't expect much more from food than that."

"I guess you're right, although occasionally we get some customers who are concerned about how things actually taste."

"Oh, screw them, there's bigger things in life to worry about."

The afternoon crowd had about all left, so Lisa had time to chit-chat with Willie.

"Hey Willie. I came up with a new way to make some extra bucks."

"Hopefully it involves keeping your clothes on".

"That wouldn't be a new way. That's the oldest profession there is."

"You're not trying to raise chinchillas again, are you?" asked Willie.

"Oh no, chinchillas had their moment. The anti-fur movement took them out. Plus, they stink to high heaven. I guess raising a couple hundred chinchillas in a two-bedroom apartment could cause that to be an occupational hazard." They both laughed at the thought of that.

"I hate to ask, but what is the plan?"

"Ok, let me tell you." I stumbled on it by accident with a bar customer the other day. I was having kind of a down day brought on by my life in general of course. This customer asked me how things were going. I thought he would be sorry he asked but no, it turned out perfect. After unloading a dump truck load or two of grief about how screwed up basically everything in my life was, which I usually try not to do in the bar, he smiled. He asked for his bill figuring I'd never see him again. He left me at $50 tip. I asked him if he was sure he really meant to do that and he said yes. He said he normally had to spend an hour on the couch and pay his shrink four times that much to end up feeling as good about his life as I had just made him feel about his, after hearing my situation. So, I told him, "Well, my couch is always available. What do you think the best way for me to make this service available to on a wider scale?" Willie wasn't sure if she was serious or not.

"I think most of your problems started with having your couch available in the first place," laughed Willie.

"Screw you Willie, you're no fun".

Then again, Willie thought, before long he may need one of her couch sessions to get through what awaited him in the short remainder of his life.

"You're too hard on yourself. How's your daughter doing, by the way?"

"Always great. She's my blessing in disguise. It looks like I may even have been lucky there. It seems like she's not going to turn into a teenager. I've always worried about that becoming a problem, but she just keeps hammering away at her studies. She's really smart you know, and it seems to come easy to her."

"Yeah, she turned out pretty well for a prom baby," Willie joked.

"Why did I ever tell you about that?" replied Lisa.

"Didn't anyone ever tell you, that you could get pregnant the first time."

"First time? You may be making an assumption there," Willie.

"TMI, TMI," laughed Willie.

"How she turned out so well, I'll never know. That wasn't the case with me. She has definite plans to go to college and I have no definite plans on how I'm going to be able to pay for it."

"Well, there are always scholarship opportunities" Willie offered.

"I have my hopes up for that, but they rarely cover everything. It would break my heart if she couldn't get into college of her choice, after all the effort she has put forth."

"You'll find a way. You always do, because you're a survivor, that's what makes you, you," Willie said.

"I know Willie. I've pretty much come to grips with my situation in life and that's Ok with me."

"I told you before you're too young to feel that way. You have a lot of life ahead of you."

"Sure, but I'm fine. I always say everyone's situation is obvious. What I have is in direct proportion to the efforts I put out. I have no one to blame. I should have stayed in college myself, but with Shannon I chose to take care of her instead of my studies, and I've never regretted it. It was a great trade off and I always believe it was karma that returned such a wonderful daughter to me for having done so.

Karma, Willie thought. "Today my karma just ran over my dogma."

"I should have listened to my dad. He always warned me not to write checks in my youth I can't cash in adulthood. Now I have them bouncing all over town."

"Well Lisa, I'm leaving you now, but I'm sure you've heard that before," joked Willie. Lisa smiled and gave him his tab.

Willie paid and left a healthy tip. "See you next time".

As Willie rose to go, he spotted a local police officer he knew somewhat. "Hey Bob, he said, as he approached the officer. I heard one of your own caught a bullet last week. How's he doing?"

"Well, he's fine. Luckily, it was a glancing blow, but thank God for Kevlar anyway. That perp was a repeat offender and luckily this time we got a judge and a prosecuting attorney who had no problem reintroducing him to his girlfriends at the federal prison. His dance card will be full soon. Yes, amazingly we actually got a judge this time who believes that there should be some punishment for committing a crime. Strange concept, isn't it? Most of the judges would make honorable fisherman though. They believe in the Catch and Release policy. We catch them, and they let them go," laughed Officer Bob.

"I'm happy for him, said Willie. I would hate to see him have to spend his nights alone. Willie and the officer both laughed at that.

"Be safe," Willie said, and he left the bar and headed for home.

CHAPTER THREE

WILLIE DROVE THE DISTANCE FROM MALLEY'S TO the entrance of his driveway without recalling a single site along the way. How can that not be dangerous, he thought as he keyed the code on his cell phone to open the gate. Willie drove up the long stone paver driveway, opened the door to the detached carriage garage with his remote and parked the car inside. He walked across the courtyard to the side entrance of his house. Willie was home. The day was ending for him a lot different than it had begun. What a difference a day makes.

Willie walked through his kitchen without stopping, heading for the rear deck where his favorite spot awaited him. His retreat. He settled into his favorite deck chair put his feet up and stared blankly at the river view before him. He was oblivious to the winter night. The house was positioned on a 100-foot bluff on the west bank of the Mississippi. It offered a commanding view of the river below and the miles of open farmland to the east. Commercial watercraft and pleasure boats were parading past, but just as on his drive home from Malley's, he saw none of it. His mind was numb, trying to process today's news. He wasn't sure if he was in shock or denial. What does one do to come to grips with the inevitable? Life doesn't exactly have a surprise ending.

There's no reason to sneak a peek at the last few pages to determine the outcome. It's not like one of those books that leaves you wondering about what becomes of the main character. He felt he was robbed of the time he needed to prepare. Yet, can anyone ever be prepared for the final chapter. Now all he could do was concentrate on what little time he had left, and that time was fleeting. Like the hourglass full of sand, when you're young and 80% of sand is in the upper half it seems to barely trickle out. When you're old, and the upper vial only has 20% remaining, the sand seems to rush out at an incredible pace. As Willie assessed his life, he had to admit he was truly blessed, even if often the blessings were of his own doing. It had not always been easy. He knew his bucket list was more complete than that of most people. That alone however, makes it even harder when the merry- go- round finally must stop. He wasn't afraid of the oncoming pain. He believed feeling anything was better than the alternative, at least that's how he felt now, while he was still without any physical pain. He was more terrified of the mental preparations he would be faced with, knowing he now had an expiration date, "best if used by." Maybe a sudden tragic death was the best way to go. Gone before you ever knew you went. So much was out of one's control.

    Willie had spent most of his life living near the banks of the Mississippi. From a childhood spent on a rented farm, too young to know he was poor, to this river bluff estate too rich to know he was happy. He always joked when his time came, he would just walk east until this hat floated. "I guess the time has come to select the hat" thought Willie. At times Willie thought life was like a cruel joke. It shows you all kinds of wonderful things, lets you enjoy some and then slams the door and the party is over. Willie, however, also believed death is what makes life worth living in the first place. Life without death would be like a child with access to an unlimited amount of candy. After a while you lose interest in it. Without death awaiting us, why would we work? Without death there would be no desire to create anything, or to even form relationships with anyone. You wouldn't need anyone for anything. There would be no passion. You would never be hurt, sick, or die. You would have no sense of urgency to do anything. There would be very little individualism. It would be numbing. Oddly, death is what gives life its zest. "If only it didn't come so soon," thought Willie.

Willie stared across the vista. The temperature was falling. After a time, he got up and went into bed. Enough of life, and death for one day.

Willie didn't need an alarm clock. He was a natural early riser and the window wall of his bedroom faced east. When the morning sun rose over the horizon it painted his curtains and bedroom windows with rays of morning hope. There was no reason to block the view. His nearest neighbor to the east was probably five miles away, across the river and the flat farmland that lay beyond it. Willie always thought mornings were God's gift for everyone to start their day and life anew. A new beginning. Now for Willie a new beginning for what was left of his life.

Willie made his coffee and started to plot his day. He needed to stop in at his office and speak to Vera. Was it too early to tell her the news already? That was going to be tough. He decided to wait a bit. There was still time for all the business arrangements to be made for things to one day carry on without him. He decided the same about breaking the news to Cherise, his ex-wife, and the kids. He felt there was no reason yet to bring this into their lives. He believed it was best to make any period of grief there might be for others as short as possible.

Telling Cherise would be strange. More of a formality. Why should she care? There was a time when a timely demise of his would have made her day. He knew she had softened though, as had he. Neither had remarried. Both came to the realization that they were each tough acts to follow and neither were the type to settle for less than what they had thrown away. Life goes on, somewhat. He and Cherise kept each other at arm's length. Willie often contemplated moving away somewhere more tropical, if it hadn't been for staying in close proximity to the kids. He was a beach bum at heart. The years had taken away the body of a Greek God. He now more resembled a God damn Greek. For his age, he was in more than acceptable shape.

As Willie drank his coffee, he made a mental list of the people he was close to that he felt he had to tell. How can I be thinking about these things? It's a beautiful day, and I feel fine. This can't be happening. I'm going to spend some time in the denial phase, Willie thought. It's not really happening. How can it be, I don't deserve this? Why me?

Willie was brought up in a religious family and his faith was important to him. Yet as he grew older, and supposedly wiser, the concept seemed to be too unbelievable. What intelligent, reasonable person could wrap their head around the whole salvation theory and life ever after. Where is it anyway? Yet, Willie chose to play the odds and believe. He caught himself thinking he'd rather be considered a fool for a lifetime than a victim for eternity. He heard a person only used about 10% of their brainpower. Who's to know what the other 90% would allow one to comprehend, or experience? What's locked away in the power of the supposed other 90%.

Willie had a near death experience when he was in high school involving a car wreck. So much for street racing. The car he was driving left the roadway at a high rate of speed. The car flipped over and left the road surface, landing on its roof in a creek bed at the bottom of a shallow ravine. It all happened in a split-second. In that second, it was as other people who have faced similar situations have said. Events and scenes from years of his life flashed before him in a great detail, unhurriedly yet and in an elapsed time frame that had to be less than a second. Willie recalled thinking as the car left the roadway crashing through the trees, that he would not be hurt from this. He realized he would be killed, and it was an incredibly calm feeling. It was the realization that life was about to be over. No reason to worry or struggle, it was inevitable. The clarity of the experience was amazing. Willie had enlisted in the Navy while in high school and was due to be inducted two weeks after graduation and even that thought process went through his mind. Well, I won't be going in the Navy, he thought. Miraculously, other than a few scrapes and bruises, Willie was unhurt by the accident. The car was totaled. In the dark of the night when the car came to a rest in the creek bed Willie was disoriented. The bump on the floor of the car was actually the dome light on the roof, as the car was inverted. Water was running in the open windows, but it was little, as the creek was essentially dry. Willie crawled out the open window, thankful for once he wasn't wearing his seat belt or he thought he would have had a hard time releasing the buckle if he was suspended upside down in the car seat. He crawled up the embankment and blended in with the gathered spectators who had seen the car leave the roadway. He recalled one person asking him if they had gotten the body out already, not knowing he was speaking to the driver of the car.

 This ordeal caused Willie to rethink the whole life after death scenario. What if heaven or hell wasn't a place but merely and everlasting state of mind. He often wondered why he felt no fear or why he was so at peace when he was convinced there was no way he would survive what was going to be a horrific crash. Maybe at the moment of your death your subconscious reacts to you if you were either a good person or bad person. Willie began to believe if it was determined that if you were basically a good person, your heaven would be an eternal state of peace and bliss. He dreaded the thought of the opposite. Willie never believed in the benevolence granted by a death bed confession. What would it be like to come to the realization at the end of your life that you could not be numbered among the good? Were you going to be subjected to pain, and experience agony for eternity, as your everlasting hell? Willie chose not to risk that. He decided to live his life for good. Come hell or high water, he would try. He wasn't going to risk the alternative, but of course like for everyone, it's not always an easy thing to do.

CHAPTER FOUR

WILLIE DRESSED IN HIS BUSINESS CASUAL AND readied himself to meet Vera. It was a clear day but not one the late Midwest winter was going to give up easily. It was crisp, but turning cold. The wind would be biting. Not the kind of day Willie normally liked, but he approached everything with a new outlook. He added it to the "list of lasts "he was formulating, not taking anything for granted. Find the treasure in everything. The sky was already hazy. The forecast called for inclement weather coming in. Probably just what Willie called a teaser snow. It comes down quick and heavy then by late afternoon it has all melted away. It just causes enough aggravation to provide some income for people who cleared his lots of snow. This time Willie hoped it would be a blizzard of epic proportions. It might be his last. Maybe, he thought, I'll fall back into it and make a snow angel, before he hoped, he might meet a real one. This would be a Range Rover Day. The classics would get to stay snuggled in their garage spaces.

Willie never kept an office at the assisted living centers he owned, one of three. Life takes weird turns and he never thought one day he would own a heaven's gate business. He came by them via a roundabout way. Years back his construction company had been hired to build facilities such as his around the Midwest area, the ownership being a subsidiary of a local bank. It was good steady work for Wille's construction company. He had to hire more people to meet the demands of the bank's expansion into these facilities.

Willie ended his local construction business to pursue the opportunity full time. The downside was, however, many of the projects were out of state. This created the need to stay away from home, his marriage, and his children for extended periods of time, but the money was good. Cherise never worried about any infidelity on Willie's part. She had known from the onset of their marriage, Willie only had one mistress and his mistress was work. She often thought the line about "forsaking all others" in the marriage agreement should have also included work. It was the hardest mistress to combat. It's tough to complain about a mistress that provides a family with every comfort, besides a husband and father of course. She complained about his absence to her lady friends and their response was basically, "Shut the hell up girl and enjoy it," as she got in her Beamer and headed for home. It wasn't that easy for Cherise. She was also a competent, intelligent woman, with aspirations of her own tugging at her. Yet she felt trapped. With Willie gone so much, she conducted the mundane tasks of keeping the house in order. All the children issues became more and more unfulfilling for her. When Willie was home, it was to catch up on things, more like a Christmas visit. Then back to another project in another state. Cherise didn't even bother to know where anymore. It didn't matter. Gone was gone, no matter where he was. Willie realized this wasn't the ideal situation also, but his options were limited. He wasn't highly formally educated. His success so far had come from sticking his hand in a box of nails and not stopping until he was a millionaire. He may not of had a college degree, but he was the valedictorian of the school of hard knocks. People refer to others as being street smart. Willie was boulevard smart and it served him and his family well.

He missed his kids, and what his marriage to Cherise had been like at one time. At times he felt guilty about being in a situation that kept him apart from his family. He knew he was missing out on a lot and the family was growing distance, but he convinced himself that that this was the best way to provide for his family. His kids lived in a nice home, went to the best schools and were able to pursue whatever sports they chose, to at whatever level they felt like competing. There was no 9 to 5 desk job waiting for Willie back home, yet he knew he couldn't keep this up forever. It would have to stop. The problem was it didn't stop soon enough.

Willie couldn't decide which news was more devastating to him, the news of his impending death or the news at the time that his marriage was over. Shocked, he thought both news flashes were undeserved. The only difference being the depression caused by the divorce had no definite ending date, his life now did. He survived the divorce financially well enough to be able to pay his monthly bills and wallow in despair. And wallow in it he did, for a long time. He subtracted himself from his friends and family that remained. He was severely deep into an abyss he had no way of knowing how to get out of.

Willie looked in the mirror one day and barely recognized himself. After months and months of self-impose isolation, he had completely lost all color to his skin. The perpetual tan he had was gone. He could never remember not having a tan. In the summer, outside work provided it and, in the winter, trips to the tropics could get him across.

When once he felt he was physically invincible now every lump or bump on his body had to be a tumor, every cough had to be cancer. He gained weight while losing muscle mass from nearly being completely inactive. This was the first-time his death was predictable. This time it was he, who was doing the diagnosis. It clearly dawned on him, that if he didn't snap out of this, he was going to die. Without a doubt he would die, and this time, not being sure if he cared or not.

Through all this, one friend remained. Dale never gave up on him. He knew Willie's true self, and he was not going to let him destroy himself. One day Dale gained access to the dump Willie was living in and told him in no uncertain terms today was the day this was going to stop. Dale physically threw him out of bed and out the back door into the yard where Willie hadn't been in months.

"It's over Willie, this shit is over. Move on."

"That's not as easy to do as you think, Dale."

"Shut up. I'm not listening to it anymore. You're going to start by staying vertical for a whole day. Laying in that bed is not the answer. Your work is what kept you going your whole life and you're going back to it, now. You still have business contacts; a good credit rating and you have investable cash. You obviously didn't spend it all on these empty delivery pizza boxes and two-liter bottles of soda. The only thing you don't have is a damn excuse to get your ass moving again. Now get your smelly carcass in the shower, get clothed in something you haven't already worn 10 times without washing and let's get out of here, and try matching socks for once."

"Dale, that's not going to happen. You know I have never worn matching socks in my life so don't push it." Willie laughed for the first time in a year. Willie, actually heard himself laugh.

"My God, thought Dale, there may be hope yet."

"Where are we going anyway?" Willie asked, as Dale drove into the street.

"I never thought I would say this to someone in your state, but you need a drink."

"This may surprise you but through my period of enlightenment, I rarely drank," said Willie.

"Well then, you definitely need a drink.

"There's a new place in town called Malley's, hot girl there too who just started. Maybe that's what you need, laughed Dale. Just don't let her see your socks." That's the day Willie met Lisa.

Dale and Willie walked into the newly opened bar and took a seat. Both were greeted by Lisa's smiling face.

"Lisa, this is Willie, an old friend of mine, even older than me. He doesn't wear matching socks!"

"Weirdo!" laughed Lisa.

"That will be reflected in your gratuity" replied Willie.

Lisa turned around and yelled to the wait staff, "hey we got one here who says he is actually going to tip".

"God knows if you don't tip" remarked Lisa.

"And He also knows who deserves one and who doesn't," jabbed Willie.

Willie and Lisa bantered back and forth, astonishing Dale as to how fast Willie was recovering from his state of enlightened, as he referred to it. The old Willie was surfacing. Dale took out his phone and dialed the number on the menu. Lisa went to answer it.

"If you are done with your nails, could we maybe get some drinks here," Dale said into the phone.

"Very funny" said Lisa as she hung up the phone.

"The things you have to go through to get service around here is amazing," said Dale.

"Ok, what will it be?"

Dale ordered a beer.

Willie said "I'll have a seven and seven and make it hurt."

"Do you mean you want it strong, or do you want me to hit you over the head with the bottle?"

"Dale, where do they get these people?"

"Craigslist, I think."

Dale was right. She was hot, but way too young, Willie realized, but she had the personality to make coming to Malley's a regular stop. Dale and Willie placed their food order and began some conversation about Willie's next move. Various business propositions were discussed. Some of them even legal. Things tended to revert to Willie's construction background. Most ideas were rejected quickly. Lisa brought their food.

"Dale asked Lisa if she was interested in raising chinchillas with Willie to make some extra money?

Lisa excitedly responded, "hell yeah, what's a chinchilla?" She laughed.

Dale told her "They were little furry things like big rats that people raised to make fur coats."

"Wow didn't know that," said Lisa. "Can you make socks out of them too?" she said.

"Your tip is diminishing as we speak," said Willie.

"Wow, you must be good at math. I didn't know a person could subtract something from nothing," joked Lisa.

"Actually, you can. I was pretty good at math until the alphabet got involved."

After another drink, Willie was getting lightheaded. He actually hadn't been drinking much recently. Dale was holding up well.

"You know what you need to do?" asked Dale.

"Yeah, get out of here before I fall off my chair."

"I heard the one person who suffered as much from your divorce as you did is the guy you used to build the assisted living centers for. I heard he had to be hospitalized himself when you stopped doing his project."

"Serves him right. He was making a killing on those things.

"As soon as you had one built for him, he put you to work on another. You were doing OK, but he was making a fortune without ever getting his hands dirty. You'd build them, he'd staff them, and move on to the next town or state to build another."

"Do you even know how many he owned?"

"Not sure said Willie, but I think my company built him at least ten.

"There's your answer. You're in a position to make more money than he did. You don't have to pay someone to build the facilities for you. That's what you do. You'd start out with a lot of equity in the property, giving you enough cash flow to build as many as you like."

"I don't know anything about running a place like that."

Dale laughed, "you think that fat ass you built all those facilities did either?

"OPW, other people's work. Yours at the time, and then his staff."

Willie had to admit, he never backed down from a challenge. He was led by the adage, "if someone else can do it, why should I think I can't."

The idea was enough to get Willie's mind snow- balling and that is all it really took. Willie was also compelled to forge ahead for another reason. He didn't have a choice. He knew if he didn't involve himself in some form of endeavor, any form, to pull him out of depression he would continue to sink and die. He was convinced of that. He had nothing to lose.

"Dale, you were right. I really needed a drink."

"You owe me, Willie.

"Think about the profit he made on those businesses. All they get to eat is chicken nuggets and pea soup which he probably made in a 55-gallon barrel. Residents either have long term care insurance or government assistance of some kind. If not, he is more than happy to have them sign over their yearly pensions, and everything they own. He already knows the average lifespan in one of the facilities is about two years. It's a no-lose situation."

"Dale, but some fail."

"That result is caused by the greed of the owner or his mismanagement. The owners can afford to walk away after they make the kind of money they do."

Willie absorbed all the information and found it hard to dispute any of it. The second half of his life's work was about to begin. Dale and Willie finished their drinks and the last of their meals. As they rose to go, Lisa told them both "she would appreciate a tip she could bend."

Willie slipped her a quarter and told her to "buy herself something nice." He quickly followed it with some money she could bend.

"Thanks Lisa said. Bring him back again sometime Dale, but stay here with him. I don't want to be alone with him."

"In your dreams" said Willie, as they headed for the door.

As they got in Dale's car for the ride back to Willie's house, Willie's mind was vacillating from planning a new adventure to fighting off the tugs of depression threatening to pull him under again. He sat quietly.

"Willie, I can read your mind. I told you earlier to snap out of it. You can accomplish anything if you try, you always could. Just get on with it." "You're doing fine."

"Sure, Sure," thought Willie.

"Hey Dale, what kind of car is this anyway?"

"It's a 1967 Dodge Coronet 500, with a 426 Hemi, with the factory dual quad setup".

"Whoa English please", said Willie.

Willie never had the time to pursue hobbies like Dale did. For Willie it was always Work! Work! While they were married Willie did have a late model Corvette, he considered his vehicle while Cherise drove the SUV. He barely knew how to open the hood on it, though he was mechanically inclined.

"Where is the cup holder?"

"Funny Willie, there's no cup holder. People didn't use to eat and drink nonstop when they drove in those days."

"Is this a window crank?" How much do I have to crank it before the ice cream comes out, laughed Willie?

"I'm sure you know you're driving in a piece of automotive history. They only sold 121 of these things."

"Well at least they came to their senses and stopped."

"Willie, you have no appreciation for the finer things in life."

"No, I actually do appreciate the cup holder in my car. How did they talk 121 people into buying one of these? No, I prefer my car."

"You don't have a car, Willie. All you have is computerized junk."

"Well maybe with all of the money I'm going to make feeding old people chicken nuggets and pea soup I'll buy some old pieces of shit like this and make you work on them," said Willie.

"You do that my friend and I'll be glad to do it. I just want you back, that's all." Dale didn't know Willie had a higher appreciation of classic cars than he let on.

At his house, he got out of the car and profusely thanked Dale for everything.
"No problem said Dale, just get your shit together and keep it together."
As Willie walked in, he was already making plans to contact his banker in the morning. Willie wasn't much for half stepping things.
Willie made an appointment with his long-time friend and personal banker for 10 AM. He was brought right into Vince's office as soon as he arrived.
"Good to see you again, Willie, you've gone kind of dormant." Vince has helped Willie negotiate various deals and was his constant companion in the past. Willie was a reliable and secure borrower, with a good standing credit rating.
"I took a little sabbatical after my divorce to regroup somewhat. You can only have so much fun though. Willie had little for almost a year. I've decided to ruin my life and go back to work," joked Willie.
"Good to hear it. I'll be glad to be of assistance, as long as it doesn't involve me getting up on any ladders," laughed Vince.

"Glad to hear it, because it's going to involve the bank's participation?"
"Well, that's why we're here, I always say "your interest is our interest." It's how we keep our lights on."
"What do you have in mind?"
Willie went right into it and kept it as short and sweet as possible. Vince was a typical banker. They prefer everything straight and to

the point, and they'd make their decision from there. They were busy people and Willie demonstrated he valued their time.

"You know my company used to build the assisted living centers for a client in the past. This deal is kind of a spinoff of that. I've decided now to build my own. I have my eye on a property just outside of town. The site has good access, the properties visibility is good and its environmentally clean. It's located on Parton Road."

"I know the site. The bank has been approached by other interested parties about the site for other developmental purposes. Are you concerned about the existing assisted care facilities just near there already?"

"No, I'm not. I've checked, and they are 100% occupied with a six-month waiting list. I considered it a plus to be close to them. A rising tide raises all ships in the harbor."

"Could be. I'm sure you know, based on the size facility you're considering, you're talking about a sizable investment. You know, from your background, as well as anyone, what the construction costs will be."

"I know upfront it's a boatload, but I feel by the time it's finished, I can have the suites pretty well committed to, so the cash flows should be pretty sufficient to reverse the flow of the money. I do realize it will take the confidence of the bank for me to accomplish this."

"Willie, you know already you have my vote, but the decision isn't solely mine."

Here comes the good cop, bad cop scenario, thought Willie.

"There's the under writers and the appraisal estimate and the board members consideration for a loan this size, to someone they are going to assess has no background in managing a facility like this." Willie knew this was all going to be a hurdle.

"I'm in a position to take care of the ground cost and the infrastructure costs with funds on hand. Of course, also my sweat equity as always."

"While I have every confidence in you, I'm not sure it's going to fly with everyone who must get on board. If you're open to suggestions, I might have something for you," offered Vince.

Willie felt a little as though the rug had been pulled out from under him, but he was prepared to listen.

"Ok, I'm open to hear what you have."

Vince began. "There's a facility in Owensville, about 20 miles away that we hold the paper on, sad to say. It was acquired in a package deal the bank was involved with that included multiple properties. The buyers were more interested in the residential rental property that was the majority of the deal, however, the assistant care facility was part of the package. It came down to a take it all or leave it all situation. The buyer didn't want to walk from the other properties, so they agreed to accept the assisted care facility as part of the deal."

"I think I know about that particular property." Said Willie. I built some homes in that area. Seems like the demographics were right for it."

"Yes, it really was no fault of the location or the facility itself. It just suffered from the non-interest of this ownership group. It had nearly 100% occupancy and a good reputation when they bought it, but they managed, by not managing it to shoot that all to hell. I think it's at about 50% occupancy and slipping from there, I hear. I am admittedly sorry I was one of the principals here at the bank that made that deal work out for them originally. In more caring or capable hands it would have done well."

"How large of a facility is it?" asked Willie.

"It's 60 units, but as I said it's down to half capacity now. It's starting to show signs of physical neglect too. There's a silver lining to the cloud though." Said Vince.

"What's that, joked Willie. Fire insurance?"

"No, said Vince, "Vera Lucas".

"And who might that be? The Patron Saint of assistant living centers?"

"If not, the closest thing to it." said Vince.

"Ok, I'll bite," said Willie "who is she?"

"Vera was the manager when the property was acquired and if it hadn't been for her efforts that place, and my job would have been on the chopping block a while back already. She's a tireless worker who generally cares for the residents, much more than I can say for the owners or some of the staff she inherited. Fortunately, she's the type that can squeeze a nickel until it shits quarters. The ownership group barely gave her enough money to keep the lights on. I know for a fact that she forgave some of her own salary, when the need was that urgent, and I am not kidding you I drove by once on a Sunday and she was mowing the grass."

"I could definitely see her as an asset of this deal succeeding," said Willie.

"Everyone has their breaking point and she's about there. I think she's just hanging on until she's sure the remaining residents will be well taken care of, if the facility has to eventually close."

"I guess we're talking a time is of the essence thing here."

"You got that right, and without Vera, I don't think in good conscience I could recommend the place to you."

"That much of a prize, is it?" asked Willie.

"Well, Willie as long as I've known you, you were the type of person who could fall into a bucket of shit and come out smelling like a rose."

"You would not be so surprised at that if you knew how much practice I've had doing swan dives into buckets of shit."

"If you're ready to head for the end the diving board I can get you a meeting with Vera and let her show you around. All joking aside, I think this will be a perfect situation for you and a test bed to see if this business is for you. I'm sure the board will be happy to see new ownership in place. It's a lot less of an initial financial outlay for you, and I think it's one you can quickly get the cash flow reversed. It may not be what you came in here asking for, but I'm sure I can get this deal done for you. If you're really confident you can always get an option contract for six months or so on the site that originally caught your eye."

"I'll keep that in mind. Ok, set it up with Vera, and the sooner the better." said Willie.

Before Willie hit the parking lot, Vince was on the phone.

"Vera, it's Vince from the bank. I have someone for you to meet who I think is going to make your day. He's old school and is interested in purchasing the property. He's proven himself capable in everything he's ever tried so I think he might be the person who can bring new life into that place."

"Well get him out here because we're on life support and about to flatline."

"Ok, his name is William Lovd. Most people call him Willie."

"If he can reverse this, I'll call him whatever he'd like to be called" said Vera as she hung up the phone. Please God let him be the answer, Vera prayed.

Willie walked out of the bank with a renewed state of options about his future. By the time, he reached his car it was already gone. His mind had already retreated to turmoil and recurring depression. On one shoulder sat a gremlin telling him he was going to fail. "Look what you've done to your life. You've lost your marriage and ruined a profitable career. You're practically estrange from your children and now you think by some miracle you're going to be able to accomplish this. You're kidding yourself. Just get back in bed and pull the covers over your head and forget all this. You'll be glad you did." They were all strong arguments rising from his subconscious.

Then gratefully in the next instant, the guardian angel perched on his other shoulder spoke up. "Don't listen to that, you can do this. Look back, you came from nothing and look at everything you've achieved. "You can do this. This is you; this is what you've always done. It is impossible for you to fail. Just get on with it. You need to do this."

Willie sat in his car outside his house knowing he would have to choose. It came down to a matter of choosing to fail or choosing to succeed. There wasn't any middle ground. It was a restless night.

The morning phone call made the decision for Willie.

"Willie, it's Vince. I spoke with Vera, and she said she was open to meeting with you as soon as you are available."

"Is late today too soon for her?" asked Willie. Willie had all the time in the world.

"I'm sure she can make midafternoon, after their lunch session has ended. "I'll tell her you will meet her at three this afternoon."

"Thanks Vince, I can make that."

Vince called Vera to let her know Willie would be there at three.

"Great" said Vera, I'm sure in the long run I'll be thanking you. "Good luck and good bye," said Vince.

Willie arrived at Peachtree Assistant living center taking one of the many vacant spaces. From the onset it seemed dismal. There were no peach trees to be seen, but a good crop of weeds was flourishing. From his car he could see the place was already screaming for help.

Willie entered the facility through the stale smelly lobby, and found the main office door. Vera Lucas, it unpretentiously proclaimed on the open door. Willie stepped in and studied the sparsely furnished office, as he waited for someone to arrive. He had never met Vera and had no idea what she looked like.

Shortly, a middle-aged woman entered the office with an arm full of files. She sat them on the desk, leading Willie to conclude that this must be the infamous Vera.

She turned to greet Willie with an easy smile and said, "you must be Mr. Lovd."

"Right, but you can call me Willie. "I'm not too big on formality."

"I seem late, but actually, you're early. It's just 2:45" noted Vera.

"I have this sickness where I've always believed if someone isn't 15 minutes early, they're 10 minutes late."

"That's one affliction I wish was contagious," responded Vera.

"I detect you may have one other sickness though," said Vera.

"Really, what's that?"

"Well, I don't know the clinical name for it, but it refers to when a healthy sensible person would want to take on a situation like this. I've heard it referred to as insanity."

"You got me there," said Willie.

"Vince at the bank spoke very highly of you so I'm hoping you may be part of the cure."

Vera and Willie got comfortable with each other about the basics of their personal lives outside of work. It was obvious, it was work that consumed her, as it had Willie in the past. He was grateful and happy for Vera though, that she could be successful at balancing her duties at work with her family life at home. Something Willie had failed at. Willie took that as a mark of confidence in her favor. Willie told her about his construction background that had a heavy focus on building assisted living centers for a past client. He was quick to assure her however he didn't have a clue about managing one. He mentioned he was recently divorced and let it go at that. Vince told me about the lack of support the ownership group provided. I've learned it's impossible to make any venture succeed if the interest level isn't there. It can be as devastating as a lack of funding. It's impossible to overcome.

Mrs. Lucas, began, Willie, "I must tell you my purchasing this is far from a done deal. Even though the bank seems to be agreeable, the lending particulars still take a little time. I'm sure I have the initial financial input needed with some for reserves of my own or either borrowed to get the place back up to shape."

"That's all normal, Mr. Lovd. Do you have time to take a walk around today?"

"I'd like that. I've never seen an occupied facility. My work in the past on these places was complete when the last nail was driven, and again it's Willie, not Mr. Lovd."

"Oh, sorry," said Vera.

"I'm ready if you are Mrs. Lucas, but one thing. If there's a need to introduce me to anyone for now let's say I work with the insurance company and I'm here for a property safety assessment or whatever crap you want to dream up. We don't need to tour the outside. I've already drawn my conclusions there, said Willie. By the way, where are the peach trees?"

"I'm afraid they died of neglect."

"Neglect? said Willie. Vera, I promise you, when I own this place, nothing outside or inside will ever die of neglect." Vera was stunned and pleased by Willie's bluntness.

Vera led Willie around the facility, stopping to greet the guests they came in contact with. Willie, noting she knew them all by name, often asking or commenting about their family members or their friends. It was apparent she genuinely cared for them. The staff members they met made halfhearted attempts to perk up a little in Vera and Willie's presence. It was apparent to Willie that the clock on the wall would never be stolen. The majority of the employees kept their eye on it. One or two were more enthusiastic. In most cases they were always the most recently hired. Their attitudes were up until they were eroded by the mindset of the long-standing employees.

Vera explained the falling occupancy rate which put the facility at about what he had been told by Vince at the bank. As the facility was allowed to decline due to lack of financial support, families chose to move their loved ones to another location. Vera saw to it that the remaining guests always were positioned in the best of the remaining rooms, the rest being closed. Attempts at re- occupancy where dismissal as no funds were made available to refurbish the vacant rooms.

There was no need to view all the vacated rooms. When you saw the condition of one, you saw the condition of all. Through all this Vera had managed to maintain a good rapport with the state review board and with all the health department inspectors. Amazingly the core business was sound, no doubt thanks to Vera Lucas.

Willie asked to see the power supply room and areas that dealt with the utilities that supplied the building. He was looking for items that could be costly to deal with if they had also suffered from neglect, or poor maintenance. They also toured the kitchen part of the facility. Vera and Willie ended up in her office via a circular route.

"I hope that little stroll didn't snap you back to your sanity," said Vera.

"No, I'm still insane, Willie answered. I didn't see anything too daunting to discourage me."

"I'm shocked," responded Vera.

"Well, you have to understand my background in construction and what others may assess as a big issue or deal breaker, I'm used to dealing with on a daily basis."

"That's good to know, because no one around here has been dealing with any issues on a daily basis."

"Don't sell yourself short Mrs. Lucas, you've done wonderfully in the area that is your specialty."

"Do you have an accountant on staff or are you the one who handles those issues?" asked Willie.

"I compile the information for him to keep his costs down, but he completes the reports and does the final filing."

"I'm going to check to see if Vince will get me the ownership's approval to allow my accountant to go over those with me. I'm not expecting the best, but I'd like an idea of what the current income and expense reports will show".

"Can't blame you for that Mr. Lovd."

Vera noticed Willie went quiet for a bit. She could tell he was contemplating something. After a bit she broke the silence.

"Is something especially bothering you, Mr. Lovd?"

"Yes, kind of," said Willie.

"Well, I'm willing to hear it now Mr. Lovd," said Vera

"I've been trying to figure out Mrs. Lucas how much I'm going to dock your pay every time you call me Mr. Lovd," said Willie.

Then Vera seemed a little taken back and was silent on her part. Willie hoped she knew he was joking.

"Is that a problem?"

"It does create a little situation of my own," said Vera.

"What's that", asked Willie.

"Well Willie, she said I can't decide if I'm going to give you one week or two weeks' notice before I quit if you ever call me Mrs. Lucas again."

They both laughed at their decisions.

As Willie rose to leave, he told Vera he would take the time the bank was doing their thing to assess his game plan, with her input of course, as what he envisioned needed to be done to the facility. He told her once he knew it was going to be a done deal, he would be back to go over those plans with her and to meet all the staff. The next time she could tell them, he quit his job as the insurance safety inspector and decided to buy the place himself.

"Sounds good." said Vera.

"And while I'm gone, said Willie, take down the clock!"

"How will they know when it's time to go home?" asked Vera.

"They'll know. It'll be one minute before they drop from exhaustion, every day until we get this place in shape, and the residents are the last people who need to know time is fleeting." With that he left.

"Holy shit," was all Vera could think of as Willie left the office.

The next day Willie called Vince about getting a look at the financial statements for Peachtree Assisted Living Center. The next day after that they arrived. Their rapid response time told Willie they were anxious to sell. That would play in Willie's favor when countering their asking price. He studied the reports to the best of his ability, then had them reviewed by his own accountant for a final interpretation.

Willie's accountant at least credited the current owner with competent filings and documentation of income and expenses. While not the goose that laid the golden egg in the present status, the goose was at least fertile and could lay again in the future. The accountant gave his blessing. Willie passed this information on to Vince to help him in the loan approval process.

Vince answered his phone on the first ring.

"Hello Vince said Vera, "he's a bit intense, isn't he?"

"Who on earth could you be referring to? joked Vince. Oh, let me guess, you met Mr. Lovd."

"You're nervier than me calling him Mr. Lovd."

But you're rich, you can afford to do so, I can only afford to call him Willie, to avoid having my pay docked."

"He does prefer Willie to Mr. Lovd, I grant you that."

"That's all fine, I'm not going to even guess what the B in Willie B. Lovd stands for."

"Good thing you didn't ask either, because I couldn't tell you. All his bank files say Willie B. Lovd. I've never asked. Other than that, what do you think of him?"

"If we all survive, I think he will be the best thing for this place."

"You've got to agree a lesser person than Willie is not your answer. I'll let you in on something. His bark is worse than his bite, but I agree a little bit of Willie goes a long way. By the way, he's made an employment contract for you. Your one of the stipulations of the deal. So, you must be loved, in Willie's eyes."

"OK, just promise me he's harmless."

"Trust me Vera, he's the man for the job and I don't know of any crime he has been convicted of yet." laughed Vince. That ended the phone conversation between the two of them.

"Is the ship still afloat?" Willie asked Vera, as she answered the phone.

"Aye, Aye Captain Blythe."

"It's already Captain Blythe, is it?"

"I figured calling you that was free," said Vera.

"Yeah, no charge for that, call me what you want as long as it isn't late for supper. I've been busy with the bank and the loan procedures. It's all going well, Vera."

"Good to hear," said Vera.

"I'd like to come see you again. How about lunch time tomorrow?" suggested Willie.

"That works, do you want me to order in lunch?"

"Why would you do that?" "I'm meeting in the cafeteria with all the guests. You're welcome to join me."

Vera was a little taken back by the thought of that.

"You know the menu is a little on the light side. Some say bland, is the word for it. I can get us something delivered?"

"No," said Willie, I prefer the dining room. If it's good enough for everyone else, it's good enough for me."

If it's not, then it's time to do something about it. So how about 12:30 Tuesday?"

"I can make that."

"Bon Appetit!" said Willie, as he hung up the phone.

The previous ownership requested meetings in town, fine dining over lunch, while getting nothing accomplished except blowing the budget, while doing so. Vera was already sure the corporate fat was going to meet the grease dumpster when Willie came to play. She smiled to herself. About time, she thought!

Willie spent the time, while the loan proceedings were in process, brainstorming his plan for the facility once he took over ownership? He had little else to do as he had let his construction business lapse while under the mist of depression following his divorce. He did however begin to contact employees of his in the past and let them know he would be having worked for them soon. They were happy to hear it. Willie was a take no prisoners employer. His people also knew he would never ask them to do something he couldn't or wouldn't do himself. He always took the lead if anything was remotely hazardous and performed those tasks himself. They respected him for that and always liked working for him. With Willie, they knew the paycheck would always be on time, even if Willie had to sacrifice.

Time passed and one day the call came from Vince at the bank.

"Willie, it's all a go. The papers are ready to be signed and Peachtree Assisted Living Center is yours for the taking. Just a small formality of stopping by and signing your life away." joked Vince.

"How about 9:00 AM?" asked Willie.

"It works for us here at the bank, see you then." Willie hung up and placed a call to Vera.

"Vera, it's done, at 9:00 AM in the morning, I'll be your new boss. I'll meet you at 11:00 o'clock to go over the new game plan. Have as many of the staff available as possible. On second thought skip the 11:00 o'clock and we'll all get together at 2:00 o'clock."

"Sounds good, lunch will be over Willie, I'm excited to get started", said Vera.

Neither knew what was in store for them. Borrowing money never bothered Willie. He'd had done it often and came to realize what other people feared. Banks can't exist without borrowers, and oddly the more you borrowed, the more they liked it. They put themselves in a position where they have to work with you, to get their investment returned. Oddly, the less you borrow the greater the fear, that they will wipe you out. If you can't make your car payment, well they just take your car and they're done with you. Borrow a million dollars, and they won't take your business, except as a last resort. They need you to keep running it so you can repay them, which often means being more lenient on their part, over having borrowed a few thousand for a used car. Willie in the past had been comped baseball tickets and travel coupons when he owed big time. He never remembered being given baseball tickets when all he had was a truck loan. Willie understood all this but never let himself get in a situation where he had to test the theory. His credit rating and standing at banks he realized were also very important. Everything went smoothly at the bank for the loan closing and Willie walked out the new owner.

Willie met Jeff Meyer in the parking lot of the assisted living center at 1:30 PM. Jeff was a longtime employee of Willie's and he would be playing a key role here with what Willie had planned for the center.

"Looks like a shit sandwich" commented Jeff as he glanced about the property.

"Well, get prepared to take a big bite." laughed Willie,

They walked in together to meet Vera in her office.

"Vera, this is Jeff Meyer. He's going to be assisting me with the logistics of getting this place in shape. He's a good man." offered Willie.

"Pleased to meet you, if you're good enough for Willie, I'm sure you'll be good enough for me."

"Nice to meet you, Vera."

"If the lunchroom is cleared, let's head that way," said Willie.

"I'll show Jeff around later."

The day shift employees were not required to be on the floor at this time and a few of the night shift employees had shown up for the meeting. All seemed nervous and apprehensive, contemplating their fate, inwardly searching for some hidden past tragedies that were hopefully long since buried. What the hell, some of them thought, I had a job before I found this one.

Willie, Vera and Jeff took their seats in front of the assembled employees. Willie noticed the bright spot in the wallpaper were the clock used to be. Good sign, Vera was listening. Vera, lightheartedly, called for everyone's attention. She rose only to be heard. She began by announcing the reason for the meeting. Explaining that the property was now under new ownership but assuring them all first off that their jobs were still secure and hopefully with the input of the new ownership more secure than ever. She kept her comments brief, as this was not her forum to conduct.

In closing she just said," I want to introduce you to the new owner, who I personally think will make us all proud once again of the facility and the fact that we work here." Mr. William Lovd.

Willie stood up and immediately worked at breaking the tension he felt. "First of all, that is the last time, I want anyone to refer to me as Mr. William Lovd. My name is Willie, you can call me whatever you want to under your breath but if you need something from me, It's just Willie. Relax, Willie said to all of them, this is not some kind of an inquisition." He quickly hoped the term hadn't exceeded their grasp of the reference. I would tell all of you I believe in an open-door policy to my office. The problem is I do not plan on having an office here. The office belongs to Vera. My office will be walking through corridors, the parking lot, the kitchen, the roof, if need be. I don't feel I can achieve my objective sitting on my ass. After all we have Vera for that and from what I've heard she does deserve to take a seat and a round of applause from everyone. She's the reason there was still something here for me to purchase, and the reason you all still have a job. As far as I'm concerned, the best thing about Vera, is her worth ethic that the rest of us are going to pattern ourselves after, myself included. Less will be unacceptable. I told you I want every one of you to remain on staff. Keeping your job will be up to you, however. Initially I was going to go over the plans for the renovation of the facility with Vera only, but that's not how I operate. You are all part of the survival of this place. You all deserve to know firsthand and openly what is planned for Peachtree Assisted Living Center, after all it's going to involve extra effort on your part, so I feel you deserve to be kept in the loop. It will benefit all of you in the long run. It will also expose you to what is to come, and if you don't see yourself in that scenario, then I'll give you the opportunity to bow out gracefully."

"I want to take this time to thank those of you who have stuck it out through the issues with the past ownership and I want to welcome and promise the newly hired that I will prove to you that you made the right decision by getting yourself hired here."

"Before I go into the plans, I have for the facility I want to introduce you to someone who will become a familiar face around here. This is Jeff Meyer. He has a few things to say."

"OK thanks Willie, about time, you were starting to scare the crap out of me," began Jeff.

"First off, as Willie said, my name is Jeff Meyer. I don't know what I'm doing at this meeting. I am a nuts-and-bolts kind of guy. Willie only asked me here at the get together for one reason and that's to assure all of you, he's basically full of shit."

Everyone laughed at that. Everyone was going to like Jeff.

"Several thoughts to begin, I have been a long-term employee of Willie. I'm here to attest to you, you can count on one thing, Willie will see that the payroll is always on time. Let me also tell you, he is very approachable. Never be intimidated to talk to him. He wouldn't want it any other way. Also, if you look up fair in the dictionary you will see a picture of Willie.

I would be amiss however if I didn't give you a few survival tactics to employ around him, just something that I've learned from the years I've known Willie." The best analogy to describe Willie is as a dog with two leashes. If you pull on one, he will roll over and let you rub his belly. Not a pretty sight, I'll admit, Jeff said, and received some laughs. But if you pull on the wrong leash, he can rip your head off. Like I said earlier about Willie, he is fair. He lets you decide which leash you want to pull on. Some people say he's the nicest, sweetest guy they've ever met. Some people say he is the meanest son of a bitch (Pardon my language) they ever met. Both people are right. Do your best to choose which lease to pull on. Hey, I've known about all this for 15 years and still I'm proud to be called his friend and employee. So, he can't be all bad. My life would be less if I had never met him."

"Ok, that's enough from you Jeff, go up on the roof or something before all these people fall madly in love with me." That will conclude the character assassination of me, now I'd like to go over plans to bring the place up to its former glory and beyond. Trust me, I seriously don't know who Jeff was referring to."

Willie began. "First off, a lot of the demise here is no fault of anyone's here. You and the facility were under- funded, and under-supported. It's no wonder it's at 50% capacity. Today will start the change. I did not buy this place to maintain the status quo. The guests remaining deserve a better living environment and you all deserve a place you can be proud to work. That is the bottom line."

"Vera has given me the opportunity for some covert observation here so I could assess what I felt needed to be addressed. To demonstrate my openness with all of you, even Vera has no first-hand info of what I plan here. We are all involved and all equal. A lot of the plan to implement this will fall on Vera's shoulders. I'm asking all of you to do what you can to help her. I realize you have obligations to the needs of the guests, and I understand that is your priority, but I'm also asking all of you to step up beyond that. I will try to make this renovation and the improvements quick. I've always believed I'd rather work hard, than long. Most of this will not involve you. I understand the guests are your highest priority. If, however, someone wants a few more hours, I'm sure I can find something for you, for which you will be additionally compensated."

"Next week the grounds will be redone. Primarily new landscaping, plants and addressing the parking lot. Thankfully this building is predominantly brick so minor painting will spruce up the rest. Curb appeal is very important in people's opinions about a place."

"I had the pleasure of dining here with Vera one day and that is where some changes will be made. I realize many of the guests have dietary restrictions so I'm not planning on converting the menu to French cuisine. The food items served, other than some minor tweaking are not the problem. We are moving away from the disposable dinnerware and replacing it with China, silverware and glassware. Vera mentioned, the expense this would entail and the added labor. I have already assessed the kitchen and will be having a dishwasher installed next week. The larger storage room also has a hook-up for a washer and dryer that was never utilized. Next week Vera will place the china and linen orders. This was a big issue. Willie said I realized there will be some upfront cost. In the long run the money spent on all these disposable products used every day will be recouped. I feel it makes a huge statement as to how we intend to treat our residents. The menu may not be fine dining but there's no reason it can't be eaten with dignity. I'll discuss this in detail with Vera, then she can implement it with the cooking staff later."

Willie continued. "In a way, we've inherited a good renovation situation. As the occupancy dropped off the former owner moved everyone to the east wing, essentially closing the west wing, leaving those units vacant. This made some sense, since both sides are essentially served by separate utilities. They were able to shut that side down, saving the expense. This at least allows us to renovate that entire wing without disturbing the guest in the occupied units in the other wing. This will also greatly expedite getting the wing restored. "Vera, next week an estate sale will be held here to sell off anything salvageable in the units. Contact the local shelters, and the thrift locations and tell them what doesn't sell is theirs for the taking. Then place an order for all new furniture for the entire wing. We will need them in three weeks, so lean towards a supplier who can facilitate that timetable."

"Prior to the arrival, all the units will be stripped of all flooring, and repainted. It's a sizable financial outlay and I need to reverse the flow of the cash as quickly as I can to keep Vince at the bank happy. He's aware of my renovation plans and approves."

Vera spoke up again. "It shouldn't be a problem to get the new units leased. Most of the other facilities in the surrounding areas have waiting lists. Seems like everyone is getting older, joked Vera. I can contact them to see if they want to get off the waiting list and come here. That should put us back to 100% capacity pretty quickly."

"Not quite Vera. As soon as we have these units ready to occupy, we will still only be at 50%."

Vera and everyone else were confused. She asked how he figured that.

Willie said, "because as soon as those are finished and ready for occupancy, we are offering them to the current residents. Vera was visibly taken back.

"It's a way to thank all the guests and their families who remained loyal to the place through thick and thin. It's time to show our appreciation for them for having done so. So, Vera, keep your game plan in place. As soon as the current guests are settled in the new suites, I'm taking the other 50% apart. I'll leave one display model in the newly remodeled wing vacant as a display model you can use to lease the second wing from. I'm sure you can do it. It also gives you an extra 30 days for logistics."

"It will be tough, thought Vera. Who would forgo 50% of the facility income even for a short period?" Everyone was quiet and Willie knew he had dropped something on them that was beyond standard procedure.

"This is my call. I believe it is more important at this stage to build a reputation than a bank account. It will pay off in the long run." Willie could not have been more right.

"One final thing in closing, and this is an area where if I actually do have a wrong leash to pull on it, this could be it. What I'm about to say goes for everyone. I never want to hear a hint about a guest that has been neglected, abused, or ignored in any way. I want every last one of them treated with the utmost respect, and I'm aware some of them may be a little challenging. That's no excuse. You knew the job was dangerous when you took it. Work with them. I myself will not be happy until I get a smile from every one of them. Think people, one day you will be more horizontal than of vertical. Consider how you would want to be treated. I couldn't be more serious about this and if anyone thinks this is too much to ask for, then let's make today your last day."

"Let's go to work people."

Willie met with Vera in private after the meeting.

"Well, am I crazy or not?"

"I guess you're intitled to be as crazy as you can afford to be, joked Vera. Actually, at first, I thought the plan was a little askew, but the more I thought about it I came to the conclusion I think you hit on the right plan for our future. Moving the guests to the new renovated rooms does give me some more time to fill the newly renovated second half."

"I know this is going to put a large share of the workload on you. I'm big on promoting from within. Its' a "kind of the devil you know thing." Do you know of an employee who you think you could move up to help you with the management and paperwork issues? "You are going to be overwhelmed without an assistant and I will be buried in the renovation work."

"There is one girl I believe might be interested. She's smart, computer literate beyond me, and seems to have the right attitude for long term commitment. Her name is Barrie Lou. She's been here a while, so she knows the daily workings of the place."

"Vera, if you think she is worth a try, move her up. Do you see any issues with the other employees?"

"Not now, really. I've already dismissed the ones that I thought were bad apples and I think you put the fear of God in the ones that are left", laughed Vera.

"They will come to see my bark is worse than my bite and I'm sure we'll all become one big happy family. Here's a little incentive for you. Pick an island. When we're 100%, you will be headed for the beach. That is of course if you get Barrie Lou to be able to cover for you while you're gone.

"Sounds good to me, but there's just one thing Willie. Some of the guests may not want to move to the newly renovated units."

"Why would that be. We will move their personal items for them with or without their families help. Then isn't it just a matter of wheeling them to their new room?"

"It may not be a problem for the guests. I'm just saying the family may take this as an excuse to move to another facility instead of just to a new room. Some of the families have expressed concern about the downward trend of the facility."

"Wow!" Willie wasn't prepared for that.

"Alright, don't mention that plan to the families for 10 days. When they see what improvements have been made so quickly, they will know what direction the facility is going in. I'll convince the families and together the two of us will convince the guests that this is where they want to stay."

"I'll just have to win their hearts with my good looks and charm."

"Oh boy, we're in trouble now," laughed Vera.

Willie and a team of laborer's were at the facility early the next morning. A truck from the local nursery arrived, loaded with sod, bushes, groundcovers and flowering plants. They began to unload everything with the help of the driver.

"By the way, where do you want the peach trees?" asked the driver.

Work on Willie's plan for the facility went right along on track. By the time the first wing was completed Vera had convinced all the current guests and their families to stay on. They were all happy and grateful to move into their new rooms.

Willie asked Vera, how she had managed to get them all to decide to stay?

"I just asked them, why not stay where you will be loved!" Not long after the last wing was all renovated and Vera had managed to get it fully occupied Willie asked her how she had managed that so quickly?"

She replied, "I asked them the same thing."

Willie had made the right decision by foregoing a quick financial return in favor of establishing a good reputation and it had paid off.

Vera had worked tirelessly, and she was deservedly proud of what they had accomplished together. She wasn't hesitant to remind Willie of the promise he had made to her early on.

"I heard it is especially nice in the Caymans this time of the year," said Willie.

"When do you think it is never nice in the Caymans?" laughed Vera.

"Well, why aren't you packing then. You have more than earned it?"

Willie spent the time Vera was gone getting more acquainted with Barrie Lou. Vera was right as usual. She was proving to be more than capable of managing the facility. That would work out well. Willie had bigger plans for Vera.

It wasn't long in the future before Willie, Vera and dignitaries of a nearby city were cutting the ribbon on a new, modern assisted living center that Willie had built. The sign said:

A William B. Lovd Assisted Living Center.
"Why Not Stay Where You Will Be Loved."

Willie acquired other existing facilities, instilling excellent management teams in them, assuring himself and his guests that they would always be treated with dignity. All was well in Willie's world. For now. While Willie rarely felt the need for a pat on his back, for things he had accomplished, he was justifiably proud of the recognition he received upon the opening of his latest assisted care facility. He decided to call Jeff, his construction supervisor to also thank him.

"Jeff, it's Willie, I wanted to thank you for the role you played in getting the latest facility opened. During the ribbon cutting ceremony they actually gave me the Key to the city."

"I know, I heard," said Jeff.

"How did you find out about that so quickly," asked Willie?

"The mayor just called me to start changing all the city's locks."

CHAPTER FIVE

WILLIE GOT UP AND AS HE WAS GETTING DRESSED, decided to have breakfast in town. He didn't feel like facing the one egg skillet this morning. It was decision time as Willie entered his garage. Just as women dealt with which pair of shoes to wear on a chosen day, Willie had to wrestle with which car to drive.

April Fool's Day had played its own joke. It was unseasonably warm today. Willie had always joked that next to Groundhogs' Day, April Fool's Day was his favorite holiday. Such an easy holiday. You didn't have to decorate the house, you didn't have to buy any useless stuff, that would be returned anyway, and no one was coming over for dinner. Willie, reflected on how he would miss any more April Fool's Days. Another thing he could now add to his "list of lasts." Oddly, he'd still felt fine. There were the usual aches and pains of damn old age in general, but nothing seemed amiss. Youth was a wonderful thing he thought, why did they waste it on children? Maybe Doctor Mike was playing an April Fool's Day joke on him.

"Hey Willie, it's Doctor Lillenberg, "April Fools", I was just kidding there's nothing wrong with you. You're not going to die any faster than the rest of us. Willie knew that was a fantasy phone call he would never receive. Mike was way too much of a professional to pull a prank like that.

Willie chose the T bird. Thankfully he hadn't put the hardtop on this winter, so it was ready for an open-air ride. He needed to drop some papers off at the bank. He could do it through the drive up.

The 1955 Thunderbird was Megan's favorite car of Willie's. They teased back and forth. Looking down into the car one day from her elevated inside window, she had remarked how she could just melt into those seats.

"Why didn't they make cars with those kinds of colors anymore?" she asked. "Why does everything have to be black or white these days?"

"It's a sign of the times Willie said, oh you mean cars," he laughed.

The two- seater T-bird painted its original pastel blue with its blue and white pleated upholstery was about as far from black and white as you could get. The wire wheels framed the car perfectly. Megan called the car, "Eye candy." He decided to make her day as he backed the car out of the garage. He needed an extra distraction for her today anyway. He needed to drive off with a deposit canister.

After breakfast, Willie drove to the bank. He took a drive-up lane where he would have to use the canister to send in his paperwork.

"Making my day" said Megan as he stopped his car. "Nice day for that. Is it the maiden voyage for my car today?"

"Your car? Willie joked," let me check the paperwork in the glovebox about that."

"Yeah, like you have a car payment book in the first place. Take me to the drive-in in that thing, suggested Megan."

"Sure thing, as soon as you're 30 years older," sighed Willie. Willie then put his items in the canister and sent them over. Megan noted the signature of William B. Lovd.

"What's the B. stand for anyway, Willie? "I'm running out of guesses." It was a little game they played whenever he came to the bank. "I know, how about Brian?"

"No."

"Benjamin?"

"No."

"Bert?"

"No."

"Buster?" laughed Megan'

"NO," said Willie "it's worse than Buster."

"It can't be Bill; your first name is William. Who would name their kid Bill, Bill, Lovd?"

"Basil?

"No, no, no, give up you'll never get it and I'll never tell you as long as I'm alive"

"Wow it must be bad," laughed Megan.

"Bart?" Megan guessed one more time.

"No."

"Am I your only customer or something" asked Willie.

"Almost, only you and the other six computer illiterate people in the world remaining. You are the only people who ever come into a bank anymore. Nobody comes here, they can bank online."

"They don't know what they're missing." remarked Willie.

"What could that be?" wondered Megan,

"You," said Willie.

"Are you home tonight?" asked Megan.

"Why on earth do you ask that?"

"Well, if you're not, I'm going to come over and steal that car," laughed Megan.

"Go ahead," said Willie, I always wanted a red one."

With that, Megan sent back the cannister with Willie's receipts.

He drove off with it as another car pulled up to her service window. Now he had the canister he needed.

His thoughts went to how he was going to break the news to his family and friends one day about his untimely departure. He played scenes over and over in his mind, usually different with each person he was filling in about the situation. He kept putting it off, but time was moving on. Some days he wanted to get it over and done with. Some days he felt like waiting as long as possible, until it was obvious something was wrong. Why burden anyone with his news. He wasn't looking for sympathy, but he still knew it would be unsettling for some. He wanted to spare them of that. Thinking about these things were at least a good reason to see Lisa at Malley's. She was always fun. Willie took a seat at the bar and waited for Lisa to finish with a customer.

"Hi Willie, what would you like?"

"Jack and coke and make it hurt."

"Sounds good," said Lisa

"Well, have one yourself."

"If I could, I would".

"Are you ordering food" asked Lisa?

"No, I had breakfast. I'll just drink my lunch."

"Ok, what is it, is she still insisting on that prenuptial agreement?"

Willie laughed, "you know there is no one in the picture."

"Just one of the very few things we have in common," said Lisa.

"I can take the lonely days," said Willie.

"Yeah, so can I, but it's the long, lonely nights that are a bitch."

Lisa turned to get his drink. Lisa return to chat after waiting on a few customers.

"How are the chinchillas doing anyway," asked Willie.

"They're fine, I have a freezer full of them. Shannon says they taste like chicken."

Willie and Lisa laughed. They both knew the chinchillas were a long-gone joke of the past.

"I know what you need, Willie?"

"What's that?" ventured Willie.

"Me!"

Willie sputtered into what was left of the drink.

"Yeah, for sure."

"How's everything with Shannon?"

"She's great. Still pouring over information from colleges she won't be attending, thanks to mom being too poor to pay attention."

"Something will work out," offered Willie.

"Yeah, and if, if's and buts were candy and nuts we'd all have a Merry Christmas. You're making me consider sneaking that drink," confided Lisa.

"Not now, with Office Bob sitting nearby. He might arrest you", laughed Willie. I didn't know the crime rate in Malley's was so high. He seems to be in here a lot."

"Police officers have to eat too you know. And I can think of worse people to be handcuffed by".

"Maybe he has some fur lined ones?

"He might be the guy for you, you never know?"

"I'll have another," said Willie.

"Jack and Coke and make it hurt right?"

"Right."

Willie read all the decor paraphernalia on the walls as he watched Lisa work. He hoped the best for her. The drinks seemed to be going down well today, and Willie had another. He took a minute to walk over to talk to officer Bob.

"How's your fellow officer doing Bob?"

"He's fully recovered and back to work. I'll tell him you asked about him."

"Great, said Willie. By the way, where can someone buy Kevlar if they wanted to."

"Are you planning on making yourself a vest?" joked officer Bob.

"No, laughed Willie, I'm not worth shooting. I just have a little garage project going on where I thought it might work for what I need.

Officer Bob responded, "well the same place you can buy just about anything these days. On the Internet."

"You're probably right, I never thought to look there."

Willie returned to his stool in Lisa's section. Shortly after she stopped by and asked if he wanted another, "That depends" said Willie, "can you drive a stick?"

"I can try, if you would like me too."

"No, I think I'm done."

"You do have something I could use though".

"What's that" asked Lisa.

"Does Bruce have any empty 5-gallon pickle buckets he hasn't thrown out yet. I could use a couple."

"I'm sure he does. People are nuts over our fried pickles. I'll ask him. You want the lids too?"

"Yes, if he has them."

Lisa returned with two white 5-gallon pickle buckets, including the lids. "Great said Willie, my gratitude will be reflected in my gratuity. See you next time," as Willie left the bar, a bucket in each hand.

Willie politely dismissed all the admirers gathered around the T-Bird and left the parking lot. Jesus, thought Willie, these cars could give a lesser man an inferiority complex. The cars were the stars, not he, he knew.

Willie made the first of his two stops on his way home. The hobby store would have what he needed. He set panels of two-inch-thick star foam, along with some slats of balsa wood on the counter. The clerk asked if he was getting an early start on making Christmas decorations? Willie replied, "you could never be too prepared for Christmas, who knows when it could be ones' last." The clerk had a questioning look on his face about that remark but bagged the items and thanked Willie for the purchases.

The joke April Fool's Day had played with the weather was rapidly coming to an end. The temperature was dropping to what Willie like to refer to as air-ish. He was betting Marilyn, the T bird, in reference to Marilyn Monroe, was starting to shiver. Willie often felt that the T-bird was a little on the feminine side and often got teased about it. He took comfort though in the fact that JFK had fifty 1955 T-birds in his inaugural parade. President Eisenhower, Elvis Presley and Frank Sinatra were all also 1955 T-bird owners at one time. Pretty solid ground. Not too many people questioned Sinatra's manhood without getting a broken nose. Willie promised her he would get her home soon. Just one more stop.

Willie pulled into the auto parts store where he was of course a regular.

"What do you need this time, Willie?" asked the attendant. He knew Willie from frequent visits.

"Just point me to the fiberglass material and I'll be good."

"Please don't tell me you dinged one of the corvettes." The salesperson knew all about Willie's cars.

"Oh no, nothing like that, just a little home repair project I have going on."

"Well, there's nothing stronger than fiberglass, so hope that does it for you."

"It will," said Willie, as he paid and left the store.

Now he had everything he would need. He keyed his entrance gate code into his phone, then hit the garage opener as he pulled up to his garage. Once inside he shut the door behind him. The garage was climate controlled, and it looked like the night would be chilly. There now, Marilyn you're home. Goodnight and rest in peace. I'll be with you soon, Willie sadly thought.

Willie could never resist a last survey of his collection before turning out the lights and heading into the house. The garage was full of classic cars and vintage motorcycles, and Willie had no logical reason for such a sickness. He often considered them a crutch that prevented him from forming more personal relationships with real people. They were like children however. They always needed something, so he could blame away the time he spent with them, instead of with living breathing people, like his kids for example. Though he thought the world of his kids and would do anything for them, he often felt they were abandoned by his ambitions. He turned off the lights and walked across the courtyard to his house.

June 14th. It was after nine in the morning when the phone rang. He could see the call was from his daughter, Hope. He answered it with glee. He didn't get this call too often.

"Happy Father's Day, dad", said Hope. "I just wanted to be the first to call you."

"Thanks, it's great to hear from you. How is everything? Are you the CEO yet?"

"No, but I'm working on it. I hope to be, even if I have to create a false sexual accusation claim to blackmail someone into the position," laughed Hope.

"That's my girl, you go for it." said Willie.

Willie quickly added this Father's Day to his "list of lasts."

The conversation was getting a little strained, he could tell, so he thought it benevolent to find a closing.

"Thanks for calling Hope, hope we can do lunch sometime soon."

"Sure dad, have a great day." With that, they both hung up.

"Hey Willie, it's Mike, how are you doing? I'd like to have you stop in once for a checkup."

"I could do that but actually I'm feeling ok, Willie lied. Are you sure you are not fucking with me about all this?" Doctor Mike didn't dignify the remark with a reply, other than to tell Willie to make an appointment with his assistant.

"Ok, OK, said Willie, I'll do it."

Willie could tell though that things in his body were changing. He no longer doubted the diagnosis and was moving beyond trying to deny it. He couldn't waste remaining time pretending it wasn't true. What would that get him? He knew he needed to handle this situation as strategically as he could, as he had always done with everything else in his life. Yet there were days when he still felt the need to retreat into himself. Willie walked to the edge of the 100-foot Cliff that marked the rear of his property to the river valley below. It wasn't the simplest thing to do, but over the years Willie had found the best path to negotiate the way down the steeply descending slope to the river level below. He made it to the bottom and walked the short distance to the river's edge and sat down on a rock beside the bank. He watched, mesmerized as pieces of driftwood and other flotations passed rapidly by him in the current of the Mississippi. Things moved on, their course or destination unknown. What must that be like, thought Willie. That put Willie in a melancholy mood. He sat on a rock and hung his head. His life was floating past him just as all the debris in the current that was flowing passed him. He finally recognized his own mortality. He would die. He stood up and headed back to the base of the cliff, up to his house. This he knew would be the last time he would ever climb it. He knew the time had come to prepare others and himself for his demise.

"Cherise, it's Willie, I'd like to come over and talk to you about something, if you have some free time?"

That took Cherise back a little. While she and Willie had remained amicable, yet rarely was there ever a need for a formal conference. Guardedly she said, "well sure Willie, I can do that."

"When works for you?" asked Willie.

"How about Saturday morning," asked Cherise.

"That's fine, I'll be over. I'll bring you a cup of your high dollar coffee, and thanks," said Willie as he hung up the phone.

Thanks? thought Cherise, there's a word Willie didn't throw around easily with her, and a cup of coffee to boot. This was being awfully sweet. No, don't let yourself go there.

Those times were over. Were they, she thought? A lot of thoughts ran through her head before Willie arrived on her doorstep.

Willie arrived at Cherise's house, coffee in hand. It was a nice house in a well to do area. The yard was well landscaped. Willie knew that was through the efforts of a hired groundskeeper. Cherise was without a green thumb. He knew the pool water was kept sparkling via a service contract and the interior of the home was spotless due to the tireless and never-ending efforts of regular maid service. Cherise was domestically, undomesticated.

Cherise had done well for herself once she broke the shackles of married life. She was an incredible mother, a so-so mom, but an unfulfilling wife. She was an intelligent woman but marriage was never for her. She considered it an anchor to what she wanted to accomplish and experience on her own. Just as Willie's work was his mistress, Cherise's aspirations were her lover. It was an un-survivable situation. They both fed off each other yet neither brought anything to the banquet table. It ended painfully, without a real justifiable reason to end a marriage. Reasons had to be manufactured, after all you can't just say it's over, without a reason.

Cherise answered the door upon Willie's ring. It had been the last holiday since he had seen her. People commented to him often about how great she looked. Willie never noticed. He only saw the ugliness of the past. He had learned however, that forgiveness was possible, but forgetting, not so much.

"Here's your coffee".

"Wow it's even still warm. And it still smells great, thanks Willie, come in. I made some for you too. Just how you like it, black". Willie walked through the foyer and followed Cherise to the kitchen, which as in every house was now the living room. They settled in and Cherise asked,

"Well, what's up Willie, this is kind of different?"

Willie sat quietly. How does one come out with the kind of news that he was about to deliver? He was at a loss for an icebreaker to begin.

Hell, the shortest path between two points is a straight line. Willie thought, so here goes.

"Cherise, I came to tell you that I'm dying".

"Well, aren't we all, Willie," laughed Cherise.

"Yeah, but I know when and what of."

"That's what you always said about your uncle."

True, Willie had always joked that his uncle was one of those people who knew exactly what he would die of and exactly when. In his uncle's case, the judge told him. Willie again became quiet and that alone was not a usual situation for Willie. He didn't speak. It began to wash over Cherise. He was being serious, as if anyone would joke about something like that. Yet she couldn't grasp it. The invincible had finally become vincible. Was that even a word, Cherise wondered. Willie had always been larger than life. He was just one of those people who you could not associate with ever dying. It just seemed like Willie would, well just always be. Now she was silent, and the silence between the two of them confirmed it.

"What do you mean, Willie?"

"I mean I'm dying!"

"Well, of what?"

"Let's just say it's not my good looks and charm that are killing me."

Cherise always recalled Willie's ability to integrate his sense of humor into any situation and it was one thing she missed about him.

"It's cancer, and before you ask how about a possible treatment program, Mike already bluntly told me the remainder of my life may be just as pleasant without going there."

"Do you mind if I ask, how long do you have to live, if you say you're dying? "I mean how serious is this?"

"Let's just say, don't wait by your mailbox for a Christmas card this year."

"Damn that's quick. How can something sneak up on you so fast?"

"Who knows, did it really sneak up on me quickly?" asked Willie.

Cherise could have said, well if you had met Doctor Mike in his office at least once every 25 years or so instead of just on the golf course with him, maybe it wouldn't have arrived at your doorstep seemingly so suddenly. This was no time for lectures though, she realized.

"You look healthy as ever, how do you feel?"

"You're starting to question the diagnosis, I can tell. Generally, I feel fine. I've lived with lots of aches and pains I've caused, by self-inflicted physical abuse, but I'm starting to feel twinges, that I've never had the pleasure of meeting before. That's how Mike said it would begin."

"Willie, I don't know what to say?"

"Don't worry about it, if you did know what to say, it would be the same thing everybody else would have to say, and I only need to hear it so often. Trust me, I will get there without you needing to do anything for me. Thanks, but you don't need to offer."

"Be sure to not let your soft side show through. if you have one Willie", chided Cherise.

"I promise not to weaken".

"Seriously though Willie, if there is anything I can do, hey for old times' sake, please ask."

"You're going there Cherise, and you don't need to. I do have one favor to ask though. Let me break the news to the kids on my time in my own way. Not that I think it will interrupt their day too badly. I'm just not in a hurry to disturb the ebb and flow of this their lives with this any sooner than I think I must. I think they will be able to deal with it well enough when the time comes."

"You're making it sound like they don't care for you at all. That's not the case. The two of us both did our share to create two intelligent, successful people in their own right. They're both maturing adults who have never caused us a problem, and neither of us would want it any other way. They moved on with this their lives like we all do."

"Well, I just don't think Reed will need any Ambien to get through the night when he hears the news about the old man's demise," stated Willie.

"He's like you. Not an expert at showing a lot of emotion, but he cares for you."

"Well, the love kind of diminishes when it's applied 2000 miles away." sighed Willie.

"That's where his job took him. It was an incredible opportunity for him at his company. He deserved the promotion and we would both have been disappointed if he hadn't taken the transfer. It was a big step up for him. What else was he to do, and he gets away when he can."

Cherise was right about all this, but there was still a lot of love lost between himself and Reed. Willie could just not come completely to grips with the fact that his kids were moving on as everyone does and should. He just was afraid that the time he had lost with them in their childhood could not be made up for in their adulthood.

"You know this will be rough for Hope", said Cherise. She is more fragile than she lets on. She doesn't like to admit it, but she worships you. The two of you are kindred spirits, both in your own way."

"Yes, Willie agreed, Hope was his soulmate. They both had a structured life, but not far beneath ran the urge to run free. She would never be cubicle bound, and Willie was happy about that. It's a hell of a big world. Get out and see it, he always believed.

One of the few words of wisdom he ever gave for his kids was, it's ok to be a little crazy, but being a little stupid can get you killed. He wanted for them too experience life on the edge, but not to fall off it. Of the two, Hope skipped along the cliff's edge much more than

Reed had. That alone created a greater bond between Willie and her, than with Reed. She was the one who would feel the pain, and Willie dreaded being the one responsible for it.

"Knowing you, Willie, I'm sure your affairs are already in order," said Cherise. You probably have your suit at the cleaners already." They both laughed at that.

"I don't intend to leave a trail of destruction for anyone to sort out. I was a big enough pain in the ass while I was alive, no need for that to carry on while I'm gone."

"Who else except Doctor Mike knows about this? Cherise asked.

"Just you, and please let me be the one to spread the joy, especially to the kids." repeated Willie.

"Ok, I get it." said Cherise, as Willie rose to leave. She still couldn't imagine, a world without Willie, even if he was no longer a part of hers.

"Does Dale know?" Cherise knew how close of a friend he was to Willie.

"Not yet. I guess he's next to know." said Willie.

As soon as Willie was out of the door, she grabbed her cell and called Hope.

It was Monday. Willie drove the short distance to the church he attended somewhat regularly. He parked and walked across the lot to the sanctuary entering the side door he knew led to pastor Ron's office. The door was open, and Pastor Ron was behind his desk. Willie waited to be noticed, then was immediately welcomed in with a friendly handshake from pastor Ron. They were of a similar age.

"Nice to see you Willie, I'm glad you stopped in, I was about out of sermon material," he joked. They both laughed.

"Happy to be of assistance," said Willie.

"I'm sorry I dropped by unannounced."

"Oh no problem, this is a Thank God its Monday, kind of business," said pastor Ron. I have plenty of time. I have the whole week to prepare damnation for all the parishioners before next Sunday."

"Willie was always comfortable around pastor Ron. Even though he was a devoted man of the cloth, he had a human side anyone could relate to.

"What brings you in today? It's not Sunday you know?"

"Well, it's a matter I think you might have some insight into," said Willie.

"Really, what might that be?"

"My impending death and with it, the passing on to the next life."

"Well, it is a shred out of my chosen profession, but I'm not promising to know it all, but I will help clear up things if I can. After all, that's why I'm allowed to stick my hand into the collection plate every Sunday."

"Is this a confirmed revelation, or just a future interest we are all preparing ourselves for?"

Willie sat quiet a moment, then spoke. "I may as well get on with it, I've been diagnosed with cancer and its terminal. I've come to grips with it somewhat, but it's still quite an awakening."

"Willie, I'm saddened to hear that. God's reward is not on this earth, but I always believed he put us here to enjoy all he has created. It's always sad when one is rushed home prematurely. I can spout scriptures to you, Willie, but now I feel you have a need to be comforted in the secular sense."

"I'm comfortable, in my hopes of salvation. Unbeknownst to many, my faith has always been an underlying strength to me.

"That will be a comfort to you, and I'm glad to hear it. What would you really like to hear me say?"

"Oh, I'm not here to make a deathbed confession. My life will be its own undoing, if that is to be my fate."

"I'm here to speak with you about bequeathing a gift to the church as part of my final wishes. Are you open to a bribe," joked Willie?

"If only it were that easy. The condemned can't take it with them anyway, so they are not offering much for what they are hoping to gain, are they? By all means though, don't let chatter like that diminish the graciousness of your offer," laughed Pastor Ron.

"Always the negotiator of lost souls, right pastor Ron", joked Willie.

"I serve in my capacity at the Lord's request." laughed Pastor Ron.

"Well, you're certainly right. What I have I can't take with me, unless of course you know of a funeral home that has a hearse with a trailer hitch. I've never seen one myself, trust me, I've checked around."

"I must concur with you on that. I don't know of one either. That would make them popular that's for sure, not to mention a great disappointment to a few expecting heirs, I suppose."

"That might serve some of them right though," laughed Willie.

Seriously though, you probably know of some of the cars I have. None of which will be accompanying me to the great beyond".

"You certainly have some beauties, that's true."

"I've decided to have one auctioned off through a charity auction and have the proceeds donated to the church. Mind you, I'm not expected to jump the line at the pearly gates, but the church has always been a stable foundation for me, and I feel it's fitting for me to do so."

"Willie, I can assure you the endowment will be greatly appreciated."

"I'd prefer to make it anonymous, but because it's one of my cars, it may be a little difficult as many will know it was mine. I know a friend, named Dale Howard who is familiar with how these auctions for charity work. I'll have him handle the details, and as time passes, I'll introduce you to him. He's good people. I trust him with my life, right now I'm trusting him with my death, so to speak. I'll be auctioning off the 1967 Corvette. That model should bring in well over $100,000. So, you can plan a use for the funds when they arrive. I only ask one stipulation on the use of the money. I prefer it go as directly as possible to local people truly in need, brought on by situations not of their own making. I don't want to look down and see a new Willie B. Lovd wing added to the sanctuary, laughed Willie, assuming it will be in a downward direction I will be viewing from."

"I'm sure we can make use of your donation as you wish."

"Do what you can to keep this anonymous, at least as long as I'm still an earthly being."

"Of course, Willie, and please come see me at any time about your spiritual health if you feel the need."

"I will, said Willie, and it's ok if you use my lifestyle as a bad example in your sermon, but please don't point me out or ask me to stand up again when you're doing it ok, pastor Ron?"

"It's a deal. Have a good day Willie".

And with that Willie left the office. Willie decided this was as good a day as any to get on with his project. Better sooner than later he thought. He didn't know what his limitations might be physically when time brought his afflictions to bear.

On his worktable in his garage, Willie had assembled all the things he had been collecting over the past few months. He took the two pickle buckets he had gotten from Malley's and cut off the handles. He applied an excessive amount of pure silicone caulking around the outside of one of the buckets and slipped it inside the other bucket, essentially making a doubly thick bucket. He knew when the silicone dried it would turn into a super strength waterproof adhesive, primarily joining the two buckets.

Next, he took the Kevlar officer Bob suggested he could order online and cut a circular mat out of it and placed it into the bottom of the now joined buckets. He applied a little spray adhesive also to hold it in place while he finished the rest of his assembly.

He cut a piece of 6-inch diameter PVC pipe to match the height of the bucket, leaving it short enough for a 2-inch pad of star-foam on the bottom and room to still close the bucket with the lid. He placed the PVC pipe up right in the bucket and packed the void around it with the star-foam that he had gotten at the hobby store. Into any voids that were created, he slid in pieces of balsa wood until the PVC tube was nestled firmly in place. He placed the canister from the drive up at the bank, that he had borrowed from Megan, into the PVC tube. He added a layer of star-foam to the bottom of the PVC tube until the inside height was the same dimensions as the length of the deposit canister. It was a good fit. The bucket lid would hold it firmly in place when it was installed. He placed the lid on temporarily for now.

Willie cut a piece of Kevlar to cover the bottom of the bucket, lapping it up the sides a few inches. He used some industrial strength contact cement to hold it in place, while he continued working.

He then cut a long piece of Kevlar the length of the bucket and wrapped it around the bucket, again attaching it with cement. After the cement had dried, he took long zip ties and circled the bucket with those. Knowing the sun's ultraviolet could eventually weaken those, he took the three narrow bands of stainless steel he had made and wrapped them around the bucket joining the ends with stainless steel fasteners.

He cut a circular mat of Kevlar to attach to the bottom side of the bucket's lid. Willie knew this may not be 100% bulletproof but with the bucket's round sides maybe it would create a glancing strike if someone was to use the bucket for target practice. He left the fiberglass material he had gotten at the auto supply store there, along with some silicone to make a permanent seal on the lid.

Willie's cell phone rang. He saw it was Hope. Not a common occurrence, but also not unheard of. Hope was evolving into a mature, successful young lady and Willie was proud of it. He would never commandeer too much of her time. He did enjoy the random calls though.

"What's up, hopeless," Willie teased her with the nickname he had given her as a teenager. It stuck and had become a joke between the two of them.

There was silence for a bit before she finally said through broken words, "dad, mom told me." He could tell she was near tears. Damn thought Willie, I had specifically told her not to tell the kids. He had wanted to do it on his own time. Now he was caught off guard. It was hard enough to deal with, even with having a pre-planned speech in place, but off the cuff like this left Willie at a loss.

"Hey sweetie, it's ok. I'm still here, and I'm coming to grips with it," Willie lied.

"I just, just don't know what to say daddy."

"Just the thought of you trying to figure out what to say is more than enough for me."

"But it's so sad, and unbelievable to."

Neither spoke for a little. He hoped she was still on the line, giving him time to come up with something to say, to ease her mind a bit.

"Hope, I've decided I'm not going to spend each day dwelling on this. Willie thought, if only that was only true. So, I don't want you too either. You have important things in your life to deal with and it makes me happy that you do."

"I'm trying to think of something I can do for you, but there's nothing I can think of."

"I told you, your thoughts are enough." Let me ask you though, does Reed know?"

"No," lied Hope, after telling me, mom said you wanted to be the one to tell Reed, so I didn't tell him either."

"Thanks for that", said Willie.

He knew even though Reed and Hope were separated by half a country that they still talked on the phone or emailed each other. Now he would have to call Reed as soon as possible, before the news leaked out.

"I was about to get around to calling both of you but was looking for a good time to do so, if there is such a time. I'm sorry I didn't call you myself. I just was hesitant to interrupt your lives. Now I need to call him, just like I should have been the one to call you."

"I know what you can do for me though, offered Willie.

"What's that?"

"Let me take you out to eat."

"Just the two of us, it's been a long time I know."

"Yeah, I think the last time was Donuts with Daddy when I was in second grade," laughed Hope.

Good, she still remembered that. It was a silly little thing her grade school did a couple times a year, where the fathers would meet the kids in the classroom, early in the day for donuts. Willie never missed it. Years later when mom put her in an expensive private high school Willie asked her, if they would be having Donuts with Daddy? She laughed and said "no, they are having Wellington with Willie."

"I think I can do better than Donuts with Daddy, let's make it special. I'll make some reservations and we'll blow the budget."

"Blow your budget?"

"What are you going to do, pay for everyone's meal?" jabbed Hope.

"Sounds good daddy, but you know I don't eat anything that had a face on it." Willie knew she was a vegetarian.

"You know, I always wondered why, if you are so concerned about the animals, why do you keep eating all their food?" laughed Willie.

"Very funny daddy, I'm looking forward to it though".

"See you soon, Hope-less."

With that they both said their goodbyes.

Hope dialed Reeds number. Upon answering, Hope said "dad's going to call you. Make peace with him."

"Didn't I ask you not to tell the kids about this. I was barely out the door before you called Hope and told her."

"Well, Willie," began Cherise, "when would that have been? I'm sure it's something you could easily put off, and I understand, but I wasn't sure if you would ever get around to it, and I believe it's best if they still have a little time to come to grips with this while you're still above ground." Willie had no intention of ever being underground. He wasn't planning on taking up any real estate when he was gone.

"Well don't call Reed, I'm calling him in the morning".

"Ok, I promise, but Willie you need to do it."

"I know, I know" said Willie as he hung up.

Willie decided to take the 1969 AMX to his doctor appointment today. It was a car not as many people were as familiar with as Camaros or Mustangs. It was also a car that surpassed the Camaros and Mustangs with its exceptional power. It was another two-seater car, of Willie's. It would not have been the ideal car for a drive-in movie in high school. At that time Willie had a car with a back seat. He remembered once taking a girl to the drive-in and when things started to get steamy, he asked the girl if she wanted to get in the back seat. Her reply was "Why no, Willie, I want to stay up here with you." He married her anyway.

Willie was early to his appointment but not earlier than Doctor Mike. Willie always teased him that he only started so early to be sure no one got in his private parking spot. They didn't today either, there was Dr. Mike's Porsche.

After the usual routine in the reception room and the nurse's checkup, he was ushered into Doctor Mike's office. Mike was at his desk looking over some charts. He put them down and greeted Willie.

"Some time has gone by but I see your still moving under your own power. How do you feel?"

"Can I lie?" asked Willie.

"Can you, or should you, is the question."

"I hate to say it, but I'm finally starting to believe your diagnosis. Maybe you aren't the quack I always took you for" joked Willie.

"Well, what in general seems to bother you?"

"Lots of aches and pains I never knew. Sometimes sharp. Nausea a lot. Some nights I can't sleep, Somedays I can't stay awake. Occasional headaches."

"Now that's strange. You always said you never got headaches. You said it wasn't your job to get headaches, it was your job to pass them out.

"These are typical and early symptoms. I can start you on some prescriptions that will make things a little more bearable yet not put you in Lala land."

"Are you sure I even need a pancreas? My friend Dale doesn't have his tonsils or his appendix or his gallbladder. Hell, I have an aunt that only has half her stomach. And look, we all know most of the politicians in Washington only have half a brain."

"That's true, but that might be why they are leading us down a path to destruction." laughed Doctor Mike.

"You sure I need it? Why don't we just cut the thing out. I'll chalk it up to a lost pound or two and go merrily about my way. Would that work?"

"Can I lie?" asked Doctor Mike.

"Can you, or should you," is the question.

"Give me the damn pills and I'll get out of here. I'm going to back into your Porsche on my way out."

"I'm not afraid of that. I know you wouldn't back into my car with one of yours."

"Ok, but we need to do the golf thing while I am still moving under my own power."

"Sounds good, said Doctor Mike, I'll set it up".

"No, it's not a Javelin, it's an AMX," said Willie to the admirers as he left the parking lot. He was in no mood to discuss cars right now as he got in the car, chirping the tires as he left.

Willie knew catching Reed on the phone during his business days was tough, but he decided to give it a shot. He dialed Reeds number and surprisingly Reed answered in a few rings.

"What's up dad." Calls between the two were infrequent.

"I thought about flying out to see you for a few days, if you can make the time?"

"Sure, maybe we can play a round of golf," said Reed.

"I'd like that, I may even let you beat me."

"You don't have to let me beat you dad. I always beat you. So often I'm even starting to feel a little guilty of you having to pay because you lose. Just a little guilty though," Reed laughed.

"This all just shows you how well I taught you the game in the first place," Willie countered.

"The only thing you ever taught me about golf was how to drive to the golf course."

"That reminds me, I am driving the cart, you still may have a little problem with the concept of stopping and steering," joked Willie.

"I drove one golf cart in the creek one time, and you will never let me forget that as long as you're alive, I guess." As soon as the words were out of his mouth, Reed figured he could have rephrased that differently.

"Well, you have to admit it was memorable. At least they didn't revoke my membership at the club. You're right though, accidents do happen."

"Are you going to bring all three of the clubs you use along with you?" teased Reed or are you just going to play with ones out of my bag. You know if you ever learn to use a driver you might shoot a decent score."

"You know what I have to say about that. A man has got to know his limitations."

"I'm pretty sure that's not what Clint Eastwood was referring to.

"How's everything else going?"

"It's going just fine," said Reed."

"OK, good enough I'll be out in a week or two. Try and get some practice in."

"Don't worry about me, just bring the loser's pay along with you."

"I never leave home without it. Hey, it's not going to rain, is it?"

"Dad, you know it never rains in Southern California."

"No, but man it pours."

"Still stuck in the 60's I see. See you when I see you dad."

That concluded one of the longer phone conversations they've ever had.

Hope's phone rang. She saw it was Willie.

"Hi dad, how are you?"

"I'm vertical. What more can a person ask. I was wondering if this Saturday works for our dining out together?"

"Sure, I can make that work."

"I'll call you later in the week with the reservation details. Be prepared to dress up."

"Dad, you know McDonald's doesn't take reservations," joked Hope.

"Ha-ha, it will be a cut above that, I promise. I might even wear matching socks. "

"No way, said Hope, wow I'm going to have to dig out an evening gown for that."

"Where we're going, you'll be glad you did. Call you in a few days. I'll pick you up. Bye, sweetie."

"Bye daddy."

"Cherise, hey it's Willie. If it makes you happy, I just wanted to let you know I called Reed and I'm flying out in a week or so to see him for a few days. Promise me you can resist the urge to tell him about my situation until I have a chance to tell him in person, ok?"

Little did Willie know; Hope had already told Reed.

"That's fine, I am glad you called him, and I hope you two have a nice visit. Tell him hello for me. How are you feeling?"

"Still among the living," said Willie, as they ended the conversation.

Willie decided it was best to get these things out of the way and out in the open. Maybe, he thought it would give him some peace in his remaining time once everyone was clued in about his departure. Then he'd only have his own demise to address. It was time to check in with Vera anyway, so he called to have her make time for him. Willie had put Vera in a position now where she had capable staff under her and she was good with delegating authority. She deserved the assistance, yet she was still at the helm and Willie respected her time. He had never established an office for himself in any of the multiple assisted living centers he owned. As always, he still believed, he served best by making his presence known and felt by roaming the halls and visiting with the hundreds of guests that he knew on a first name basis. It amazed many of the staff and family members of his guests and they appreciated the care they knew he insisted on in all of his centers. He realized now many of the guests were not longer for the world than he was so he could be empathetic with them.

Willie dialed Vera's direct number, that only he knew, as to sidestep her receptionist.

"Vera, it's Willie, how is everything, fine, I'm sure."

"Everything is normal and normal in this business is good". Said Vera.

"Well, I need to come in and discuss the abnormal with you Vera. It's time we sat down and planned some preparation for my imminent demise."

"God, Willie I'm still not sure I've come to grips with this all. It's so sad."

"Yes, I guess it's sad, but also true and inevitable. I've decided I need to get prepared about a few things while I still am capable of it. I think it will make my "exit stage left" somewhat easier for me."

"Of course, Willie. You alone would know, and you alone have the right to make the decision you feel best. I'll make time for you whenever it is best for you to come in Willie."

"Thanks Vera. I'm flying out to spend a few days with Reed in a week or so. I'll call you to set some time up when I get back."

"That's fine. Have a good visit with your son and enjoy the surf and sun. Call me when you're back."

They both hung up in silence.

"Hope it's dad", how's your day going?"

"Fine so far, too early to tell really since it's only 7 AM," laughed Hope. "Sorry, you know me. The early bird gets the worm."

"Yeah, but the second mouse gets the cheese" countered Hope.

"You're right there, sweetie, I'm calling to see if Saturday night works for us to have dinner together?" Hope mentally scanned her appointment calendar and determined that yes, Saturday was open.

"Sure, I can make it, where are we going anyway, so I know how to dress?"

"How about The Grill at the Ritz Carlton?"

"Sounds good to me, you may have to wear matching socks then daddy."

"I'll start digging for a pair. I'll pick you up at 7:00 if you can be ready by then?"

"I can make that."

With that, they both said their goodbyes.

Willie sat back, pleased with himself that he had that set up. He would make it fun for both of them. The phone rang while he was relaxing on his rear deck scanning the river for pleasure crafts that would soon be making their trips south to warmer waters. It was Dale on the line.

"Hey Willie, I heard the news."

"Hell, had Cherise told him too, wondered Willie?"

"I've been meaning to talk to you. It's not great news."

"You're taking this way to hard. Hell, everyone deals with it. Lighten up."

"You know yourself I have the exact same issue and I deal with it. You'll get over it. We might as well enjoy it and live it up, there's nothing we can do about it." Willie could not confess to this level of gaiety about his situation.

"You seem a little down, it's only another birthday for the two of us. Let's go to Malley's and pester Lisa. We'll get our free birthday beer." Willie laughed, when he realized Dale had been talking about the birthday they shared.

Yeah, a birthday was definitely not as bad as dying. Willie was really regretting adding October 2nd to his" list of lasts", but a visit to Malley's would do him some good. He could add the self-medication to the pile of drugs doctor Mike had prescribed for him. He would still have to pick a day to tell Dale the real story though. Though not today, today was his last birthday.

"I'll meet you there after the lunch crowd, so we have plenty of time to give Lisa hell."

"She's not bad at fending for herself," said Dale, as he closed his cell phone.

Willie decided to take the Harley to Malley's. The best riding weather would be over soon, and over soon forever for him. Friends of his had asked him before when he would ever decide to give up riding especially at his age. He just told them, you don't stop riding because you get old, you get old because you stop riding. He knew there was some truth in their advice though, especially nowadays with all the distractions of texting and driving. He knew an "oh shit" situation in a car was survivable, but the same situation on a bike could make you the guest of honor at the local funeral home. Yet, he couldn't give it up, nor did he bother to explain the appeal to non-riders. They would never understand. Yes, it was a risk reward type of activity, but there are lots of those. Maybe he thought, the risk could become his reward and take him out. Wouldn't that be something, not living long enough to die of cancer.

As Willie pulled into the parking lot of Malley's he saw Dale had arrived before him. He parked the bike and went in. Dale was just positioning himself at the bar as Willie took the stool beside him.

"Happy birthday buddy," Dale said to Willie.

"Back at you. How did we ever get this old?"

"Well said Dale, we didn't fucking, die."

"Die? That's the last thing I'll ever do," joked Willie.

Lisa approached the two. Willie could tell she was in a mood for sass. Good.

"We'd like two beers and I'm telling you now, we're not paying for them," Dale told her.

"That's a new one, you guys never tip for shit, but you usually at least pay for what you drink."

"Well, we're not paying for these two. These are our free birthday beers."

"I see old people trying that crap all the time. One guy comes in here and claims it's his birthday once a month. He'd have to be about 200 years old if that were true."

"And why 2 beers. Don't tell me you two have the same birthday."
"Stranger things have happened, said Willie, but you got it."

"That might explain why you both are equally obnoxious. "Who's the older one here anyway?"

"That honor belongs to Willie, I'm the youngest here."

"Right, you're both a pair of fossils, the combined age between you two must be about 190."

"Willie, did you hear that? Combined age, wow, there is a chance she might pass her GED test one day after all.

"I think her daughter Shannon is probably just reading her bedtime stories about what happens in school after 5th grade."

"Better late than never I guess," laughed Dale.

"Fuck you guys," she said as she set the beers in front of them.

"Do you two need bibs, in case you start dribbling while you're drinking? I can't believe you two were born on the same day."

"It's true, I'll admit they did lower the flags to half-mast that day."

"That's right, when my great- great grandmother was a child, she distinctly remembered there were only about a dozen stars on the flag that day," laughed Lisa.

"Go to work, you got a customer waiting."

"I hope he's a paying one, finally."

"Really Willie, how have you been? I haven't been to your Taj Mahal lately."

"I need to have you stop by soon because there's something I want to talk to you about."

"I'm telling you right now, no matter who she is don't marry her. It might not even be your kid", joked Dale.

"What would I do without your advice. It's car stuff so find an open day."

"Let me guess, its fall and you need help putting on all the hard tops."

"Yeah, that's it," said Willie.

"I knew there was an ulterior motive. But what are friends for? I always say a friend in need, is a pain in the ass."

"Ah, Dale, you know I have all the friends I can use."

"Just pick the day. A day when you'll have a few beers in the fridge."

"It will be a week or so. I'm flying to California to see Reed and play a little golf, and this weekend I have a dinner date with Hope."

"Good for you, what's up? "Your birthday making you decide to connect with the kids a bit?"

"No just thought it was time to do it. Birthdays are ok. No biggie."

"Yeah, they're ok every now and then, but too many of them can kill you."

"She's coming back, let's give her some more shit."

They spent their afternoon having a good time, like lifelong friends will do.

CHAPTER SIX

WILLIE CALLED HOPE IN THE MORNING TO TELL her he was looking forward to their dinner this evening and to remind her he would pick her up at 7:00 o'clock. He was sure this call was too early for her, especially on a Saturday morning but what the hell. get up and face the day he thought. She could always go back to sleep. Willie had mixed feelings about their dinner together tonight. It was something that they didn't do often. People could say there were fathers who had closer relations with their kids than Willie did, but no one could say they cared for their children more than Willie cared for his. With Hope he knew there would be moments of laughter and tears, teasing and inner reflections. Cherise was right, he and Hope were closer kindred spirits than he and Reed were, and he really didn't know why. She was more of a free spirit than Reed, and Willie could closer align himself with her, though he cared for them both equally.

Cherise was wrong. His best suit was not at the cleaners in readiness for his funeral. He still had it and he put it on. Some would say snakeskin boots don't go with a suit. To that Willie would say, Why Not. There were people who cut a more dashing appearance, but Willie believed every day in life was a compromise. So, he traded the six pack abbs, for a few indulgences, to which he would say. Why Not. You only live once, and that realization had been made to him clear enough. Though he stayed in shape, the body of his youth was gone. Actually, he still looked fit, somewhat.

He had decided to pick up Hope in what he knew was her favorite car of his. Earlier in the day he had gone in the garage and verified its readiness.

He raised the full forward folding bonnet of the XKE, exposing a meticulously maintained engine. The inline 6-cylinder, 4.3-liter, dual overhead camshaft engine was a thing of beauty. The twin polished stainless cam cover boxes on top of the engine with its multiple side draft carburetors was a thing of engineering awe. The car was unconditionally red with polished chrome wire wheels that were blindingly bedazzling. It was the 2+2, XKE coupe model that represented the epitome of Jaguars one-time dominance of automotive excellence. The engine was mated to what the British referred to as a gearbox, a four-speed manual transmission. To Willie, an automatic in a car like this would literally be sacrilegious. The leather interior was incredibly supple. Its hides were taken from pampered cattle, raised on farms where the perimeter was fenced without barbed wire so their hides could not be scratched in preparation of their readiness to one day adorn the seating of the finest cars that England could produce. The car reeked of opulence and sophistication yet the engine still provided a throaty sound from its exhaust, reminiscent of the car's racing heritage. It truly was the special occasion car. It was the one car in Willie's collection, that although admired by the true afficionados, he often received the," You rich prick, salute," to which Willie just smiled, tipped his head, gave the two finger wave and continued to motor on.

His other cars, some of them equally valuable, were given a pass because of their representation of true American muscle cars. This foreigner had only it's expanded pedigree to defend itself with. An off the rack Porsche had nothing on it.

As the afternoon passed, Willie was almost relieved that Cherise had done what he told her not to. At least Hope already knew the news. He would be able to bypass that icebreaker in the conversation. God, how he loved his kids. He often felt guilty burdening their young lives with his issue. Sure, kids were meant to bury their parents, not the other way around, but is the time really here already for that. Fuck, I'm going to die. Willie knew he needed to step up and keep his inner most thoughts about all this to himself. After all, whose problem was it other than his own? The time had come to pick up Hope. He entered the garage. He smiled as he glanced at the personalized license plate, a WHY-NOT. He got in the jaguar and fired it up. The mechanical sound of the historic engine was music to his ears. He didn't care if others didn't appreciate it or understand this thrill. It was a thrill to him. He backed the car out of the garage, drove down his long driveway, out his gate to the street and headed for Hope's home.

He parked in the street in front of her condo and walked to the door. He rang her bell, and she immediately opened the door.

"Hi daddy, I'm ready."

"Wow," said Willie, but no you're not. You look incredible, as she truly did, but you need to hang a sign on you that says "I'm his daughter," to save the embarrassment of people thinking I am paying for your company by the hour. You are stunning. Where did my little tom girl go?"

"Do you miss her?"

"More than words can say, but the transformation is acceptable."

"I'm glad you approve daddy."

"What's not to approve? Brains and beauty and all rolled together."

"You look kind of nice too daddy."

"Well thanks for saying so," responded Willie.

"I'm glad you do look nice. Then I won't feel so odd being with an old buzzard like you."

"The approved term is fossil. You know what I always liked about you Hope?"

"No, what might that be?"

"Nothing. laughed Willie, let's go."

When Hope saw the Jaguar, she admired the honor it was. She immediately approached the car on the right side to enter the car.

Willie quickly said, "that's OK, I'll drive," he laughed. True to its British heritage the car was right hand drive. Hope walked around the car to the left side and got in. She had known this about the car, but it seemed so unnatural that it was an easy mistake to make. Driving a right-hand drive car on American roadways creates some unique situations. Driving the car wasn't that strange once you got used to the fact that you also had to operate the gear shift with your left hand instead of your right. One issue boarded on being dangerous. If you were on a Sunday drive on a two-lane road behind someone who had decided to take their car out for a walk, passing them could be interesting. To get a good viewpoint if the road was clear to pass you had to creep the car crossed the center line until you could see if there was oncoming traffic. More than once, Willie had to quickly return the car back to this right to avoid being side swiped while he was taking his look. Worse of course would be a head on collision. This was the primary reason Willie rarely allowed anyone but himself to drive this car. Hope had been with guys who had the "look at me" cars, as she called them. They had them to appease their own ego, but she knew with her dad that was not the case. He truly enjoyed and respected his cars for what they were. With him, she knew it had nothing to do with himself. Looking for Mr. Right was going to be a tough act to follow, sighed Hope.

As Willie negotiated through traffic, Hope said," I think I'm about to cry already."

"If you do that, I'm going to make you pay for dinner."

"Well, you offered up the right deterrent, since I probably couldn't afford to pay for this excursion."

"You don't have to worry about that, but from what I hear, you'd be more than capable of it." Willie knew she was doing well. I'm especially proud of you for having pulled yourself up by your own bootstraps."

"Daddy, we both know you helped fill the boots when it was needed, and I'm grateful even if I have never told you so."

"That does make me wonder about something though?" asked Willie.

"What's that?"

"Do high heels have bootstraps?"

They both laughed. Seeing his daughter laugh. Priceless he thought.

Willie eased the car under the portico of the hotel near the valet stand. The valet approached and mistakenly opened Willie's door first. An honest mistake, not expecting the car to be right hand drive. He quickly circled the car and opened the door for Hope. Once out of the car, Willie opened his wallet, removed a large denomination bill and tore it in half. He handed half of the bill to the valet.

"Bring her back tiptop mate, and the other half is yours. Keep eyes on her as if she were truly Her Majesty's own. Willie and Hope headed for the awaiting doorman.

"Sir? Willie turned and said, "of course, as he flipped the keys to the already salivating valet drive".

"Good one daddy. Bond right, James Bond, right? asked Hope.

"Ah sweetie, I'm afraid my 007 days are far behind me."

"Don't sell yourself short. In this all-inclusive world we now live in, it might be time for a secret agent in a walker."

"That thought alone, I'm sure would keep everyone shaken, but not stirred, and do you know what I always liked about you Hope?"

"Yeah, I know nothing," laughed Hope as they entered the alcove of the restaurant to the reservation desk.

Willie knew the table spacing in the dining room was gracious, but he had still requested a corner table to hopefully provide as much privacy as possible. They were led to a table he requested. As always, Willie took what he called the gangster seat with his back to the wall, facing the entrance. It wasn't that he thought he was worth shooting, it's just had always been a quirk of his. Whereas William Randolph Hearst always chose any seat at a formal affair, foregoing the seat at the head of table where he would always be welcome and be expected to be placed. His reply was," wherever I sit is the head of the table. "

As soon as they were seated the Maître D arrived at their table with a vase of fresh cut flowers. A little confused the Maître D said, "My note says these are for the hopeless one."

"Well, this evening that would be me, but the flowers are for my daughter, Hope."

The Maître D placed the vase of flowers on the table, much to the envious glances of other female diners.

"Really daddy, flowers too?"

"Why not?" said Willie.

A waiter approached their table.

"Mr. Lovd, I'll be serving you this evening."

"First, call me Willie. When you say Mr. Lovd, I expect to turn around and see my father, and secondly you are not expected to serve my daughter and I. All you need to do is help me navigate the trappings of the evening."

"Sorry, Mr. Lovd, I mean Willie, but as you might suspect we cater to a somewhat haughtier clientele."

"You can rest easy. We're not haughty, just hungry."

All three chuckled at that. "We're just Willie and Hope, and what did you say your name was?"

"It's Glenn."

"Well Glenn, I'm sure you're going to do just fine."

"Can I start you off with some drinks?" He took Hope's order first.

"I'll have a gin martini, very dry, shaken not stirred." Hope winked at the waiter. Glenn grinned as he caught the reference. Willie ordered a glass of house Merlot with a rock glass of ice on the side.

"Very well," said Glenn, I'll be back with those and some menus."

"I'm sure I'll be dining from the carnivorous selection, but Hope will have to see your offerings of all things to eat that never had a face."

"Ah, a more common request every day. And our chef can accommodate. We are renowned for a few items specifically," said Glenn.

"Yes, it amazes me what can be made delicious out of weeds and twigs," said Willie.

"Very admirably of you Hope, someone has to save the world and if the young won't do it, who will? asked Glenn.

"Nice drink pick, Hope."

"You know dad, you're probably one of the two last people on earth who still drink Merlot, and definitely the last person who drinks red wine over ice."

"To which I say, who's drinking it and who's paying for it", laughed Willie.

Glenn returned with the drinks and the menus, explaining a few new items offered.

"I'll be back to take your orders."

"Thanks Glenn, no rush."

"Of course, Sir, sorry, Willie, I mean."

"Glenn, never apologize for your professionalism, it's just that it's wasted on me."

"I can tell it will be a pleasure to be your waiter this evening," said Glenn. He left the two to themselves.

An uncomfortable silence, fell over them. Both their minds were in search mode wondering how conversations about what brought them together tonight would begin.

"Tell me about your latest man quest, Hope, there must be many."

"Not as many as you might think."

"That has to be a situation of your own choosing."

"I called Reed. I'm flying out to see him in a week or so. I'm really looking forward to it."

"I'm sure you two will have a great time catching up."

"Do you see your mom often enough, as a loyal daughter should?"

"Oh, yeah, often enough, but she can stay pretty busy herself."

Both knew the small talk would not sustain them. Glenn brought the menus, and they made their selections.

"All good" said Glenn, as he headed for the kitchen to turn in their request. It was quiet again. Then Willie spoke.

"Let's dance."

Hope laughed, "in here, we can't dance in here," to which Willie replied, "Why Not?"

"Well for one thing, there's no music."

"Sure, there is. There's always music."

"Are you serious? It may not even be allowed."

"Then let's not ask for permission."

Willie rose and extended his hand to help Hope rise from her seat. She looked about questioningly.

The two stepped between the widely spaced tables. Willie put his hand on the small of her back as he glided her through the open spaces. There was faint background music playing.

"See, I told you there was music."

"I'm surprised you can even hear it," said Hope.

"I can hear it plenty well."

The two slow danced to the music. Initially much to the dismay of the roomful of diners. Soon however the looks of bewilderment turned to glances of awe.

"You know daddy, I don't think we've ever danced before, at least not since I was three or four and just stood on your feet as you led me around the living room."

"Then it's time we did. I'm not about to be denied the father daughter dance with the bride one day." Hope knew what he meant. As the song was ending, Willie gave Hope a kiss on each cheek.

"I also can't remember anytime you ever even gave me a peck on the cheek."

It was true. It just wasn't in Willie's genealogy to show open displays of affection with his kids. He always blamed it on it being a "German thing".

"I still haven't given you a kiss."

"I believe you most certainly did, two as a matter of fact."

"No Hope, they weren't for you. I want you to pass them on to my grandkids one day, when I'm long gone. Tell them they were from their grandpa."

"You'll promise to do that for me, won't you Hope?"

"Of course, I will daddy, as she sniffed back a tear."

"I am glad you stopped with two kisses though." Two will be enough for me."

"I thought once myself two were enough for me too but, when I discovered how wonderful you two turned out, I often wished there would have been a dozen."

"I doubt mom would have gone for that." They both laughed as the dance ended.

They returned to their table amid light applause from the crowded room to which Willie bowed from the waist, floating his arm as Hope curtsied to the crowd. They took their seats.

Glenn approached and asked if they'd like a new round of drinks. To which Hope said, "after that, hell yeah! "

"Actually, it was quite touching. I hope you are celebrating a joyous occasion, said Glenn. Your meals will be ready soon."

"A monumental one," said Willie.

"I don't know why I was ever surprised you would ask me to dance in a dining room full of people. You always did the things that others would have thought were insane, but you did them anyway. You seemed to have this, who says I can't attitude, not in a pretentious way, but you always had this larger-than-life attitude, that allows you to pull off stuff others wouldn't consider doing. It's refreshing and I feel myself trying to lean that way in my life sometimes. I mean after all we only live …" Hope caught herself before she finished the sentence.

"It's just one of those things you taught me daddy."

"Stop the presses. You mean I taught you something. Who would have thought it?" joked Willie.

"You taught me more than you know. You don't think that is something a know-it-all teenage daughter would ever have admitted to her father, do you? It's like what Mark Twain said, "when I was 14, I thought my father was the dumbest person on earth, it's amazing how smart he got by the time I turned 21." Willie was touched by this revelation. He never thought he was the teaching type with his kids. It was in a trying time once in my career, and I was unsure if I could fulfill my obligation. It was all to new and foreign to me. Then I remembered something you had said once.

"What might that have been, pray tell?" asked Willie.

"Quite simply you told me, "If someone else can do something, why do you think you can't". "It really rocked me to action. That's right, I thought if someone else can do it, I can do it too.

"Don't get too big a head though. There was plenty of silliness to go along with your words of wisdom. You always did have a way of reducing everything to its lowest common denominator though. You would just cut through all the crap that seems to surround everything and get to the heart of the matter. That's a gift I'm trying to unwrap for myself," said Hope.

"It's true, I guess, but sometimes when getting things to their lowest common denominator, you can lose something in the subtraction process. Things that can't be recovered."

Their meals arrived and they ate in relative silence.

"How are your weeds? asked Willie.

"Incredible" said Hope, "Are you enjoying our four-footed friends."

"Arf, arf." replied Willie.

"At least your meal selection should leave you room for dessert."

"Not sure, I am up for that," said Hope.

"Oh yes you are. I pre-ordered it and I'm sure Glenn will have it here in a bit."

After their tableware was cleared, Glenn appeared at the table with two individual presentations of Creme Brule'. Willie knew it was Hope's dream desert. Glenn placed them on the table and from his server cart he produced a stainless butane torch and asked Willie if he should?

"Oh yes", said Willie, let's burn the witches. With that Glenn let the torch and lightly turned the topping of the Brule to a golden hue, warming the insides to a decadent level of heat. "Bon Appetite" said Glenn as he left the table.

"This is too much daddy,"

"No, it's not, and Why Not?"

Upon finishing their desert, Glenn approached and asked, if there was anything else they would like?

"I think we're finished, Glenn, just bring the damage."

"Of course," said Glenn.

At the check presentation Willie left a generous gratuity. "Buy yourself something nice Glenn, you were fantastic."

"With the amount of your generosity, I will actually be able to do that."

"It was well earned," said Willie.

"But beyond my expectations! I do hope we will see you all again sometime soon. I'll have the valet bring up your car."

"That would be wonderful," said Willie as they rose to go. Hope picked up the vase of fresh flowers and they headed for the exit. The Jag was already parked at the curb waiting for them. From his pocket Willie produced the torn matching half of the bill and handed it to the valet as he went to open the door for Hope.

"She looks fine," said Willie.

"Thanks, she's a dream, she must be a joy to you?"

"She sure is" said Willie, and the car is an enjoyment to me also."

"Of course, Sir."

"It's Willie, just Willie," said Willie, as he got in the car to leave.

Thankfully this was the 2+2 model and not a Jag roadster. He told Hope she could place the flower behind the seat if she liked.

"No, I want to hold them" she said.

"Ok" said Willie, it just looks like you're being swallowed up by a botanical garden or something."

"I'm fine. They're beautiful, and I can't begin to tell you how wonderful of a time I had. I'll remember it as long as I live."

"I will too, said Willie, it just won't be as much a strain for my memory as it will be for yours."

"Dad, you seem to be able to joke about all this. I don't see how you can."

"Hope, what else can I really do?

"I know, but it must be hard for you."

"What is?" asked Willie.

"Well, the fact that you're dying, of course."

"You seem to be able to reduce everything to the lowest common denominator, wherever did you learn that?" asked Willie.

"I'm sorry, it's just too sad to comprehend, and too hard to imagine it's true. You have always been larger than life."

"Well Hope, I'm not. I'm sorry Hope, I didn't mean for that to sound so, well mean."

"Your forgiven, I wouldn't know how I could ever be able to conduct myself if the shoe were on the other foot," said Hope.

"You know daddy, in the restaurant I told you just a few of the things you ever taught me. Now once again, you know more about a subject than I do. I wish you were able to help me understand what it's really like.

"Knowing, what it feels like to know you're going to die?

It's not something I'm thrilled to be able to teach, and no one living could tell me, if I were right about it or not. Discovering the fact that you are dying is really about discovering life in a way. Dying makes one think about living."

"I'd still like to hear your thoughts, dad," pleaded Hope.

"You don't need to concern yourself, with thoughts about dying, Hope, you need to concentrate on thoughts about living, please," said Willie.

"All I've learned is what everyone has always been told their whole life. The same things that you and I have been told and heard many times, but we don't listen or take the advice, nor does the person who's even giving the clues. The lessons are too simplistic to be given any weight. Life is way bigger than death, then one day it isn't."

"Haven't you ever been told or heard life's smallest pleasures are the best. That the most important things, are not things, they are your family and friends. Haven't you ever been told to slow down, stop and smell the roses. Treat others as you would want to be treated. Look for joy in your life, not hate. Be a friend, not an enemy, help your neighbor, do some random acts of kindness. Such simple things, if they were more complicated then maybe people would take them more seriously and put them into action, yet all assume they are too simple to possibly mean anything. Well, Hope, they do mean something. They mean everything."

"Surely you can give me a greater revelation than that."

"Well, Hope there is no greater revelation."

"Do you have regrets, dad?"

"Yes, I have regrets, but I have learned to forget the cringe- worthy moment of life that everyone has had, or most people will have. I've learned to let them go. Where once they held sway over me, thinking they defined me, I've come to the conclusion they didn't. They were just a part of my life, shit that happens. Hey, I made a mistake or two."

"I regret not spending more time with you kids most of all. Family is everything, maybe the only thing. Hope, do you realize of the billions and billions of people on earth a family is an oddity. That a half a dozen people are thrown together by fate. They spend their lives together amid billions of other people they will never meet. It's just them. To not cherish that, or to do anything to jeopardize that is pure insanity.

Hold onto each other for the speck of time you're blessed with. My greatest regret might be that I have to die to realize this myself. Don't let that happen to the family of people you take the ride through life with. I should have been closer."

"Dad, you were always there when we needed you. Maybe you weren't there to help me find my socks in the morning before school. Maybe you weren't in the house every morning when I got up or every night when I went to bed, but I never felt I was ever without your love and protection if I needed it. That's a lot more than many of my friends can say even with parents who weren't divorced, but maybe should have been. The world is going to miss you, you daddy."

"Don't be silly, no it won't, why should it? Soon I'll be gone, and the world will go on just fine without me. What have I ever done for it? Maybe I did more good than harm but, I didn't exactly spend my life rescuing everyone on the planet."

"Really daddy, not everyone is sent here to save the world, but look at all the lives of people you've improved. Think about all the jobs you've created for people. You gave them jobs to feed and house their family and send their kids to school. They had jobs so they could care for relatives when they were sick. You strengthen the bond of so many families so they could enjoy the thing you call an oddity, a group of people among the billions. I won't let you think your life didn't serve a purpose here."

"They would have gotten a job someplace else."

"Yes, they might have, and they could always have chosen to leave you if they wanted to but very few did. They did have a choice of where to work and they chose to work for you."

"You're too kind, Hope."

"It's true daddy."

"I still regret not having made a more profound impact on people's lives." Willie parked the car, as they arrived at Hope's condo. Hope started to cry.

"Please don't cry, Hope."

"I can cry now, you already paid for dinner."

"I'll tell you one other thing I've just come to marvel at in the past few months that I never would have if I hadn't found out about my untimely demise."

"What's that?"

"Again, with life being all consuming it's not going to seem like a great discovery but I'm basking in it, and I wish I would have done so my whole life. I guess it goes hand in hand with not taking things for granted. It's really just the marvels of the physical world itself. Think about it. Can you imagine if the sky was any color other than blue? What other color could it possibly be? The same for the ocean waters. Could you imagine an orange sea, or grass not being green, or the night sky not being black, sprinkled only with glowing stars. This had to be by Grand Design. Colors to me are now so vibrant. When once I saw a tree, all I saw was a brown stick with a clump of green on top. Now I stare at a tree so intently I can see a trail of ants marching between the bark. This world is incredibly beautiful, making it much sadder to be leaving it. I wish I could have you see it, but I think it's a gift only death can grant and wonderfully it's not your time. Do what you can to see it for yourself now. Strain your eyes, and your mind. It's there and it's beautiful."

"And Hope, live more. No one on their death bed ever said, "Gee I wish I had made another million. I've had a great life, better than I deserve, so I should be content. And Hope, don't waste time hating. If you plant bananas, you harvest bananas, if you plant hate, you harvest hate."

"It still seems ungraspable. All the things you've done, and even now are still doing. How it must feel knowing that it is all coming to a close. I'm going to miss you daddy. No matter how nonchalant you seem about it." Then came the question. "Aren't you afraid of dying."

The silence hung in the air, before Willie said, "No Hope, I'm not afraid of dying. I'm just afraid of not living anymore." He knew, she knew what he meant. He had taught her the difference between living and just existing.

"Come on, grab your petunias and I'll walk you to your door."

"Yes Bond, James Bond, right?"

There was still some night left so Willie decided to stop at Malley's. It was Lisa's turn to work the night shift.

Lisa barely recognized him in his attire.

"Whose funeral," joked Lisa.

"Mine" laughed Willie, seven and seven short, piece of lemon and make it hurt."

"You got it. It's been a special night in here too."

"Dale, it's Willie. I'm flying out to California to see Reed in the morning. Let's get together when I get back. I'm only going for the weekend."

"OK buddy, sounds good, and if you're not already a member of the Mile High Club, take a shot if it presents itself, but I'm afraid membership has been closed for you. See you when you get back."

Chapter Seven

Reed waited in the terminal pickup area for his dad to come out. Willie had called and said his plane had just landed, so he would be outside in a few minutes. Reed knew it would take his best poker face, to pretend he didn't already know the real reason for Willie's trip to see him. Hope had already told him.

Reed felt sorry for the old man. He knew his dad had probably spent many sleepless nights trying to figure out how he was going to break the news to him, news Reed already knew anyway.

Willie spotted Reed as he stepped out of the terminal door. Reed had gotten out and opened the rear hatch for his dad's luggage. Reed knew at least his car would offer the icebreaker.

"At least it's not a tan minivan," joked Willie, as he shook his head at the car.

"Oh, just fine, and how are you, welcome to California dad," laughed Reed.

"I'm good, and it's great to see you. It's been too long."

"What is this anyway?" Willie asked, as he got in the vehicle.

"It's a car dad, just a car. It does everything a car needs to do. It got me here, and it will get us there. That's all a car is for," laughed Reed.

"Bite your tongue, where's the thrill?" asked Willie.

"I'm thrilled I rarely have to go to the gas station."

"Don't worry, I have a friend who has a dealership in Anaheim. I'll have him send you something without a back seat or a roof, maybe something red. You need a trunk?" They both laughed. Willie knew Reed had not adopted an interest in cars, other than one that will get him from point A to point B. They had long ago agreed to disagree about cars.

"You look great dad. Willie always did, and he still had a spring in his step that belied his age. Reed could not think of a single time his dad had ever been sick of anything. I guess he was saving it all for the grand finale. His dad was the type who would be just fine until the very end, until one day he would wake up and be dead, but now, like a lot of people Willie still seemed outwardly to be too well to be dying and supposedly soon. Jesus, how is he going to bring this up, wondered Reed. "Great putt son, I'll be dead by Christmas. Let's eat."

Willie had taken Reed's advice and had set his arrival time, when traffic was lighter, if you could call this light. Reed had no problem negotiating the drive to his condo. Not surprisingly Reed's condo was in the minimalist style. Reed was never one to hold onto or collect things. People say everyone collects something. It would be a mystery to try and tell what Reed collected. It represents an efficiency that made life simple. If you don't need it, get rid of it. Willie often wondered if that included himself. Where Reed and Willie were alike was in holding their thoughts to themselves. Reed had to grow up mostly without a father in the house and it made him self-sufficient. It wasn't the easiest of times. He never developed a relationship with Willie that some of his friends had with their dads. Something always seemed to be missing and Reed, just like Willie, could not figure out what it was. It wasn't the best, but then again, Reed also new friends of his who had relationships with their fathers that were way worse than the relationship he had with a somewhat absentee dad that he had.

Reed wasn't incredibly close to Cherise either. They just weren't that type of family. He never worried about not being cared for or feeling unprotected. He knew both parents were always there for him, yet it was subversive. Everyone kind of fended for themselves until help was needed, then it was always there. Reed had long ago decided this was fine. Others had way more things to complain about than he did. While there was always money in the house when he was growing up both parents took the position, that they would always give their kids everything they needed but not always everything they wanted. Reed was glad it worked that way. Now all his achievements were his own. He was already reaching a point of self-actualization, as was Hope. She had also been exposed to the same upbringing.

"Nice place Reed. I like it better than the last one. Is the day trading kicking in a little bit too? "

"Somewhat, but I mostly stick to my assigned duties at the brokerage."

"I gave up on the market awhile back. My strategy wasn't working out," admitted Willie.

"What strategy was that?"

"Buying high and selling low," laughed Willie.

"Yeah, not the best game plan for sure."

"Now I'm into investments that accelerated," joked Willie.

"Great kitchen, but don't fire it up. Let's go out. Take me to your favorite place."

"I'll pretend I'm not you dad."

"I'm not ruining a hot date night, am I"

"No, I'm good to go tonight," said Reed.

"Great, I'm ready. You are driving that thing though?"

"You just love giving me crap about that don't you?"

"Not to worry, the red heart throb from Anaheim should show up soon," joked Willie.

Reed and Willie walked to the car. Nice area, great condo, no garage. Impossible situation, thought Willie.

"Are you sure you don't want to drive," offered Reed.

"I would try it but I'm not risking the paparazzi getting a photo of me driving that. My reputation would be history."

"Where are we going?" asked Willie as they drove off, not that Willie really cared.

"It's not far. A local place, you'll like it"

"Why is that? Is there stuff on the menu I'll recognize?"

"Believe it or not, you will think it's kind of normal."

"Yeah, I'm amazed everyday about what is now the normal," laughed Willie.

Reed parked and they went in. It actually did seem normal. The bartender asked for their drinks. Reed said," I'll have a corona." And my dad who will be dead by Christmas, but can't figure out how to tell me, will have a seven and seven, short with a piece of lemon.

Actually, he did order a corona and Willie took a beer also. The bartender placed the check receipt down and Willie saw the two beers came to 19 dollars.

"Damn that isn't normal," laughed Willie.

"Now I'm really glad to know you're doing well. I think it's a matter of necessity"

"Everything is kind of relative to where you are. The prices out here are high but so are the salaries. Everyone is just playing with bigger numbers."

"How the hell can people afford to get drunk out here?" They looked at the menu. Willie commented that you can actually eat cheaper than you can drink.

"You're acting a little impoverished dad. Do you need me to loan you a few bucks?" teased Reed.

"No, I'm good," laughed Willie. It's just sticker shock sometimes. It's caused by being cursed with a good memory, recalling when you could get the whole cow for $24, and the farmer's daughter was included."

Willie picked up that Reed was a regular here. Occasionally a friend would stop by and Reed actually introduced Willie as being his dad. Of course, his dad who lives in some backwater swamp, just to tease Willie.

They ordered another round of drinks. Willie was glad to see drinking was a controlled situation for Reed. There was so much to be proud of, with both his kids. They talked about everything and nothing. Reed had set a tee time for the two of them in the morning, so they decided to call it a night.

"I better get you in the sack, so you'll have even a remote chance of beating me tomorrow," said Reed.

"Don't worry about that. Just get me to your place before the paparazzi starts hounding me."

Reed was glad Willie saved breaking the news this evening. It had been a lot of good-hearted fun. That was a rare occasion between the two and Reed knew opportunities like this would soon be gone.

"I borrowed a set of clubs for you to use dad." Who's this Nancy Lopez player, anyway?"

"Real funny Reed, and she was before your time."

"What does matter. You only use the irons anyway."

"That's all I'll need to beat you.

"Dream on dad, dream on."

Reed and Willie walked out of the pro shop to their cart and headed for the first tee. As Willie teed up his ball, Reed commented, "it's 450 yards dad, you sure you don't want to use a driver?"

"No sense starting anything new now." Willie did place a long shot to the center of the fairway however. Reed's shot with the driver flew far past Willie's. The game was afoot. Willie played with earnest, but he could care less if he won or lost. That conclusion had already been foredrawn anyway. He was just there to spend time with Reed and enjoy the beautiful surroundings and the perfect weather, and to tell his son, he would soon be more father-less than ever before.

After a few holes, Willie announced proudly that at least he hadn't lost a ball yet.

"I guess not, said Reed, "you don't hit them far enough for them to go out of sight."

"I think the problem is, you have home course advantage."

"Yeah, I'm sure that's it," said Reed.

"How do you find time to play this much golf? Aren't you supposed to be working out here?"

"Keep swinging dad, keep swinging." Reed could tell that Willie did have a little check to his stride, and occasionally stopped to catch an extra breath of air. That was different from normal but then he had gotten older since they last played. He could be fine, if Reed didn't already know he wasn't. Reed was enjoying this outing and for once didn't have awkward feelings between the two of them. In a way they were both letting go of the past.

"Where's the scorecard dad?"

"You're not going to believe this, but while we were both away from the cart, a pelican actually came up and snatched it from the cart. I'm serious, but I think the score was pretty close. You know in the Midwest we don't have many pelicans and I had no idea they did shit like that."

"That's it! where's the girl with the drink cart?"

"Little early for the drink cart, isn't it?"

"I'll just drink a mimosa."

"Mimosa, that's a tree, isn't it? "

"No dad, you're thinking of a Formosa. "

"Doesn't matter. Still wouldn't drink it."

It was obvious to Reed, that they would be finishing the 18th hole before Willie delivered the news. It was hard to tell who the tension was greater for. They finished this game, and Willie admitted defeat. "I really thought I might beat you this time," joked Willie. "Let's get your winner drinks in the clubhouse." Here it comes, thought Reed, as he swallowed a lump in his throat. Damn, how is he going to go break the news, wondered Reed?

They took a cafe table on the elevated veranda overlooking the course. A waitress came for a drink order. She asked if they wanted menus and Willie said he was good for now. Reed also declined. Willie ordered his usual and told her to make it hurt. Reed was sure it would. He settled in for a tea. Willie settled for a moment of silence. Reed started to prepare his poker face. When the drinks arrived, Reed saw his dad take a big swig of courage. Who wouldn't, thought Reed? Here it comes.

"You know, I'm flying back tomorrow. I wish I could have stayed and spent more time with you. I've had a great time. I wish I could say I came out here just for this reason, as I should have had more often but it's not the case."

"I need or have to tell you something Reed, that I've been dreading and probably should have told you already." Reed felt it was best not to interrupt his dad as he probably spent a lot of painful time working on a delivery.

"You're not the first person to get this news, so I have found the best way is to just be blunt and come out with it. It's kind of a nonnegotiable situation anyway." There was a pause before Willie spoke. "Reed, early in this year I was diagnosed with cancer and its terminal. I don't have a lot of time left. I understand your silent response and it's probably the most appropriate. Everyone asks the same questions. Are you sure, is there some kind of treatment for it? Have you gotten a second opinion, etc, etc. Your pause about what to say, is the very reason I was hesitant to tell anyone. It hurts me to put people in a position where they don't know what to say. They feel like they need to say something to comfort me. It pains me to have them try to think of something. There's nothing to say, that everyone hasn't already said. I've come to grips with it. No one should have to struggle with it but me. The diagnosis was from my friend Doctor Mike Lillenberg. You know him, he did a few sports physicals for you. Trust me, he beat the bushes to be sure before he told me the news, and I could tell it tore him up both as my doctor and my friend."

"I sometimes thought about just dying without telling anyone, to try and maintain the status quo, if you will, as long as I could, but then I wasn't sure if that wouldn't just have caused more pain or confusion."

"It's OK, Reed, I've been blessed with a half dozen lifetimes compared to a lot of people. I just have been given the insight into knowing when I'm leaving, but trust me, sometimes I think I would have rather been run over by a bus," laughed Willie.

Reed was searching for an emotion, as well as a response. His dad was right. What was there to say about news like this, but he had to say something. Again, his dad was right, it was painful for someone to come up with a response. What really could someone say?

"Well dad, you nailed it. I can't imagine anything I can say that hasn't been said, I'm sure. You've probably also already heard that the news is almost impossible to believe. I'm sure you've gotten offers of help, but I can't imagine how someone can really reverse the situation as you say. I'll say this, I'm stunned though." Reed truly was, even though he had already known the news.

"Both your mom and I wish you could have stayed back home. We would have had more time together, but we knew this was a good opportunity for you."

Reed thought, and if I had stayed would we really have spent more time together or would we both just be living in the same town.

The waitress came and asked about another round of drinks and this time Reed took her up on a real one.

"Dad, right now my mind is racing, and I don't know what to think." Reed's mind had been racing for a week since he first found out, but that hadn't helped him come up with anything either.

"Reed, I love you, so please stop trying." That was a rare expression from Willie, so if Reed had any doubt this situation was as real as it could be, that confirmed it.

"Let's get out of here, before that Pelican drops off the scorecard," joked Willie. And with that they got up to leave.

They drove back to Reed's condo in silence, interrupted only by meaningless small talk. Fuck I'm dying, thought Willie.

"Don't worry Reed, I'm not really having my dealer friend from Anaheim send you a useless red car."

"I know dad, but I appreciate the thought."

"Dad, I don't know if I will ever be able to express how I feel about you.

"Nor me you, but do we really have to?"

"I'm sure I don't have to tell you; you mean the world to me. If I had to tell you, it would come out as trying to convince you it's true, when I hope you already know it is."

"Ditto dad."

"That's good enough to last me a lifetime," said Willie.

"I do have to tell you one thing though dad."

"Yeah, what's that?"

"You suck at golf."

They both laughed, until they both almost cried.

At midafternoon they arrived back at Reed's condo.

"Dad, I hope you don't mind but I have a little something planned for the evening. My girlfriend is going to come over and we were planning on barbequing, I hope you'll join us?"

"What the hell else am I going to do? Take your car for a ride?" laughed Willie.

"I'd enjoy meeting her, but with one promise from you."

"What's that?" asked Reed

"That you don't tell her what I'm sure the three of us all have in common."

"And what is that?"

"First of all, our good looks and charm and secondly the fact that we are all dying, me first."

"It's a deal, let's forget that for tonight." Like that would ever be possible for his dad, Reed thought.

"Do you have stuff here to make margaritas?"

"I'm sure I do."

"Ok, I'm on it," said Willie.

They had a great evening together. Reed could tell that his girlfriend was a little enchanted by his dad, and she made Reed promise to turn out just like him. Willie told Reed, he thought his girlfriend was a keeper, and was glad he had met her.

Willie turned in first, to pack for his return flight in the morning. Willie was up early and had amazed himself by figuring out how to work Reed's space age coffee maker. He had two cups ready to go for the drive to the airport.

"I'm ready when you are," announced Willie. Reed came into the kitchen, grabbed his coffee and they were out the door.

"Last chance, dad, you sure you don't want to drive it?"

"Why not," said Willie, as he accepted the keys from Reed to drive.

"The hell with the paparazzi. They probably aren't up yet this morning anyway." Their last few moments turn to silence again, as Willie followed the signs to the airport.

"Reed, if you can make this work out, I hope you can come back for Thanksgiving. It will probably be my last hurrah, and it would mean a lot to me with all of us being together one more time. I'll have it at my house over the river. Bring your girlfriend if she can escape her own family. I'll have mom there too."

"I can make that work," said Reed as Willie pulled to a drop off spot in front of the terminal. Willie quickly got out and retrieved his luggage before the parking Nazi showed up. As they shook hands to part, Willie handed Reed an envelope.

"I don't need anything dad, really."

"Well, it's not money, said Willie, why would I give you money anyway?"

"It was great seeing you dad. I'm glad you came out."

"I loved every minute of it, said Willie, see you at Thanksgiving," as he turned and walked into the terminal. This he was sure put California on his list of lasts. Before Reed drove off, he opened the envelope. Inside was the scorecard from their golf game. Across it, Willie had scratched, "You'll always be a winner, love Dad."

CHAPTER EIGHT

Dale keyed the number to the entrance gate at Willie's driveway into his phone. He was one of the few who had the code. As the gates swung inward, Dale put his car in gear and drove up the long driveway parking in the courtyard between the two matching garages. Dale had been to Willie's home often. This invite struck him as different though. Willie had had a strange tone to his voice. Who knew, maybe just one too many or one too few beers?

Dale entered the garage. He knew Willie would be inside.

"What the hell is all this?" asked Dale, as he saw Willie's bucket project on the garage's wide workbench. You planning on kicking the bucket soon?" laughed Dale. The silence was too long to be comfortable, for both of them.

"Well Dale, began Willie, I have to fill you in on a little something, and decided it's best to just rip off the bandage and get it out in the open. You're not the last to know, but one of them."

"What the fuck are you talking about? jabbed Dale. Don't be messing with me, one of the last to know what?"

"Dale, I've known for a while that I have cancer, and don't make me have to explain it to you like I have already done to everyone else.

Yes, it's terminal. Being the good friend that you are I was torn between telling you sooner or keeping you out of the loop. I didn't somehow want you to hear it from someone else. I feel you deserved to at least hear it straight from me."

"You're being serious, aren't you? Damn, I guess that explains you getting together with your kids, and now I do recall you backing out a time or two for a drink, to see Doctor Mike. I really never put two and two together. I just thought you were being a regular "old fuck".

"Something we both have in common," joked Willie.

"Yeah hell, I wonder sometimes how we ever got this old in the first place."

"Well, we didn't die," laughed Willie.

"And who you calling old?"

"You've got to give me a minute Willie. This is coming off as one hell of a kick in the gut."

"Yeah well, it has been for me too, trust me."

"How long have you known this anyway?"

"Over six months already, but just started to let the news out lately." I told Cherise first, then Hope and Reed. Vera knows. Strategic planning, you know and my pastor, Ron. You know him."

"Oh yeah, I see him sometimes on Sunday's, usually at the gas station in town," joked Dale.

"Everyone has pretty much honored my request to let me tell people in my own time and in my own way, but time is not something I have a lot of."

"Damn, damn," sighed Dale as he shook his head. I'm speechless., Willie."

"It's best that you are. It pains me to see people struggle to come up with something to say."

"No, no, this can't be."

"I wish it wasn't so, Dale, but I'm afraid it is."

"How are you dealing with all of it?"

"Some days I can't believe it, but I'm starting to come to grips with my early demise. There aren't many alternatives, other than to except it after a while."

"Jesus", said Dale, excuse me while I raid your refrigerator for a beer."

"You may as well grab me one, no sense leaving them behind, said Willie. Everyone asks if there's something they can do for me. I just wonder, like what, thank them and say no."

"They don't need to do anything for me. You my friend, are not going to get off that easy though. I have things that you can and need to do for me."

Dale stared around the garage and asked, "what the hell are you going to do with all these cars?" Realizing the other garage was just as full as this one.

"That's one thing I'm going to need a little help with and who better than you. You know all these cars and motorcycles as well as I do."

"Well, at least you didn't let it get out of hand, laughed Dale. I can't believe I'm cracking jokes after what you just told me Willie. Damn, if you're bullshitting me, I'm going to kick your ass!"

"That would be an ass kicking I would gladly accept, but I think it's best if you accept it as truth as quick as you can, so we can concentrate on still having some laughs."

"Ok. now tell me about this bucket shit."

Reed saw the call was from Hope. He didn't answer but he texted her to tell her he would call her after his workday was over. It was late in the evening before Reed finally called Hope back.

Hope answered when she saw it was Reed. "What's up brother? How is everything? I've been wondering how it went with you and dad on his visit out to see you."

"We actually had a good time".

"Glad to hear that."

"It was a little tense. The waiting for him to pick the time to tell me what I already knew. I felt a little sorry for him, knowing he was struggling with how to open up about his situation, but I had to let him do it in his own way. Even though I already knew, it did still shock me more than I thought it would. It's hard to believe. He carried it off well and did his best to make light of it for me."

"We had a good round of golf. I beat him, he still sucks at it," laughed Reed. Later my girlfriend came over and we barbecued at my condo. He played the cool dad. They got along well."

"How did you handle it all?"

"Really just kind of numb, about the whole thing. In the end, it left me kind of terrified."

"Terrified, why that?"

"Hope, I wish I could find something touching to say about him, but I just can't. It's not that I don't like him. I certainly have no reason to not like him. I sometimes wish I had a reason to not like him, but I don't have that either. You and I both know we were separated from him a lot. The problem is, I really don't know the man all that well, and that's what terrifies me. I think his passing will just leave me void of any deep feeling one way or another, but what terrifies me is I'm afraid sometime later in my life it will dawn on me, what I had and lost, and then will never be able to do a thing about it."

"Maybe now is the time to express your feelings for him then."

"That's probably not going to happen, no matter how right you may be, in that regard. I'm too much like him. He made a valiant effort, but I'm afraid we are both just going to slip away from each other."

"That's sad, Reed."

"I know it is, but you know that's how our family always dealt with things. We can feel it, but we can't express it".

"We will have another chance to try. He wants us all to get together for Thanksgiving at his house."

"I know. I told him I would fly back for that. It's only a few weeks away."

"Ok, I'll let you go. Look forward to seeing you on Turkey Day and bring Mrs. Right along. I've never met her."

"I'll ask if she can get away from her family for the holiday. I think she will try probably more for me, because she knows it will probably be his last."

"We got to make sure this isn't a "cry in the gravy kind of thing." I don't think he wants that."

"Ok, we'll just drink ourselves silly then". said Reed.

"You bet, see you then," Hope said, as she ended the call.

Willie knew it was time to pick up the pace. There were lots of things a person had to do to get ready to die and he would get it all done, even if it killed him. Willie didn't even note the irony in thoughts that like that anymore. There were so many jokes and references to dying in one's lifetime, it's like life was just one big joke in the first place.

Cherise answered her phone when she saw it was Willie calling. "Hello, she said."

"Just called to let you know I've asked the kids to come to my house for Thanksgiving Day. If you want to skip that split holiday thing this year, you're welcome to come over also. Next year you can have them all to yourself, I'll be out of town."

"Are you going to be up for all that preparation?"

"Hey, I'm not dead yet, but actually I'm having it catered in. I told the service though, I wanted it to appear as traditional as possible, as though I might have actually made it, laughed Willie. Someone will still have to hack the bird to pieces, just like a Norman Rockwell painting. If you want to bring something, you can pick up a pie at the gas station.

Please don't try to bake one yourself. This is my last Thanksgiving and I'd like to make it to Christmas."

"Very funny, I made a pie once."

"Yeah, I still remember it, and so does the fire department."

"It wasn't that bad."

"It wasn't that good."

"Are your brother and sister coming?"

"I gave them a pass. With family of their own out of state and everything, it will be too tough for them. I told them I would call them on Thanksgiving."

"Do they know, Willie?"

"Yeah, they know."

"Surprised they wouldn't make the effort then."

"Cherise, you know, we all got along but, still we were mainly C&E relatives. T- day never factored in that often. It's all good between us, no drama."

"But still", …

"Forget it, they won't be there."

"It will be nice to have Reed come in for this."

"Yeah, I'm looking forward to it all. I'll let you go and remember, don't try to bake a pie."

"I could try," said Cherise."

"That's about all you could do, try." laughed Willie, as he clicked off.

"Willie, it's Mike, how are you holding up? "

"I was going to call you. Some days definitely better than others. Some days nauseous. Other days I feel almost too weak to get out of bed. A brain fog sometimes, but I always had that, joked Willie. Then some days, I actually think I might live. "

"I have a few different scripts for you, that may help a little."

"How about I just make a house call?"

"Do doctors still do that?"

"Just for you, buddy, just for you. How's tomorrow sound, about 2:00?"

"That's fine."

"OK, see you then."

"Thanks Mike, I'll be here. I'll have the driveway gate open for you, just come on in the house. I feel one of those bedridden days coming on."

Mike arrived at Willie's house and drove up the driveway. As told, he just let himself in the house with a shout.

"Honey I'm home," yelled Mike. He wished.

"I'm in the study, I made it to my desk chair. Keep walking, you'll find me."

The house was so huge it didn't have hallways. It had corridors, but eventually Mike found the study.

"At least I know you're getting your exercise just by walking around inside this place, said Mike, as he entered Willie's mahogany, raised panel study. This place is beyond nice."

"It's a sickness like many I have, and I've seen your place too Mike, not exactly poverty row either."

"Ok, but nothing like this."

"You know what this house was all about? It's like the jeweler who wears the $20,000 watch or the fashion designer who wears $3000 suits. This is what a builder does just once. It's a testament to the epitome of his trade. It's a self-accounting thing. To prove to himself that he had achieved the top of his game. Other than that, it's like I said, it's just some kind of sickness to live in a house like this, with its major taxes and upkeep, but I had to do it once."

"Mind if I ask what's going to happen with it?"

"Well, I'll take $100 off for you if you're interested in it, joked Willie. It will be sold. No one in the family wants it. It's too extreme. It wasn't their dream. At one time, I thought I was building a family compound, like Kennebunkport or Hyannis Point, that would be in the family for many generations, but those days are over. People nowadays want to be more fluid and not tied to an edifice like this. I'm sure there's a hip hop star or a rapper with newfound wealth that will love it."

"Yeah, probably more than the neighbors will after he moves in."

"Won't be my problem," said Willie.

"Personally, I enjoy the cars more. I've built too many houses to fall in love with what is really just a pile of sticks and stones in the first place."

"Yeah, but this is one hell of a pile."

"I'll tell you a funny story. Long ago I spent time below decks on a navy ship in a bunk where I could touch the edges of my domain without getting out of bed. One time I lived in an apartment so small, I had to sleep in the fetal position. My mom came to visit, and she asked how I could live in someplace like that. After I had this house finished, she came, and I gave her a tour of the place. "Mike, you know what she said?" She said, "how could I live in some place like this," laughed Willie. "I've always said a house is just a place to keep your things and sleep in. You don't live in it. You live in the very small plot of land between your ears. If you're not content there, no amount of square footage is going to correct that situation."

"Well, I'll say this, you didn't half step it.

"I'm sorry we never got that golf game in we spoke of."

"Not a problem, I went to see my son in California, and he embarrassed me enough to last a lifetime, at least my lifetime. Hey, but you're here now. What do you have in your little black bag for me?"

"Just some things to ramp up the relief a little. I'm going to take a blood sample back with me too."

"You actually know how to do that? I thought you left that to all your able-bodied assistants."

"I think I can still handle it."

"Ok, I'll give you one shot to hit a vein. We're not talking urine samples here also, are we?"

"That does remind me of another funny story. You want to hear it too? This one is provided curtesy of your medical profession. Mike could tell Wille was rambling on, probably good therapy.

"Sure," said Mike.

"When Cherise and I we're having fertility issues we both had to be checked out. I had an appointment to make my contribution for analysis. The girls at the reception counter gave me a cup and sent me down the hall to a private room to do my thing. I took the happy ending back to the reception counter and the girls laughed. I thought hey, that's not so bad. Sir, they said, "we meant a urine sample!" Mike laughed. I was almost embarrassed, but they said not to be, because it happens a lot. I told them maybe they should put up a sign that says "DON'T BEAT OFF IN THE CUP!" To this day, I don't know why they wanted a urine sample instead of a sperm sample. What the hell, we were trying to conceive a kid, not a piss ant!"

"At least no one can say you're leaving this world without some wonderful experiences," said Mike.

"I feel it's my duty to tell you, Willie the time is going come when you are going to be too weak to get around and I hate to tell you, you're going have to consider not driving anymore. That's for your own good, as well as mine in case I'm on the road the same time as you."

"I know this will be coming. I've spoken to Vera and probably after Thanksgiving depending on how I feel, my bedroom will become my hospital room. I'll have live- in full time medical help. She said she will be sending me the best we have, she said she would just bill it to the company. Of course, that's me anyway. I've been able to afford to live as I like, and I can afford to die as I like. I did always joke when I built this house, it would be my last one and I was only leaving by being carried out. Kind of ironic isn't it"?

"Just promise me, you'll stop driving when you know you are no longer able to. You, yourself might think that might be a preferred exit out- strategy but the people you may encounter may not agree."

"You're right, as soon as I start driving like you, I'll stop."

"If you don't need anything else Willie, I guess I'll head back to the office. Call me about anything, anytime. Try and stay vertical as much as you can and as long as you can."

"Thanks Mike, now get that Porsche off my driveway before the neighbors think I'm going bankrupt. That thing doesn't leak oil, does it?"

"See you again soon, Willie." He never would.

Willie took the Range Rover to the bank. It was a crappy weather day. He pulled up to the drive-up window, and there of course was Megan.

"Do you ever miss a day? You know you're going to end up owning this place one day," said Willie.

"I'm working on it. I must confess something to you, Willie."

"What's that?" asked Willie.

"I cheated."

"Don't tell me, tell your boyfriend."

"I thought you were my boyfriend?"

"Yeah, uh, huh!"

"What did you do?"

"Since you won't tell me, I asked Vince, if it didn't violate any privacy issues, if he had any paperwork that showed what your middle name was?"

"OMG, as you would say, that is really driving you crazy, isn't it? Maybe it's just B., as in Willie B. Lovd. With a first name that can already be Willie, William, or Bill, maybe I have enough names already. What did you find out?" Willie knew she didn't find out anything. He never signed with his middle name."

"Nothing, darn it. You're still a mystery wrapped up in a riddle. Why don't you just tell me?"

"Never as long as I live. It's too much fun to keep you guessing."

"Well, I'm done guessing, I give up".

"You're not the type to give up, you'll figure it out one day. Your world is too perfect, you need a little turmoil."

"Gee thanks. Are you ready for Thanksgiving?"

"Except for going out in the woods and shooting a Turkey, I'm set," said Willie.

"I guess you have "Marilyn" bundled up for the winter?" I'm going to miss seeing her until spring."

"She's snuggled in for her winter's nap, but I'll tell her you asked about her, laughed Willie. Enjoy the holiday." With that, he drove off.

"Hey Dale, it's Willie," he said, as Dale answered the phone.

"How are you feeling today? OK I hope."

"Yeah, not too bad today,"

"So, I am wondering if you had this afternoon free to stop over? There are some things I need to go over with you, and today is as good day as any for me. When I have a good one, I try to not waste them."

"I can make it today. Do I need to bring anything?"

"No, just your charming self."

"I never leave home without it." said Dale

"How about one, if you can make it by then."

"I can do that, see you then," said Dale, as he hung up the phone.

Dale had no idea what was in store for him. When Dale arrived at the entrance to Willie's house the gates were open. He drove up the driveway and let himself in the garage. He guessed Willie would be in one of them, and he was right.

"Grab a beer out of the fridge if you want. This might take a bit."

"That bad huh?" asked Dale.

"Let's just say I have some final details to discuss that I would entrust only to you, for various reasons. I need you to give the family a hand by unloading these cars and motorcycles.

"You know, this all still seems so surreal to me. I still struggle with it sometimes Willie. Too damn sad to even grasp it."

"Well, the time has come, where for me, I have no choice but to grasp it or leave one hell of a mess behind for the other people to deal with who wouldn't know how or where to begin. You're my best option. You know these cars as well as or better than I do. You know their values. I need someone to handle the sales, so my family doesn't get taken for a ride, if you'll excuse the pun. You also know every last detail about these cars to best market them. We both know values are not an exact science, but I trust you to use your best judgement."

"I know someone who would take that Hemi Roadrunner off your hands right now."

"Yeah, Fuck you, Dale. I can guess who the buyer is for that one".

"Yeah me," laughed Dale.

"That is exactly the kind of losing I'd like to avoid. But I will take $100 off for you, and let you have it for 100 K and that's a lifelong friend's discount."

"Gee thanks, I may have to pass on it though."

"I have a file folder with maintenance records and registration paperwork on each vehicle. I've always kept up the best I could on the value, and I have that in each file also. I hope that helps as a guideline for you to work from, but again something is only worth what someone else is willing to pay for it. I've already explained to Cherise that I was giving this job to you and told her there is no way I or you can guarantee an end value to all this stuff. I told her I trust you over anyone to give it your best shot."

"What did she say to that?" asked Dale.

"Well in a word, she said "Hallelujah!" laughed Willie.

"There's a few I have specific purposes for, and I'll fill you in on that before we're done. I do have to tell you, I have already spoke with my pastor and I have donated the 67 Corvette to the church to be auctioned off. I have to tell you I have already offered your services to him to assist with the details working with the auction company.

You've met my pastor before. Ron's a good guy and will be easy to work with."

"I've ran into him a few times in town, not exactly in church, but I'm sure we can get it done. Letting go of that one has to hurt a little, I would bet. The least it should do, is get you a pass into the pearly gates."

"Letting go of any of these is going to hurt a little, but I'm not trying to bribe my way into a lofty eternity. I figure that's already been decided for me, so I'll end up where I end up. I never believe in that whole death bed confession thing."

"Grab a beer and get me one too, said Willie. Let's take a walk and see if anything jogs your mind about something you should ask or need to know to help get rid of this junk."

Willie and Dale walked from car to car, just reminiscing about the good old days.

"This one is going to take a special buyer. You know that don't you Willie? They were besides the fender- less 33 Ford roadster with the monster engine. Willie would admit it was one of the less practical cars in his collection. Yeah, it just doesn't play well with others. Willie referred to this car as the valedictorian of summer school. Rules were meant to be broken and the car broke all of them. Willie built the car to be enjoyed, sparing no expense. The car represented a freedom by escaping adhering to any Judges verdict about what was correct or incorrect about it. The car just didn't give a damn.

"It might not be as big a problem to get rid of as you think, Dale. I'm thinking about sending the valedictorian off to school to get its GED. I'll fill you in on that later."

"Damn," said Dale, this one's a killer. The GT40 Ford was beyond perfect. A car, so exotic Willie rarely drove it. It was a reproduced version of the original car that beat the Ferraris, one-two-three in Lemans in 1966. The car was still worth at least $500,000, cheap compared to a six million dollar original one. I'm sure, I can get a sale for it that will make your heirs smile for a long time."

"Where's the Jag XKE coupe, by the way?"

"She's having a little procedure performed on her. She's due to be discharged next week. I had the parts on order that she needed, so it was only a labor issue. I had them put a rush on it anyway. It was something I didn't think you or I wanted to tackle doing, at least not with my limited time."

They finished their stroll through the garage and walked across the courtyard to the matching other garage. It was a cold November day, but the heat was on, so it was comfortable walking among the cars and motorcycles.

"You got to love that GTO. The father of the muscle car movement. At least John DeLorean got something right." said Dale.

"Dale, this is what you really need." said Willie as they stopped in the bike section and looked at the 1971 Triumph Bonneville.

"It just screams Steve McQueen. doesn't it."

"I don't think I could deal with a kick start only bike at my age.

I've seen people try to kick start those things until the cows came home, before they finally started."

"Well, let's see," said Willie. Willie turned on the ignition and tickled the two AMAL carburetors. He set the choke and sat astride the bike. He cycled the kick start lever to the top of the downstroke position. It was true, the compression the 650CC engine could kick back and blacken the back of your leg. Willie raised himself off the seat and with all his might thrusted his weight and foot down on the kickstart lever. The engine caught, but did not start.

"Are you sure you're up to that Willie?"

With that Willie recycled the kickstart lever to the top again raising his whole body off the seat for the downward thrust. This time the bike sputtered, and Willie quickly feathered the throttle and brought the bike to life.

"Only two kicks," said Dale. " If anything in these garages says this shit is all good to go, that does it." Willie let the throttle warm up the bike to idle as smoothly as old triumphs were ever meant to. "Take that Steve McQueen!"

"You know Dale, if you want to ruin it, it can be fitted with an electric start motor. Sacrilegious! Please don't do that until after I'm dead."

The 1968 Hemi Roadrunner was in this garage. Willie knew it was a favorite of Dale's. While Willie had no preference for car brands, Dale was a Plymouth and Dodge fan all the way. For Dale it was Mopar or no car.

"Can I," asked Dale?

"Of course," said Willie. Get your jollies." Dale reached inside and tapped the center horn button of the steering wheel. Beep- beep the horn sounded. Chrysler had paid a reported $50,000 to obtain the rights from Disney to use the beep- beep sound from the Roadrunner cartoon for their horns. Dale, some kids never grow up do they?" "You got to love it, though. Can you imagine a white-collar designer even thinking of a marketing something like that nowadays?"

Dale, finally couldn't resist asking, "what really brought on a sickness like this Willie? Hell, I get it, I like a beer too every now and then, but I don't feel compelled to buy the whole fucking brewery!"

"Dale, you know how I grew up on a farm in a family that was too poor to pay attention. I used to say my dad, worked 11 hours a day, ten at work and one hour every day on the family car, just so it would make it to work and back. We drove a two-lane road every Sunday to church, all the while I was in the backseat praying. I still remember the prayer. "Dear Jesus, we got up early, we're heading for church, can you please see that the car doesn't breakdown on the way there. I'd rather like to avoid the embarrassment of "there's the Lovd's again, broke down on the way to church," Amen. Ironic, praying to God, to help you get to church. From then on, I always told myself, no matter what the sacrifice, I would always see that I drove a nice car, even if it was all I could afford at the time."

"Well, Willie, I got to hand it to you, you sure didn't half step it."

Willie just shook his head and laughed, "I guess not."

"It's still a little insane though," said Dale.

"I have something else to talk to you about over in the other garage. Then you'll really question what sanity is or isn't."

"Sounds like this will take a stop at the fridge," said Dale.

"Might not be a bad idea," replied Willie.

Willie led the way into the garage, and headed for the workbench, where the bucket was. Willie first handed Dale two power of attorneys.

"This one, said Willie, is granting you the power to handle the sale of the vehicles. And after a pause, he said, "and this one is granting you the power to retrieve my ashes from the funeral ceremony and bring them here."

"And to do what with them?" asked Dale.

"I'm getting to that."

"Why do I think it would be more convenient to have the bucket closer to where the beer is?" asked Dale.

"We could, but it will be easier for me to explain your duties here at the workbench."

"Duties? You sure this isn't above my pay grade."

"I told you before, you're all I got."

"Is this when I should say, lucky me?

"Say what you like. I'll admit to a little insanity, but your task is really quite simple, but I can't do it myself, because I'll be dead."

"OK, heading for the fridge," laughed Dale.

"OK, then, what is all this shit anyway?" asked Dale, as he motioned to the work bench.

Willie explained how he had bound the two buckets together and wrapped them with Kevlar to make them virtually bulletproof. He showed Dale how he had filled the interior of the bucket around a 6-inch diameter tub of PVC tubing with star-foam and slats of balsa wood. Willie then picked up the bank drive-up canister and showed Dale that it was a perfect fit inside the cavity he had created in the bucket's interior.

"All right, said Dale, what am I supposed to do that you can't?"

"That will be obvious. I need you to bring my ashes home from the funeral service, pour me, or my former self, into the bank canister, snap the lid shut and slide me into the center hole. Then take the lid, apply a heavy bead of silicone caulk to the rim of the bucket and tap it onto the bucket to seal it. Then take the fiberglass mat I have here for you and make a triple pass of fiberglass to seal the lid to the bucket. I know you're capable of that. You've helped me with fiberglass work here in the garage before."

Dale, just stood there in silence as Willie was relaying what he was sure was a well-rehearsed speech to him.

"That's it," said Willie.

"That's it? asked Dale. Then what the fuck do I do with you?"

"Let's go back to looking at all your cars, you're right, this is a lot more insane."

"Actually, I'm just asking you to gather a few friends and my family together, have them come down to the little waterfront part on the bank of the Mississippi and throw my ass in."

"You're insane."

"No, the bucket is doubly strong and watertight. I'll be fine, very fine actually, laughed Willie. It's wrapped in Kevlar in case some kids feel like taking a potshot at me. I should be good to go for a long time. I even took the handles off so I wouldn't get hung up on anything. Then I'm good to go."

"Where the hell you plan on going?"

"That will pretty much be out of my hands," said Willie.

"I have to ask, does your family or anyone else know about this already?"

"No, not yet, just you."

"Now is this the time for me to say, lucky me?"

"You sure none of the meds you've been on aren't making you a little, how should I say it, FUCKING NUTS?"

"Really Dale, maybe I should ask Cherise if she would like me sitting on her mantel like a flowerpot, she never waters. Or, here Hope, I'm sorry I wasn't the perfect father, but I think you could use some extra Kitty Litter, or here Reed, if you really sink one deep in a sand trap, maybe sprinkle a little of this around to get a good footing."

"I could end up like crazy Larry, who carried his wife's ashes around in his work truck, then got stuck in the ice one winter, and sprinkled her under his tires for traction."

"You know he never liked her anyway," said Dale.

"Well, I'm not going to waste a lot of real estate by being buried. That doesn't seem right and, places are running out of plots. That's why they are burying spouses on top of each other."

"Yeah, I heard about Larry. He survived so many ex-wives when it finally came to plant him the hole was so deep, they hit oil."

"See, that's what I'm talking about," said Willie.

"Is floating the waters of the world, crazier than spending eons 6-foot underground, in a place where people feel compelled to stop and see you but won't. I won't be a part of causing that guilt" I don't know want to be sitting around, to be just another thing to dust.

"Dale you've got to do this for me. Hey I'd do it for you."

"Now I know it's time to say, lucky me! Is that it," asked Dale.

"That's it, said Willie, nothing to it, seal me in the bucket and throw me in the river. Even a kid could do it."

"Yeah, but I bet your kids won't."

"Well, I'm not asking them to do it, I'm asking you."

"Wouldn't it all be simpler, if you just didn't die," Willie?

"Yeah maybe, but I'd hate to mess up such a perfect plan."

"You're crazy, said Dale, but I'll do it."

"But I have one question?"

"What's that?" asked Willie.

"Did you steal that canister from the bank?"

"No, I just borrowed it for a really long time."

"Let's get together one day at Malley's before Thanksgiving."

"Fine with me, but you're buying after what you unloaded on me today."

"For sure, said Willie. I'm sure Lisa is missing us anyway."

"I'll call you on a well day, they're getting fewer and farther between."

"Hate to hear that, hate to hear it."

The next day wasn't one of Willie's best. He knew he wouldn't be leaving his home or even his couch today. He told Vera the way he was feeling it might be best to set up his in-home care soon after Thanksgiving. This saddened her. He spent the day phoning people and wishing them a happy Thanksgiving. He called Vera and Vince at the bank. He called Dr. Mike. He called Reed and Hope telling both of them he was looking forward to seeing them next week on Thursday and thanking Reed for coming all the way from California for the holiday. He called Cherise and reminded her she was welcome to come to Thanksgiving, teasing her again to not try to bake a pie. He even called Dale, just for the hell of it, which was kind of weird for the two. He was only up for hearing voices today other than the ones inside his own head. After a few journeys to the bathroom, he decided a vomit bucket beside the couch would be more practical. He knew Thanksgiving was going to be entered into his "book of lasts." That would be ok, he just prayed for the health and strength to get through this last one. Some days were definitely better than others, and it wouldn't take much for one to be better than today. He could almost understand when a person's pain or sickness was so severe, that they welcomed death. He wasn't there yet, so he decided to just enjoy the pain a little longer.

The phone rang early in the morning, and much to Willie's relief he felt fine, or at least way better than the day before.

He saw it was the European car repair service. "Mr. Lovd, we have the Jag done, and we thought you might like us to bring it over while it is still dry today."

"Great idea and thank you for getting it done so quickly".

"It's really just a bolt and unbolt procedure. After all, a lot of them were shipped that way. You having the parts really expedited things, good thinking."

"I had considered having it done for quite some time, I'm glad it's finally done. I'll be home. Bring it whenever you can."

"Ok, we'll have it there before noon."

"Thanks, said Willie, as he ended the conversation.

Willie piddled around the house waiting for the car to be dropped off. He had the space in the garage open for it when the service arrived with the car. Once the car was in place, Willie secured the garage and called Dale.

"Hey, it's lunchtime, let's go pester Lisa."

"You sound a lot better today than you did yesterday, I was really spooked by how you sounded on the phone."

"Well, that was yesterday, gone and forgotten."

"I was going to tell you. I had the weirdest dream last night. I dreamt, you wanted me to stick you in a pickle bucket and throw you in the river."

"No shit, that's crazy," said Willie.

"What the hell, it must have been something you ate before bed, laughed Willie. How about one o'clock at Malley's?"

"Sounds good," said Dale.

"If you beat me there, just start in on her till I get there."

"You got it buddy, and bring your wallet, you're buying remember?"

"Are you still dreaming Dale? See you at 1:00."

They both arrived in the parking lot at the same time

"Nice to see you 're vertical," said Dale.

"Nice to be vertical."

They walked in and both smiled in unison, as they caught Lisa's eyes. They could see her mouth "oh shit," when she saw the pair. Her day was about to begin in earnest. They took seats at the bar and let her pretend she had other customers. She could only pull that off for so long, so finally she approached the two.

"We're closed," she said.

"Right, then why don't you go home?" Dale said.

"A beer please."

"One beer, or do you mean you'd each like one of your own?"

"And what would you like pops, and sorry, we're out of Geritol."

"Well, I'll just have a water then."

"What, is that some kind of shit to get out of tipping me? What are you going do with water?"

"I thought I would drink it if that's ok with you." said Willie.

She got Dale his beer and sat a cocktail glass of water with a lime wedge and a swizzle stick in it in front of Willie.

"What, no little umbrellas?" teased Willie.

"I thought I'd better make it look like a vodka tonic or someone might think you're dying."

Dale cringed a little at that, but Willie just replied by saying "yeah that will be the day." Dale wondered how he would handle stuff like that.

"I know you're not dying because you're already a fossil who can't handle his booze anymore."

"Happy Thanksgiving to you too, said Willie. Do you have big plans for it?"

"Actually, I'm going to see my sister in Blytheville, for the holiday."

"Blytheville, uh, I know it's not the end of the world, but I hear you can see it from there." Dale had spent a few years stationed there when he was in the Air Force.

"It's working out ok for my sister. She married a guy whose dad has about 3000 acres of cotton. I should have married the geek."

"If you had done that, you might never have met us."

"Now I really wish I had married the geek."

"You love us, and you know it," said Dale.

"I'll be back, I have to wait on some customers I actually like."

"She sounds kind of testy today."

"Holidays for a single girl and a kid that you're trying to figure out how to get in college, can sometimes bring out the demons."

"Maybe we should brighten up her day?"

No way, she would really think you were dying if we did that." "Sorry," said Dale.

"Why are you drinking water anyway?"

"Some days the booze hits my stomach kind of hard."

Yeah, I have the same thing when I drink too many the day before, said Dale. Here she comes."

She sat another beer in front of Dale and asked Willie if he'd like another gin and tonic. "Yes, please and make it hurt.'"

"Funny, really funny."

"How's your daughter, by the way?"

"The smarter she gets the broker I am."

"It's kind of like the cliché, the drunker I get it the better you look," teased Dale.

"Borrow some money from the cotton picker in Arkansas and send her to school." suggested Willie

"I can't do that."

"Why not, you're always begging us for tips?"

"Yeah, and look where that is getting me.

"Well, if it makes you feel any better," said Willie, I would like to say I think you look rather bodacious today, Lisa."

"Bodacious? Is that good or bad?"

"Ask your daughter when you get home, she's the smart one, you said."

"You know, we're just funning with you."

"Funning with me, now who's been to Arkansas?" laughed Lisa.

"You know, I actually appreciate you guys coming in here and breaking up my day. Some of these people take their drinks too seriously to enjoy them."

"What do you all have planned for Thanksgiving?" she asked.

Dale said he was visiting family out of town.

"My kids are coming to my house for Thanksgiving."

"Kids, you have kids? How did that ever happen?"

"Yes, I have kids, I'll have you know. I was quite the stud-muffin in my day."

"How long does it take to turn from a stud-muffin into a fossil, anyway?" asked Lisa.

"Actually, it goes quicker than you think," said Willie.

Dale asked Lisa if she was cooking the Turkey?

"Really, do I look like I cook?"

"Yeah, silly question, I guess."

"How do you expect to catch Mr. right if you don't cook?"

"It's not my cooking that ever got me in trouble."

The three bantered back and forth, each enjoying every bit of it until they had finally had enough. Willie paid for the drinks and left a pair of Franklins on the bar, when Lisa had her back turned.

"Best gin and tonic I ever had, Happy holidays" said Willie,
as he turned to go. He would never see her again.

CHAPTER NINE

"THERE IS A GOD," THOUGHT WILLIE AS HE WOKE up early on Thanksgiving Day. It seemed like this was going to be a doable day, as far as his health was concerned. Now he only had to survive the social interactions and the day would be a success. There wasn't much the house needed in the way of sprucing up. Willie only lived in about 10% of it.

Willie went to answer the door and it was Cherise. "I know I'm a little early, but I just wanted to see if you needed any help making this appear as you've actually had a hand in creating this feast. Here, I baked a pie."

"You shouldn't have, really."

"I just wanted to."

"Well, you shouldn't have, really," laughed Willie.

Willie accepted the pie, from Cherise. When she wasn't looking, he put it safely in the back of the broom closet. He knew that would be best for everyone.

The house was clean, just as the cleaning girl had left it. Cherise helped Willie with the final preparations. The service had it all mostly staged and ready to present. With the additional efforts of Willie and

Cherise, they almost made it look traditional. Going against Willie's lifelong beliefs against rushing each season, Cherise noticed Willie had his tree up already. Willie saw her looking at it.

"I know I'm early this year, but I had a well day recently and I thought I better do it now while I still could. Book of lasts entry number, who knows how high?

"It's nice and it is always such a rush to Christmas, after Thanksgiving. It's hard to get everything accomplished you need to, in that short of time."

"Yeah, I know, tell me about it," said Willie. Cherise went silent when she realized what Willie really meant by that.

They nibbled on the assorted crackers and cheeses. They talked about the kids.

"Let the fun begin, announced Willie. Would you like a drink?"

"Sure, why not."

"That's my line," said Willie.

Willie grabbed two cocktail glasses, made two seven and sevens, short with pieces of lemon and made them hurt. It was the family drink, or it once was the family drink. Cherise accepted hers from Willie, and took a sip.

"Really got my money's worth on this one," she said.

"They tend to get a little softer as the day goes on."

"I'll take your word for it."

"They will, you'll see." said Willie.

"Reed got in late last night. He and Hope made the Thanksgiving Eve bar rounds, visiting with old friends."

"He's coming with her. He didn't rent a car for this visit'" said Cherise.

"Makes sense, he won't be in town that long. It's nice to see them get along with each other."

"Yeah, better than when they were kids. I thought some days they would kill each other. Two teenagers in the same house, you're lucky you missed out on some of that."

"Funny, right now I don't feel lucky about that."

"I'll get some of the stuff warmed up in the oven."

"OK, I'll alert the fire department."

"You know I did learn to cook. A little."

"Wonders never cease.

The doorbell rang. The offspring's have arrived," said Willie as he headed through the foyer to the front door. He opened the door and welcomed them in. Both were bearing a customary offering for the host. Hope, with an incredible side dish that Willie knew would be delicious. She could cook, and Reed with a bottle of Willie's favorite wine, Merlot, just plain boring old Merlot.

"Come to the kitchen, mom's in here warming up the food."

"I'll alert the fire department," said Reed.

"Don't bother, I already have."

"You guys need to stop teasing her about that. Look at it this way, at least she kept her youthful figure."

"Yeah, can't argue that, not sure if it's worth starving nearly to death though, just because you can't figure out how to light the burners."

"Why are my ears ringing?" shouted Cherise from the kitchen.

"It's probably the drink," said Willie as they entered the kitchen.

Cherise gave Reed the mandatory hug. "It's nice to see you, it's been a while since you visited us rednecks here in fly over country."

"You know your own description makes me want to go back, pack up my avocado trees and move back here," laughed Reed.

"Do it, I'll get a heat lamp for them." The fire department is going to be busy, thought Willie.

"Hope, I think you look nice, but a little woozy."

"Thanks, that's nice, but those Thanksgiving Eve get togethers can be brutal. Too many friends and too many drinks."

"Well, I'm glad to see you both survived that. You all need to be careful on the roads after a night of that. You might run into me," said Willie.

"You didn't happen to meet a plus one during all that I suppose," asked Cherise.

"It was close, said Reed, but I rescued the guy from it at the last minute."

"Hey, he was cute."

"Yeah cute, very drunk and from what I heard, very married."

"No way?"

"Yes way," said Reed.

"That's ok, Hope. He probably didn't deserve you anyway."

"That guy didn't deserve anyone." laughed Reed.

"Oh, he wasn't totally bad."

"Wow, sorry he couldn't make it today, laughed Willie.

"Speaking of love stories, how's your girlfriend? I wish she could have made it here with you."

"She's good, but she has a big family that she can't escape so easily."

"She shouldn't try to escape, lucky girl," added Cherise.

The four wined and dined and chatted the afternoon away. It was nice thought Willie. Gratefully, everyone avoided the elephant in the room, with barely a question about Willie's state of health. The ones that were, Willie reflected quickly. Today wasn't for that. It was late afternoon. Reed had an early flight, and everyone was going to give

Hope an excuse to leave and recover after two days of dealing with the fruit of the vine.

Willie let the two out the front door. As they were walking to the car, Willie called Reed back. Reed returned and walked across the courtyard back to Willie.

"Reed, I'm glad you came, it was nice to see you, but you need to do me a favor."

"What's that dad?"

"Don't come back for the funeral. No one likes funerals. I never did. I always said I would skip my own, unfortunately I never figured out a way to do that."

"I feel I should."

"Well, feel somehow else."

"Play a round of golf that day instead. I'm sure the weather will be nice, even at the end of December in California."

"I love you too much to ruin your day," said Willie.

"That soon?"

"Yeah, I'm afraid so."

Willie then extended his hand and Reed took it. "And remember, don't come back."

"What was that all about," asked Hope as Reed got into the car.

"It was nothing, just drive." said Reed.

"It didn't look like nothing to me."

Hope brought up the subject of their parents.

"You know, those two seem to get along so well together. It's a shame they never got back together."

"Hope, do you still harbor that dream? If you do, finally it will be one you can bury along with dad.

"Those two are like an iceberg, seemingly harmless above the surface, but below, well, let's just say, it could lead to a calamity of Titanic proportions," said Reed.

Willie came back into the house to the kitchen. Cherise could tell he was downtrodden. Cherise had seen the exchange from the window.

"That was a little rough," said Willie.

"Here," said Cherise, as she handed Willie a flute of Merlot with a rock glass of ice on the side.

They talked as the two packed up the leftovers. There was probably enough to last Willie for the rest of his life, which wouldn't be long. Willie went to the broom closet and brought out the pie Cherise had made.

"Here, take your doorstop home with you."

"I wondered what happened to that?"

"The thought was nice, next time think of something else," laughed Willie.

He actually thought it might be nice if there would be a next time, but there wouldn't be. "Before you go, I must talk to you about a few things. First, I've talked to Vera, and she is sending over equipment and will be starting to schedule a home health care nurse to monitor me here. Basically, I'm turning my bedroom into a hospital room."

"You sure this is something best handled from home? And by the way, you seem fairly well today."

"I missed my calling. I should have been an actor. I'm starting to have more bad days than good."

"If the nurse she sends doesn't work out, I can always fire her, she already works for me anyway, laughed Willie. It's what I want. I never liked hospitals and have been fortunate to have never spent a night in one. Why start now?"

"I see you're not going to be talked out of this." Said Cherise

"Very observant of you," said Willie.

"Another thing, I already told you Dale is going to handle the sale of the vehicles."

"He's the most knowledgeable, trustworthy person for this job. The will dictates how the sale proceeds will be dispensed."

"You want one?" offered Willie.

"Is there one that isn't a stick shift?" laughed Cherise.

"Not sure, I'll have to check, but I doubt it."

"You can have the Range Rover. I'm about done with it I'm afraid. It's an automatic. I've given Dale a power of attorney to

act on my behalf on selling the cars."

"I've also already spoken to Tim and Fancy Girdon about handling the sale of the estate."

"They were always the best realtors we ever worked with," admitted Cherise.

"Tim has it as a pocket listing right now. I told him to market it as not being available until Dale has had time to dispense with the cars. He did say a property like this with that much car storage may attract an auto collector anyway and possibly, they may have an interest in a few of the cars or motorcycles. He did mention that often those people already had their own collection, and were just looking for a place to house their own, so it might be a long shot that many of the cars will be included in the sale of the property. Dale still says at the right price, they will become separate from each other fairly quickly."

"Sounds like you got it all figured out. You probably have your suit pressed and ready to go."

"Yeah, I will look hot in that, at least for a brief time period. I've decided on a Cremation service."

"Wow, I always pictured you underground."

"Thank you, that's nice," laughed Willie.

"No, I already have the arrangements made at Tutist and Sons. Isn't it odd you never hear of a funeral company called say, Fitzgerald and Daughters, it's always So & So and Sons? That's a question I guess I will leave this world unanswered." "Here's one little detail about that. Dale also has a power of attorney to accept my finely powdered self from the funeral home."

"Why Dale? Cherise asked, rather astonishingly.

"Didn't figure you wanted me sitting on your mantel, said Willie. That would mess with your image of me being 6 feet under."

"Well maybe the kids?" suggested Cherise. "Oh yeah, I guess I could have put myself into two Zip-Lock baggies, giving each kid one."

"Here Hope. Here Reed. Gee uh, thanks dad."

"It's been decided, yet Dale will be talking to you about it all later, after I'm talcum powder."

"What's he going to do, sprinkle you in the river?"

"Stranger things have happened," said Willie.

"You know a lot of people are going miss you Willie, even me a little."

"Yeah, well for how long really. Everyone's life goes on. I'm not even expecting a large funeral gathering, nor do I want one.

I've always thought anyway the number of people who show up at your funeral is still primarily decided by the weather."

"You know there may be more than you think. Your life has affected a lot of people."

Willie laughed, "hopefully they won't use my funeral service as a way to get even with me."

"This is starting to sound like it's time for you and your pie to head for home."

"Yeah, I guess it's getting late. I have to start getting ready for the next holiday myself. "Thanks for the invite, it was nice to have us all here today." Cherise and her pie left for home.

The afternoon was fun while it lasted, but it hadn't lasted all that long. It was still late afternoon as Willie entered the first of the two garages. He opened both large overhead doors on each garage and turned on the exhaust extraction system. He flipped on all the lights as he left the first garage and repeated the same process in the other facing garage across the courtyard. He stopped for a moment turning to face the collection of cars and bikes in each garage. Megan at the bank was right in asking why they don't make cars with colors like that anymore. They really were a kaleidoscope of colors. He then walked from vehicle to vehicle, from bike to bike and started every one of them, even managing to kickstart the Triumph Bonneville to life. He let them all come to idle. The exhaust extract system did its job, the air was clear, at least as clear as Willie liked it. He returned to the courtyard between the two open garages, and he himself was overcome with the array of cars all running one last time, just for him.

The sound from all of them at once, was like an orchestra to him. Low rumblings of the base section type, the smooth hum of the mid-section, the whines of some, like a violin section, of course there was a percussion section.

Standing in the courtyard he raised his arms and sang out at the top of his lungs. "I hear a Symphony. I hear a Symphony." The only words from the Supremes' 1960's hit that he really knew, but to him no truer words were ever sung. Repeating the refrain until his voice was hoarse, and just long enough for the neighbors to declare him insane or drunk. That was something that had never concerned him, and he wasn't about to start letting it now. He entered the garage and one by one began turning off all the engines. He had always left the keys in place, knowing an old car not having a key was the least obstacle when stealing one. He closed the doors as the vehicles were shutting down. The exhaust system was extracting the last of the noxious fumes. It crossed Willie's mind that maybe this was the answer. Turn the exhaust system off, fire up some cars, pick a seat, turn on a radio station and just relax until he ceased to exist. But that wasn't Willie. Willie had always believed suicide left a trail of guilt for those left behind. Willie knew in his case everyone was blameless, and he would never leave them wondering about it.

Willie was more the Dylan Thomas type. Rage on, Rage on Against the Dying of the Light. He locked the doors to both garages and entered the house through the side door. He would never see or hear the cars again.

On Wednesday the medical service company came and set up his bedroom with monitors and IV equipment to administer whatever meds he may need if required. Except for the evenings, Willie now avoided his bedroom. The room was large enough to accommodate both the hospital bed and the king size bedroom set. He just instructed them to place his new nest in the center of the room, facing the windows.

He set up camp in the living room, in his most comfortable recliner instead. To rule like a king for as long as he could. He placed a small refrigerator within reach of his Kingdom too eliminate some long journey to the kitchen. He went to his library and chose a dozen books from those on the shelves he hadn't gotten around to. Though Willie was an avid reader, these few he hadn't read. Willie wasn't much for science friction as he called it. He preferred historical novels, and especially biographies of way past artists, and discoveries of well, almost everything. He was fascinated by the people who were the first to present groundbreaking discoveries about the world. Sometimes Willie himself wondered, especially now, what the big interest there was in the great masters of the Renaissance. Why read about them now, at the end of his life. If he had wonderings about them, shortly, he would be in a position to speak with them one on one. Reading had always been a form of escapism, and when could that be more soothing than now? Willie read on, often awakening, with the book having fallen from his hands and laying on the floor around him. He dozed often. His phone was always at his arms reach. He still had details both business and pleasure to attend to, which he could do that quite well from the comfort of his recliner. Every day he got up and took a walk outside around the estate. He knew better than to attempt the climb down the cliff to the river's edge. It dawned on him that he had always been right about one thing. A person may surround themselves with greatness, but you still exist in this small space between your ears. People spend their whole lives expanding their horizons, but at the close of life everything retreats, until you are just a world only to yourself. Gratefully Willie was content in his.

One morning Willie heard lawn equipment operating on his yard. The mowing season had ended weeks ago. He was sure Danny was just here for the end of season wintering of the grounds. He went outside, took a seat and waved hello to Danny. Danny ran the dethatching mower over the grounds, bagging clippings as he went. He moved on to clear out the annuals from the flower beds, dressing up the mulch as he finished each area. He clipped and pruned the many bushes and trees that could best take a winter trimming. Willie avoided getting the lawn serviced by the large commercial service companies, who filled his mailbox all season long, offering one service after another. He preferred to use a local service. Danny had taken care of the grounds of the estate for as long as Willie could remember, ever since Willie stopped handling the job himself. Now Willie only took care of the pool service on his own. Time always was and is definitely a precious commodity. When Willie could see Danny was about finished, he walked across the expansive lawn, with his wallet in his hand. He paid for services when they were rendered, and he knew it always helped Danny out by doing so.

"Looks great, as always," said Willie, as Danny turned off the equipment.

"Thanks, I'm a little behind on your winter service this year, but since it has been so unseasonably warm this fall, I think it will all still take."

"I'm sure it will," said Willie, as he handed Danny the charge plus a healthier than normal end of season bonus. When Danny saw the amount, he was given, he almost refused it, gesturing to return part of it.

"That's too much Mr. Lovd, or Willie." He remembered Willie didn't like being called by his last name.

"No that's good, and hey it's Christmas time. Enjoy it. You always make me proud to pull up my driveway."

"I owe as much thanks to you, Willie. I can't tell you how many yards I've picked up just by mentioning that I do the service at River Valley Vista."

"You deserve it. I can tell you treat this property as if it were your own."

"In my dreams Willie, in my dreams, said Danny. I guess that will take care of it until early spring. I'll see you then."

"For sure" said Willie, all the while knowing he never would.

"Hey Tim, it's Willie. Strongly, recommend to any new buyer that they consider using my lawn service guy." He wished Tim and his family and their office team a Merry Christmas. With that he hung up the phone. Willie spent this valuable remaining day enjoying his reading. Occasionally, Hope called and spoke for a few minutes. Sometimes Vera, about this or that, but Willie could tell she, as always had everything under control. Jesus, he thought the amount of time she had provided for him to enjoy himself, through her trusted efforts was amazing. At times Dale called. Nothing from Reed. Willie knew he was always busy.

The day nurse prepared meals for him so all he had to do was heat them for himself. He could handle that, but he could tell the couch was becoming an anchor to his body. The day nurse coordinated things with Dr. Mike, yet he and Willie still spoke on the phone at times. There wasn't much more Willie had to do, except die. He actually tried keeping himself from reflecting on his past life, it had been a great life, so the more of it he recalled, the more of it he felt he missed it. He decided to just embrace the void that was left between life and death

The day nurse was coming on a daily basis now, as Willie's needs we're increasing. She herself was a joy. They laughed and joked a lot. She was the epitome of all the employees that Willie had insisted on, for everyone at all of his assisted living centers. He hoped they all enjoyed this kind of friendly service, even if it wasn't being providing to them as if they were the boss. He could fire them, they couldn't, but he could fire them for them, something fortunately he rarely had to do, but he couldn't say it never happened.

Cherise and Hope stop by one day to see Willie. They weren't sure if he knew they were there. They spoke with the day nurse about his condition. "I have to tell you, it's basically a hospice situation right now. You did come on one of his more down days. A lot depends on how he reacts to the meds Dr. Lillenberg has prescribed. I know his dosage has been upped to relieve some pain. That always creates a problem with how lucid someone maybe at any given time. I'm sure he knows you came by though." Hope and Cherise weren't sure about that.

"Mom, it's just sad as hell," said Hope, as they were leaving the house

"I know it is sweetie, but I think he has prepared himself for the inevitable as best as he can."

"It does make someone wonder if being run over by a bus might not be a better way to go. It's over and done with. He has been dealing with this for a year and without telling anyone until recently," said Hope.

"That's the way he wanted to handle it Hope. He told me as much, and I didn't know much before I told you, and he hadn't even wanted me to do that then."

The next day some of the fog had lifted for Willie. Hope had told him he was always able to reduce everything to its lowest common denominator. Now life was doing the same for him. His world and life were shrinking inward. There was no longer a reason to deal with problems. What by now hadn't been done, would forever remain undone. There was nothing to plan for, and now very little to worry about, being well past the part of worrying about dying anymore. All he could do was focus on a single thought at a time, and Willie decided his final thought would be to prove Doctor Mike wrong. He had resolved to see one more Christmas. That would be Willie's last goal in life, and since there was nothing else to accomplish, he decided, with all his mind, what was left of it, that this would be his final accomplishment. To see one more Christmas even though a year ago Dr. Mike had basically denied him of that.

"We'll see," said Willie to himself, we'll see about that." There was nothing else left to live for, there was nothing else left he could control, save this one final goal. He felt if he didn't attempt this, then he may be as well die today, but he decided his" book of last's" was going to include one last Christmas. It would be an earnest, but short struggle.

A couple days before Christmas Dale called and asked if Willie was up for a visit.

"I can be," said Willie, with a little help.

"How does late tomorrow morning sound?" asked Dale.

"Sounds great, said Willie. I'll start trying to get up now."

In the morning when Jesse the nurse brought in his breakfast. Willie told her he wanted to get out to the living room this morning, so she needed to unhook him from all the monitoring crap.

"Are you feeling up for that today?"

"I feel pretty good today, I want to visit with my friend Dale."

"Sounds like a plan. I'm sure we can make that happen."

"Nice to see you up anyway." said Jesse

Later in the morning Jesse entered Willie's room and saw that he was able to get out of bed unassisted, though rather slowly. Willie wasn't sure if he was stiff from lying in bed too much, or merely from the fact that he was dying. He walked around the house a bit to see if he could limber up a bit. The doorbell rang and Jesse was headed for door, but Willie stopped her saying he'd rather get it himself. He figured right that it was Dale. Willie opened the door, and Dale stepped into the marble foyer.

"Your vertical, that's great."

"It is better than the alternative said Willie. Come on in you're just in time for lunch. Jesse makes the best strained pea soup I bet you've had." Willie negotiated his way back to his recliner.

"Are you ready for Christmas?" he asked Dale.

"Ready as I'm going to get."

"How about you?" ventured Dale.

"Same here, said Willie. Bring it on."

"I wanted to tell you I've gotten a few hits on some of your cars but I feel a little uncomfortable pulling the trigger while you're still, still…"

"ALIVE" helped Willie. "You can say it, While I'm still alive."

"Yeah, ok, I also have been talking to pastor Ron about auctioning the 67 Corvette. Seems like best thing would be to take it to the big buck auction in Las Vegas. It will mean shipping it but fortunately a member of your church owns a towing service business and he volunteered to move the car out there. That saves quite a few bucks. Since it's being picking up with no return, at least he will only have to transport it one way."

"Pastor Ron stopped by last week and he told me the two of you had gotten together already. I don't know how I can thank you for all your help, Dale."

"Don't worry about it. Other than that, how have you been feeling?"

Willie was quiet, a bit before answering. "Some days better than others but the outcome is inevitable. I'm in good hands here. I'm glad I decided to ride it out at home."

"How's Lisa? Did you tell her? "Asked Willie

"Actually no, I see now why you held out so long to tell people. It just throws people for a loop. What's the hurry to do that?"

"She was always fun. Hope everything turns out well for her, but I'm sure it will, if she's nothing else, she's a survivor." said Willie.

"Have you been in the garage lately?"

"No, not at all, but your project is ready and waiting."

"Definitely something I'd like to not think about," said Dale.

They made small talk for a while, but there's only so much you can say to a person who you know is about dead. Willie started to steer the conversation towards a comfortable exit for Dale. He didn't need to linger. Willie could tell he was at a loss for words.

"I hear the dinner bell; the pea soup is ready. You sure you don't want to stay for a bowl?" offered Willie.

"I think I'm good, I'll let you have all of it. Maybe I'll stop by Cherise's and have lunch with her."

"Personally, I think you'd enjoy the pea soup more," coughed Willie.

"Don't get up. I think I can find the front door on my own. Hope to see you soon." He never would again.

They both wished each other a Merry Christmas, as Dale turned and headed across the foyer to the door. He didn't and couldn't look back.

CHAPTER TEN

It was the morning of Christmas Eve. Willie called Jesse into his room and assured her he was fine. He wanted her to spend time with her family. "Just stock me up with some goodies and don't be into a big hurry to stop by in the morning. Enjoy some Christmas Day with your family and kids. I have everything I need by my side. I feel fine."

"You sure?" Vera would be mad as hell if you needed something, and I wasn't here.

"I'll call her and tell her I fired you." laughed Willie.

"I'm fine, honest, I'll spend some time making some calls. Cherise and Hope are supposed to stop by for a bit this evening anyway. They can let themselves in and out. Now go, and Merry Christmas."

"OK, but I'll still stop in for a bit in the morning."

"That's fine if it will make you feel better."

Reed called to wish him a Merry Christmas. That was nice. Reed already told Cherise he was sitting out Christmas, but would have them out after the holiday. That's a lot better than a Midwest winter. Cherise came with Hope. They helped him get another meal together and thanked him for the gifts he had sent to their homes.

"Sorry we came a little empty handed." Said Hope.

"We weren't sure what would be appropriate, except our company."

"You have that right. I stopped buying green bananas last week already," joked Willie.

"I can't imagine what someone could give me, or need to give me, except your smiling faces."

As with Dale, he provided an exit for the two. He pretended being tired. There was no reason for them to just sit by his side. They promised to call and check on him in the morning. "Merry Christmas to all."

Willie dialed Dr. Mike's personal cell phone. When Mike answered, Willie said, "I'm not going to keep you from your family. Its Christmas Eve. I just wanted to tell you I plan on proving you wrong. I'm going to live to see another Christmas after all."

"Go for it, Willie, I'll gladly be proven wrong. Enjoy tomorrow." With that they both hung up.

Willie could feel the bright sun of Christmas morning before he even opened his eyes. When he did, he could see it was going to be a crystal-clear day. The sun had just risen over the horizon and the rays were already flashing across the river and into his room. He smiled. He had beaten the odds. He did live to see another Christmas, that's all he had asked for. He was reminded of Zorba, in the Kazantzakis novel. On the day of Zorba's death, Zorba grabbed the sides of the window frame and shouted, "a man like me should live a thousand years." He wouldn't and neither would Willie. Without a whimper or a sigh, Willie closed his eyes and died.

CHAPTER ELEVEN

Jesse let herself into Willie's house a little after 10 A.M.

"Willie, it's Christmas," she said as she entered his room. It was obvious though, that Willie had passed away. She would never know if he fulfilled his commitment to himself to see another Christmas Day or not. She called Vera to let her know Willie was gone.

"OK Jesse, I'll take care of this from now on.

"I want you to know Willie told me how happy he had been to have you looking out for him. You did all you could. You were a comfort to him."

"I have a list. I'll get the phone chain started. Go enjoy the rest of your Christmas."

"I don't envy you making those calls, Vera, especially today."

"It really won't be that bad. Willie had done his part to prepare everyone. No one will really be surprised. He had given them time to prepare. I also know he took care of the funeral arrangements. I'll call Tutis to start the process for Willie's service. I'll fill you and everyone in on the arrangements as soon as they are known."

Vera called Cherise, "Cherise, I wish I was calling you to tell you Merry Christmas, but unfortunately that's not the only reason."

"I have a feeling I know what you're going to say."

"Yes, Willie died sometime Christmas Eve or Christmas morning. He was gone when Jesse got there at 10:00 o'clock this morning. I'll let you tell your kids. That's too private between you three. I'll take care of the funeral arrangements that Willie had requested."

"Being in this business keeps me in familiar territory with that. So, don't trouble yourself about that. Of course, I'll let you know about the arrangements."

"Even though it was expected, I'm still sorry, Cherise. Hope this news doesn't ruin your whole day."

"No, I'm fine, and thanks for calling me, and for the help you've offered. I'll call the kids, and yes, it's still sad though, that it's finally over."

"Yes, it is" said Vera, as she hung up the phone.

When Vera got into her office the next day, she informed the employees, and she prepared a note to be placed in the lobby of all the assisted living facilities. Willie was not a stranger to them. Many of the residents would be saddened. He had always treated them with respect.

Hope called Reed. Reed could see it was her on the phone. He answered it by saying "I already know, mom told me earlier today."

"You may as well come for Christmas because you'll be coming now in a few days anyway?"

"No, I won't be, I'm not coming back for the funeral".

"What do you mean you're not coming?"

"On Thanksgiving you asked me what dad and I talked about. He made me promise not to come back for the funeral, so I'm not going to."

"You can't go by what people say at a time like that. You don't know how clearly, he was thinking."

"No, he was quite clear about it. I'm not coming."

"Mom will never understand. She'll be upset."

"She'll get over it. She always does."

"What are the arrangements?"

"What do you care if you're not coming anyway?"

"Hey, I'd still like to know."

"Alright, visitation starts Saturday at noon. I still I think you're being a jerk about this."

"You can tell me all about it when you come out to see me after the New Year has begun. Now goodbye."

Hope hung up on him, without a word.

"Hey, its Reed Lovd, can I get a tee time for 10:00 o'clock Saturday?"

"Sure, the golf pro told him. "Is your dad playing again?"

"No just me, he can't make it this time."

"OK I've got you down, it's supposed to be a nice day."

"Thanks" said Reed, as he hung up the phone.

"Come on mom, we should go, we probably need to be there early.

"You think anyone will even show up? It's a Saturday, so people are off work, and some may not be willing to screw up their day for this."

"Whatever, we still should get going, only you mom, will be late for your own funeral."

Cherise and Hope drove together to the funeral home. When they got there the parking lot was already full.

"I can see it now your parlor will be full and the funeral director will say Cherise will along shortly."

"Who are all these people? I thought dad was the only guest of honor today?" asked Hope. You got me, just park and let's get in there."

The Tutis funeral director unlocked the door for them, as it was now the start of visitation time. He looked outside and commented that it looked like it might be a good turnout. People were starting to stream in, with barely enough time for Cherise and Hope to get themselves situated to receive well wishes and condolences. They were at a loss as to whom all these people were thankful most introduced themselves. Gratefully, soon Dale came in, and joined them in the receiving line giving them some comfort, as did Vera when she arrived. Off to the side Cherise asked Vera if she knew many of the people? Vera said, "she did. A lot were past and present employees and family members of the residents at the facilities.

Dale recognized probably more of the visitors than Hope or Cherise did. He made small talk with the ones he knew as more continue to stream in.

Outside the funeral home parking attendants were being overran with trying to park everyone in an orderly fashion. When the lot was full, many people began to park haphazardly on the adjoining street and along the road to the funeral home. It wasn't long before it came to the attention of the local police and they took over the ordeal. Officer Bob, Willie's friend from Malley's, was at the forefront to get everyone parked, somewhere, somehow, safely, though even after a bit he told his fellow officer to just let people park wherever they liked, as long as it was safe. He had never experienced a parking situation like this before. Damn it's just Willie, not JFK, he thought.

The funeral director approached Cherise and told her a problem was about to present itself.

"We are exceeding the occupancy load of the entire funeral home, not just Willie's parlor. I hope the fire department will be benevolent, or people are going to have to speed up their goodbyes." Vera overheard this and said, "I got news for you, there is a bus coming from each assisted living center with residents who are coming to see Willie off."

"How did they talk their families into even allowing that?" asked Hope.

"Don't underestimate the power of the matriarchs and patriarchs who still holds the purse strings." It's amazing how quickly the families approved things once faced with the threat of being cut from the will If they were not allowed to be here for Willie, one more time."

Cherise remarked to Dale, "Willie always said the numbers of people who attend your funeral is still pretty much determined by the weather."

"Have you looked outside recently Cherise?" Cherise went to the lobby and looked outside.

"It is storming now," she told Hope.

"Thank God, I can't imagine this if it was a clear day." Oh yeah, and by the way Dad, she said, as she looked upward, you didn't make much of an impact on people, did you?"

Cherise and Hope were greeted by Willie's brother and sister from out of town. "Quite a turn out, they said. We weren't aware Willie had that many friends?"

"Neither were we."

Cherise never thought Willie did have that many close friends. The friends he had were close, but very few she remembered. Willie always said, "he had all the friends he could use, and joked "a friend in need is a pain in the ass."

Dale talked to Cherise. "You know this is all a gift from Willie. There are so many people here with nothing but well wishes. It's impossible for anything to bring a tear to their eye. As Cherise looked around, she could see that Dale was right. Most people wore smiles and many were laughing at memories now long past, that included Willie in some way. He ordered this fiasco all on his own for our benefit."

"That is a little like Willie. One last joke". Yeah, like farting in the crowded elevator and getting out at the next floor leaving everyone to deal with it." Now they too, found themselves laughing at Willie's wake. No one would have expected this. Least of all Willie.

"Serves Reed right for missing out on this, said Hope. He should have been here, no matter what dad made him promise."

Towards closing, Cherise said to Vera, "I'm glad it's not like in the past where you were expected to feed all these people a meal afterwards."

"Mom, you could have made them a pie."

"Oh, please no, one funeral in a week is enough" joked Vera

"I guess Willie must have spread the news about my cooking skills."

"Let's just say, he said you were no Betty Crocker."

With that they all prepared to leave after a long day.

Dale caught up with the funeral director, and they spoke separately.

"Sure, come by Monday and I'll have him ready to go." Dale said he could do that. He said his goodbyes and left. Dale's work was about to begin.

Reed was keeping his promise to his dad. At 12:00 o'clock central time, the start of Willie's funeral, Reed was in position on the first tee. Maybe Willie had suggested he do this, so it would be impossible for him not to think of him. It's the kind of thing Willie could scheme up, and it was now impossible for Reed to dismiss the whole thing from his mind.

Maybe he should have gone back anyway. Well, it was too late for that now, he thought as he teed up a ball, for his first drive. He took a few practice swings. He felt at ease. This was after all what he was asked to do, and he was doing it. Obedient son, that he was. Reed had always been a natural athletic and had developed a long straight drive. Rarely missing a fairway, always surpassing his dad's iron shots. He felt suitably limber as he set his footing for the first drive of the day. He brought the club head down from a long backstroke. He made solid contact with the ball. He could tell he was going to get good distance out of the effort, and he did. The ball sliced deep into the rough. He couldn't believe it. "Seriously dad," he laughed as he looked skyward. He pulled his tee. He smiled as he got in the cart, driving off in search of a golf ball, and of lasting memories of his dad. Both searches were illusive.

A few days after the funeral, Dale called Cherise. "How are you surviving in a Willie-less world?"

"Dale, you know I've been in a Willie- less world as you say, for a long time."

"No, you haven't, but skip that. There's something else I called about. It's something we can best take care of in Willie's garage, and you probably should bring Hope along too."

"Any hint," asked Cherise?

"Let's just say it's about Willie's' final request, but you still won't believe it if I told you. This we need to deal with in person."

"When works for you and Hope? It can be an evening if Hope is working during the weekdays."

"Not sure, but I'm sure, she can make Saturday work. Is that soon enough?"

"Sure, said Dale, this is one thing where time is not of the essence, but it's important and needs to be dealt with."

"Ok, we'll both see you on Saturday, and again thanks for all you're doing."

"No problem," said Dale as he hung up wondering how they were going to deal with what he had in store for them. "Wow," he thought people always said a little of Willie goes a long way, but he was really outdoing himself with this one.

Dale arrived at Willie's garage on Saturday well ahead of Cherise and Hope. He had some prep work to take care of before they arrived. Dale let himself in the garage and headed for the workbench, package in hand. He had stopped at Tutis Funeral Home to pick up Willie in his now finely powdered self. Dale didn't know what to expect but he was a little surprised to be handed just a box, with the inscription Willie B. Lovd on it.

Dale thought it might be more dignified, remembering he had taken home a pair of newly purchased work boots in a box that was well, just about as impressive. Yet he hadn't asked for anything special, and he was sure Willie hadn't either.

He sat Willie on the work bench next to the awaiting bucket. Dale just shook his head as he reached inside and pulled out the borrowed bank deposit canister. He couldn't help but wonder what kind of day his old friend was having when he dreamt all this up.

As Dale twisted the cap of the canister aside, he noticed a vanilla envelope inside. He pulled it out and, on the outside, was written only the words, "Dale, beep- beep." Dale opened the envelope. Inside was a title signed over to him and the keys to the original 1968 426 Hemi Roadrunner. There was also a bill of sale made out for $10,000, with a separate note from Willie. It read. "I saved you a few bucks registering the car, when you pay sales tax to get the plates. Really how much can a 50-year-old 2 door Plymouth sedan really be worth? Tell them you got it cheap because it needs a little work."

"It didn't though and, and yeah legally he would have to add another zero and then some to the bill of sale, but that would never happen. Missouri would survive." "Fuck Em". Willie ended the note by saying "now pack my ass in the pickle bucket like you promised you would. And I expect to hear you burn the tires in that thing for me at least once. They were meant to be driven".

Willie.

Dale knew Willie didn't believe cars were just supposed to be garage art, and he was well respected for actually driving his. At a car show, Dale overheard a person tell Willie that he couldn't believe how much he actually drove his cars. Willie had a classic response. "Having cars like these and not driving them, is like dating a centerfold and not having sex with her because you want to keep her nice for the next guy." The guy just laughed and walked away, but it said it all. "OK, Willie, said Dale, here you go, but I'm robbing a beer from your fridge for this."

Dale opened the box of Willie's remains and carefully poured him into the drive-up bank canister, being careful not to get any of Willie on himself. Sure, they were friends, but still in all, thought Dale. When the dust of his friend settled, he snapped closed the lid and slid the canister into the center cavity Willie had created for himself. Then, following Willie's instructions, he siliconed the lid shut, then followed that up by making an impregnable seal around the lid and the rim of the bucket with the fiberglass material Willie had left for that purpose. No one would get in, and no one could get out, least of all Willie.

Besides the bucket on the workbench, were more envelopes similar to the one Willie had left for him. They were unsealed. Dale looked in each one and just smiled. Willie had left him a few special deliveries to make. A little of Willie could go a long way and there would be people who would grateful that he did.

As Dale finished his beer, he heard Cherise and Hope pull up in the courtyard between the two garages. He met them in the courtyard and lead them into the garage, to the workbench, where the bucket sat. It stood out a bit from the automotive items.

"First Cherise, I have to tell you, just so you know this is all above board, since Willie has me handling the sale of the cars, I need to tell you Willie signed the road runner over to me. Listen, I was as stunned as anyone, but he left the paperwork, I can show it to you."

"Dale first, I already knew he was going to give you the Roadrunner, and I feel you deserve that much and more. Think about it Dale. That car doesn't even represent 10% of what you saved Willie by selling these cars for him."

"Secondly, I'm a little offended that you think I would think you would ever be anything but honest about all this. I'm just amused I was told something before you too old wives got together about it," laughed Cherise.

Hope was distracted, staring around at all the cars. She had been in Willie's garage often but was still always a little overcome by someone's dedication to all this.

"Ok, sorry" said Dale, I just wanted to be in the clear with all that.

"Shut up Dale, you are. Now what the hell is in the pickle bucket?" asked Cherise.

"Well, it's not what, it's who," said Dale.

"What do you mean who?"

"Well actually, Willies in the bucket, at least his ashen self is."

"What the hell is he doing in a pickle bucket?" They both asked in unison.

"He's getting ready for a trip", said Dale

"Does he still have any beer in the fridge? asked Cherise. I'm ready. Now why again is he in the bucket?"

"I put him in there."

"Well why did you do that?"

"Because he told me to."

"When?"

"When he was still alive, of course." laughed Dale.

"Is this some kind of ongoing contest between you two, to see who is the craziest?" asked Hope.

"Well, what I'm about to tell you will prove that Willie would definitely be the winner of that contest."

"Make my day," said Cherise.

"This has been in the works for a while. He just didn't want me to tell anyone because he was afraid people would think he was crazy."

"Well, he's right so far."

"You know he had his ashes assigned to me?"

"Yeah, he told me that, said Cherise. I did kind of wonder what that was all about."

"Did you want them?" asked Dale.

"We're past that point, move on."

"You probably also know, how Willie felt about spending extended time underground?"

"Not sure how a pickle bucket would be a lot better," said Hope.

"Well at least the pickle bucket won't be underground," said Dale

"No, then where will it be?"

"That's why I brought you all here today."

"Again, make my day," said Cherise.

"Maybe it would help if you stopped thinking of it as a pickle bucket and more of as a ship."

"Headed back to the fridge, you want one Hope?" asked Cherise.

"Any tequila in there?"

"This was getting more difficult than Dale ever thought it needed to be, but he had the luxury of having had this all sink in for a while, they didn't. He decided, right out with it was the best strategy."

"He wants you and some close friends to meet at the park by the river and I'm supposed to throw him in the river."

"Were there any limes in there, Hope?"

"Did he say where he planned on going by chance."

"I asked him the same thing and his reply was basically he didn't care as long as he kept on going."

"I guess it's too late to have him committed to a psych ward?" asked Cherise.

"Were you planning on putting him in the room that says, WHY NOT?"

"Wow", said Cherise, "well when are we having the Bon Voyage party?"

"I think he'd like to get on his way as soon as possible. I'd say assemble the troops at the riverbank as soon as you can, and let's launch him per his final request."

"Dale, do you see why I had a problem or two being his wife for a spell?"

"No, I see how you must have been truly blessed."

"We're leaving, we'll be in touch" said Cherise as she and Hope left the garage. Promise me, this is the last surprise from Willie B. Lovd."

"I would think it is, but I can't guarantee it."

The minute Cherise dropped Hope off at her condo, Hope immediately called Reed in California.

"What! Is that even fucking legal?" Hope wasn't sure if anyone had contemplated that.

"And they say people in California are the crazy ones. You guys back there need to stop drinking out of the public water supply, Jesus. Fly over country, hell yeah as fast as you can and as high as you can. Thanks for the news, send me a video of this, I'm sure I can get it to go viral."

"This is for real. You have to come back for this."

"Oh yeah, I'd like a ticket to Saint Louis so I can watch my dad, who happens to be a in a pickle bucket, be thrown in the river."

"Would you like coach or first class?"

"I am not coming back for that."

"You have to. I'm sure you're not going tell me dad made you promise to not come back when we throw him into the river."

"Well, you got me there. I think I will come back, but merely to search the public records to see if there's any chance I was adopted as a child, so I can disavow myself of all of this shit once and for all.

"Will you send a letter to my boss, telling him to excuse me for a few days so I can go home and throw my dad in the Mississippi?"

"Can I email it to him? Just be here next week. Bye."

Dale called Cherise and advised her to keep this to as small a gathering as much as possible.

"Yeah, the less witnesses to appear in court the better."

"When will Reed be in town?" asked Dale.

"In a few days."

"Let me know when, and we'll pick a day so he can get back."

"Alright, I'll be in touch."

"Is this all starting to seem less insane to you?"

"No," said Cherise, but it is starting to affect Hope. She seems strange about it. She said, more than once, that she thought we shouldn't do it, that we should keep Willie around, maybe, she said, then she wouldn't miss him so much."

Sadly, it's kind of late to form a relationship with Willie now, if it doesn't already exist for her."

"Not sure about all that," said Cherise as she hung up the phone.

Cherise answered the door. It was Reed. "Ok, I'm here now. Let's get this over with so I can get back to La La land, as if I haven't landed here in it today."

"We were all just waiting for you. Dale, your dad's friend has been orchestrating most of this. I'll tell him you're here. It's only a small group. He can probably set it up with everyone for tomorrow."

"The chosen few, how lucky to be part of it."

"Reed, you need to lighten up a bit. It's a small thing in the overall scheme of things, and since you didn't bother to come to the funeral, it's the least you can do to be a part of it."

"I was asked not to come."

"Yeah, I heard," said Cherise.

It was a bearable winter day when they were all gathered at the small overlook by the riverbank. They were alone, it wasn't picnic weather by any means. Vera was there. Cherise had brought Reed and Hope. Dale was there with a shapely young woman, not much older than Hope. And of course, Willie was there. They all greeted each other. Cherise approached the unknown girl and asked, "who she might be?"

"I'm the bartender from Malley's Bar and Grill. Willie was a regular and a friend. Dale thought Willie would enjoy me being here.

"And who might you be?" asked Lisa.

"Well, I'm Willie's ex-wife."

"Ah, the chef, sorry we're not hiring." It was obvious to Lisa who Willie's son was. Though they were decades apart in ages, the resemblance was there. "Not bad" thought Lisa, "not bad at all."

"Granted it's a strange one, but we're here today to honor Willie's final request. Yet again, I'm not so sure about how strange a request it is. Willie always wanted to keep moving. He was always on the go. Can any of us picture Willie at a standstill? It's sad. We all know it's sad, but Willie brought us here for a reason. He wants you all to be sure, so that you all know, he would always be on the go."

Hope started to tear up. Dale passed the bucket to each of them to hold one last time. Hope seemed to refuse to let it go. She knew this was the end, and she would never see anything of Willie again. She was the last to hold him, and reluctantly gave Willie back to Dale.

Without a lot of fanfare Dale threw the bucket well into the current. All watched in silence, straining their necks to watch as Willie was rushed downstream out of sight. As intended by Willie, Dale had managed to cleverly keep the small stainless-steel placard attached to the bottom of the bucket from everyone's sight.

Reed left for California on the red eye the next day. Cherise and Hope headed home. Vera and the few employees she brought along drove off together. Dale and Lisa, headed for Malley's. It's just seemed like the appropriate place to go. "I'm going to miss that old fossil," said Lisa.

"Yeah, so will I," said Dale.

Dale was at Willie's garage early. The instructions said you've got to be there before he arrives so you can take his spot. Dale grabbed the packet off the workbench, opened the garage door and backed out the 67 GTO. With the car spending time in the heated garage, it didn't take long for it to warm up. Dale put the four- speed in gear and drove it into courtyard of Willie's estate. Some guy was about to become a lucky son of a bitch!

Dale pulled into the parking lot of the medical facility and aimed the car right for the designated parking spot marked "Porsche Parking Only, Doctor Michael Lillenberg." Sorry doctor, your car is about to be upstaged, as he put the GTO in the Porsche parking spot. Dale didn't know how much time he had before Doctor Mike would show up for work, so he hastily put the keys to the car in the vanilla envelope, sealed it, and put it between the driver's bucket seat and the console, partially hidden, but easy for Dr. Mike to spot. Dale got out, just as his Uber driver pulled up to take him back to Willie's house.

As Mike pulled on the nearly empty morning parking lot at the medical complex, he immediately spotted the car in his space. He parked in the space beside it. What the hell, wondered Mike. What was Willie's GTO doing here in his parking spot? He went around and opened the unlocked driver side door. The interior was empty except for the vanilla envelope between the bucket seats and the console. Mike got inside and sat in the driver seat. He was quickly overwhelmed by the nostalgic feeling the car presented. Damn this is as legendary as it gets. He pulled out the vanilla envelope and saw his name on it. He opened it and inside was a note along with the keys and the title. The note read.

"Dear Mike, I'm leaving you this car to enjoy for the day you stop practicing medicine. By the way, how long can you keep practicing medicine anyway before you finally decide to give up? This seemed like the best way I knew to convince you that there was no one else I would rather have had delivered the fateful news to me than you. I always valued our friendship as much as this car, so it's yours, but I expect you to give it its own parking spot." Willie.

"That doesn't look like a Porsche in your spot this morning" remarked an orderly Mike knew. Whose is it anyway?"

"It belonged to an unbelievable friend of mine. A truly unbelievable guy."

A man walked into the bank lobby and approached the reception credenza. "I'd like to speak to a teller. Her name is Megan Sheepley." Not recognizing the person, the receptionist asked, "if it was about a banking matter?"

"Not exactly," replied Dale.

"Maybe I can have you talk to the bank president, Vince Coleman, first?"

"Sure," said Dale as he was led to Vince's office. The receptionist left the two, but she could see from her credenza that the conversation was turning lighthearted, quickly. After a few minutes, Vince summoned Megan to his office to meet with Dale.

"Megan, this is Dale Howard, and he's told me he has something here for you. It's ok to step outside with him for a bit." The three exited the bank through the lobby, into the parking lot. There parked broadside in a few spaces, was Marilyn, Willie's 1955 T-bird. She hadn't seen it or Willie in months, thinking it was due to winter weather, she recognized the car instantly, yet wondering where Willie was? When they were at the car, Dale handed Megan the vanilla envelope with her name on it. She opened it and inside were the keys along with the title assigned over to her. There was also a note to her.

"Megan, now you can melt in the seat all you want, but you'll have to clean up after yourself because the car is yours now. You and Marilyn were meant to be together. You always made me laugh."

Signed,

William Bartholomew Lovd.

Megan knew with that, Willie had died. He had told her he would never tell her his middle name as long as he lived. Now she knew it, but wished she didn't. It was a poor trade. "Bartholomew," she said to herself as teardrops dotted the note. It wouldn't be the last time for tears remembering Willie, caused both by sorrow and by laughter.

People now up is lot number 42. As you can see it's a big block, 1967 Corvette roadster from the private collection of Willie Lovd.

Pastor Ron and Dale stood off to the side of the auctioneer platform as he went into his rendition, describing the car to its awaiting bidders.

"From previewing this car, you all know it's a much sought after 1967 four speed, 427 Tri-power car. It's complete with both tops, power steering, power breaks and windows. It has leather seats with the rare headrests offered only in 1967. Even more rare, the roadster has factory AC. It is one of the highest production numbers we've ever auctioned off, and also the highest optioned one we have ever come across."

"As perfect as it is, Mr. Lovd drove this car regularly. It was always maintained in a climate- controlled garage. Obviously, it couldn't have been more loved. The car is being offered with no reserve and the funds from the sale have been donated by Mr. Lovd to his home congregation, whose Pastor is with us here today." Pastor Ron raised his hand in acknowledgment. This is as fine an example of a 1967 as exists, so when you're bidding remember, "you can live in your car, but you can't drive your mansion."

"The bidding opened at $75,000 and raced into the six figures. The bidding was intense. It started to ease around $140,000. Telephone bidding took it past $150,000. The hammer dropped at $190,000 to an in-house bidder. Not bad for a car that costs less than $6,000 when new, thought Dale. He wondered who would have been more pleased, Pastor Ron or Willie. Dale knew he would never see the car again.

As Dale seated himself at the bar, Lisa put the beer she knew he wanted in front of him, and a seven and seven short with a piece of lemon to his side.

"Who's that for," asked Dale

"Just a force of habit. We can pretend he's here, can't we?"

"Don't tell me I have to pay for his drink even now that he's dead and gone. It was bad enough when he was alive," joked Dale.

"I'll just mark it up as one I fucked up and comp it off or slam it when no one is looking.

"What's been keeping you busy?"

"Mostly dealing with unloading Willie's cars."

"How's that going?"

"Pretty well. I told his realtor, the Girdon's that the garage will probably be empty by Easter. Those type of cars and motorcycles move quicker when the weather warms up, when people tend to enjoy them more. The auction in Las Vegas went well. Willie's Corvette sold for $190,000. His pastor is still on his knees thanking Willie for the donation. Willie had some designated he wanted to give to special friends of his, so I started spreading them around."

"I knew he had some money, but he never seemed like the kind of guy to drive around in $200,000 cars.

"You didn't happen to see one in the corner somewhere with my name on it did you," laughed Lisa.

"No sorry, I can't say that I did. Probably best for you. Those cars can suck some gas and you'd be stunned at the registration and insurance cost. You're better off without one. Too bad he wasn't into Gremlins. One of those would have been perfect for you."

"I'd take it. My pride and joy is about on its last leg, then I'll be on mine. How do people react when you hand them one of Willie's cars, anyway? "

"Well, how would you react?"

"Before or after I passed out? laughed Lisa. I'd probably be stunned shitless."

"That's about what it's like. The one's I've given cars to were caught speechless. It was a big surprise to them. I don't think they could contemplate such an incredible gift out of the blue. I'm sure it will take a while to sink in."

"Well that keeps my inheritance record in check, ZILCH!" said Lisa.

"I have to say I'm ahead of you there. I went to the reading of my rich uncles will and it read to my favorite nephew Dale, who never had a pot to piss in, I leave a pot." It hadn't even sunk in yet even to Dale, that Willie gave him a 1969 Road Runner.

"Well, you're one pot ahead of me."

"Sneak that drink, put it on my tab, consider it an advance on your inheritance from me."

I did make arrangements to sell one car this week and started negotiations on another." Surprisingly to Dale, he had sold the 33 Ford Willie called "the valedictorian of summer school." He also knew now why Willie had said that the car was in line for a proper education. It also surprised him somewhat, how much it sold for.

CHAPTER TWELVE

"Hey Pepper, this is dispatch. Figured you'd be out on the boat today, it's almost warm. Need you to run up the Red River tributary about a mile. They're calling about a car half submerged in the water from the westside bank. Can you check it out? Over."

"Got it, I'll head that way." Pepper enjoyed his job with the conservation department, primarily fish and game enforcement. This kept him outside along the streams and fields where he grew up. He liked fishing and hunting and drinking, but not necessary in that order. Being alone most of the day allowed himself the freedom to enjoy his favorite of the three, and it wasn't fishing or hunting. He never let it get out of hand in fear of jeopardizing his job. It was the only work he knew, but that didn't stop the temptations. People said they rarely ever saw Pepper drunk, nor did they rarely ever see him sober. He'd been known as Pepper for most of his life. A barmaid once asked him why he was called Pepper. He replied by saying "it was because people always think I was a little salty." Which made no sense at all, but to Pepper it sounded better than Paul, his given name. "Spicier" he thought.

The weather was starting to warm up. Today was one of the gifted unseasonably warm, late winter days. That made it beautiful to run the water in his open John boat. There wasn't a lot of activity this early in this year, but Pepper liked to get out early to make sure the streams and riverways would be safe and ready for the soon approaching fishing season. He checked for water blockages, either made by nature or made by man. It never ceased to amaze him what people thought was ok to just toss in the river. He wasn't far up from the mouth of the main river before he spotted the car. Sure enough, the front end was submerged under water, and the rear end being was held to the bank, due to brush and two tires sunk in the mud, to the axles. There was no way he would be able to clear this, so he got LeAnn in dispatch on the cell.

"Hey LeAnn, I'm at the site. It looks deserted, but you might want to call the local police to come and check this out for a missing vehicle situation. Tell them to send a tow truck too, I don't want this thing slipping off the bank into my river.

"Your river, huh Pepper?"

"Well, when my prop hits someone's abandoned pride and joy, it will be your bill, that's for sure."

"Ok," said LeAnn, I'll send out the men in blue. Hey, and Pepper, do I smell alcohol," laughed LeAnn.

" Impossible, I haven't had a drink since this time an hour ago." Pepper knew it stayed between the two of them, mostly. Pepper continued to dart his boat around the half-submerged car looking for any signs of life. There were none. Then off to the side ensnarled in the bushes along the bank he spotted what appeared to be a bucket. Not an unusual site, but this one seemed a little different than the normal junk people threw in the river, or that of something a fisherman might have lost from his boat. He worked his way to the bank until the bow of his boat held fast on the sucking river mud. There was no handle on the bucket, so it took a little extra effort to get it on board. The find of the day.

"Vera, it's Barry Lou, there's something over here I think you need to come and see."

"What is it?"

"I think it's best if you saw this for yourself. It's making quite a stir among the residents. Just come over."

Vera was perplexed as to what could be going on. She cleared a few items from her desk, grabbed her keys and headed for the other facility, all the way wondering what the issue could be. When she arrived, Barry Lou met her at the lobby entrance.

"You need to see this," she said as she led Vera down the corridor towards the dining area.

Though it wasn't lunchtime, the dining room was full of residents, some having arrived by wheelchair some by walkers, some unassisted. All were smiling, laughing and making small talk among themselves as they all stared at the glass wall to the al Fresco dining area outside. Vera made her way through them to see what the issue was. The al Fresco dining area was empty of all chairs and tables as the weather was still too inclement this early in the year to be used for dining. In the middle of the dining area sat a bright red, 1965 convertible Mustang. Vera unlocked one of the sliding doors that opened onto the outside dining area and went over to the car. The door was unlocked. She opened the door and inside saw a vanilla envelope, that simply said "Vera," on it. She opened the envelope and inside were the keys and the title to the car. There was also a note:

"Vera, it said, I hope it's as nice as the one you once said you had in college. You've forsaken a lot of life assisting me in all that we've accomplished. I could never have done it without you. This car comes with one stipulation. You have one year to find a replacement for yourself that can fill your shoes, and trust me I know that will not be a small task. It's time for you and your husband to pack up, drop the top and start smelling the asphalt. I've left you a little advance on your retirement package also. Vera opened a second envelope and inside was a check for $100,000. I miss you already,"

Signed, Willie.

Vera turned and with watery eyes, faced all the guests and said, "it's from Willie," as she held up the keys for all to see. All the residents broke into cheers and applause. From off to the side, Dale took it all in. He had one car left to give away.

Pepper negotiated the boat to a spot downstream where he could tie up. He began to examine the bucket. He could tell someone had put a lot of effort into making this ship-shape, for what reason, and what if anything was it. Upon turning it over, he read the plaque that was fastened to the bottom of the bucket. Even this engraved plaque was stainless steel, never to rust. For some reason the plaque, and what it said on it, especially attached to this bucket, began to make Pepper reflect inwardly on his life so far. What drove a man to do something so bizarre? To be so dismissed from his family as to have himself placed in a glorified pickle bucket and tossed into the river, certainly meant to carry him away. The engraved message was something he might have heard before and dismissed it but this time it was delivered to Pepper personally.

Cherise saw on her cell that it was Dale calling.

"Hello Cherise, how are things with you? It's been a while since we've talked."

"Yes, it has, and all is well here. Just put a pie in the oven, come on over, have a chunk", laughed Cherise.

"No, I'm good, but I was checking into coming over to see you about something?"

"Sounds serious?"

"Not really."

"OK I'm open tomorrow evening if that soon enough?"

"Sure, that works, replied Dale. See you then. Can you see that Hope is there also? Oh, and clear a space in your garage." Dale hastened his goodbye before Cherise had a chance to question why.

When Dale arrived at Cherise's house the next evening her garage door was open. Dale shut off the engine and glided into the awaiting empty space. He left the garage and went around to the front door, rang the bell and waited for Cherise to let him in. It was Hope who came to the door.

"Come in Dale, mom has something in the oven. Dale looked worried, Hope laughed, I'm just kidding, she's here though." They all gathered in the large kitchen area. "So, what brings you over," asked Cherise.

"I'm glad you could make it too Hope, because you're the real reason I came over."

"Really, why is that?"

"There's something in the garage I have to show you. Let's take a look."

The three left the kitchen, entering the garage from the inside door. Inside the garage was the Jaguar XKE that Willie had taking Hope out to dinner in. "Take a look, Hope it's yours." Hope, as well as the others who had received cars from Willie, was speechless except for repeatedly saying "OMG, OMG, OMG." Upon opening the right-side door, Hope immediately spotted something different. Willie had converted the car back to left hand drive. She also saw a vanilla envelope with her name on it. Inside were the keys, the title, and a note to her:

"Dear Hope, it's yours, I could never sell it, too many memories. It's as impractical as hell. It's meant for people who understand the best part of life is found when you color outside the lines. Now, get in and have a seat. She did, and it took her breath away. On the now passenger seat beside her was a single rose, as red as the car itself. I left this world knowing you would be the one, who would actually see all of it for yourself and for me."
Love Dad.

Hope couldn't get herself to get out of the car. She just leaned back and closed her eyes to hold back the tears.

"Finally, Cherise said, come on get out. I have dinner ready."

"No, stay in the car," joked Dale.

Hope got out and the three reentered the house, not without turning back to stare at the car one more time. Cherise was as much overcome by the gift as was Hope.

"You're going to have to let me keep it in your garage, said Hope. I don't have a garage at my condo and if we really wanted to see if dad could come back from the dead, all I'd have to do is let that car sit outside for one night."

"You can keep it here. That space is always empty."

"What are you going to do with it anyway?"

"I'm clueless."

"Well, if you sold it, said Dale, you could buy half a house that has a garage with the money you would get from that thing."

"I don't know if I could ever do that", said Hope.

"I would love to stay and eat," said Hope. She really didn't. I have a dinner date tonight and I'm a little behind already. "Dale, thanks for bringing the car over. I know you've been a great help to dad with all this, and I know that rose hasn't been in there, Dale, since dad died."

"No, but it was his idea, as was switching the car to left hand drive. He knew it would be a bit safer for you to drive that way. He had that taken care of already last fall."

"OK, see you all," said Hope as she left, thru the garage to take another look at the car she now possessed. Unreal she thought."

"Well, it's just you and me then Dale, let's eat," said Cherise.

"Sure, why not." Dale could think of a lot of reasons for not doing so, but he decided to brave the meal.

"Wine first?" asked Cherise

"Yeah, that might be best," answered Dale. Something to dull the taste buds, he hoped.

They made small talk as they ate. Cherise didn't have a handy dog under the table or nearby flowerpot, so Dale nibbled away at the offering.

"Hope seemed a little in a rush to leave?"

"Oh, she has a new plus one and amazingly she actually treats the guy like he's a deserving human, laughed Cherise. I've met him, and he seems kind of nice, but it's going to take more than nice."

"She's not the type to suffer fools, nor should she be, said Dale. She's not the type, to be tamed."

"Tamed, hell, most guys are afraid to go into the cage with her. Whoever the chosen one is, it's best if he knows most dreams are a nightmare waiting to happen."

"You make her out to be a beast. Anything worth having is worth working for. I'm sure she is capable of being on a two-way Street.

"Yeah maybe, said Cherise, just have the wrecker on speed-dial,

"Cherise was shocked. Dale did eat the food, but waved off the seconds and wasn't about to risk desert.

"Something just dawned on me. You're here without a car. How are you going to get home?"

"Delivering all these gifts for Willie has made me customer of the month with all the Uber drivers."

"You don't have to do that, I'll run you home. I'm a better driver than I am a cook." That was only slightly reassuring to Dale, but he was happy to accept the ride. They got into Cherise's car. As she backed out of the garage, they both stared at the Jaguar and just shook their heads, still in disbelief.

"Just drop me off at Malley's if you would please. How are the kids handling Willie's departure?"

"Reed in California is hard to read and a long way away. Those two both carry the male Lovd trait. Never too many outward signs of affection. Reed didn't get to spend a lot of time with Willie growing up, but inside I'm confident it's all good between them. Hope is a different matter. I believe the loss is starting to sink in a little. They were close in mindset. A lot of people thought Willie could be a little out there, as people say. I could always see Hope there too, maybe not. They both lived in a world of color, Reed did too, but the only colors in his world were black and white, with maybe a hint of grey. Divorce is harder for a father and son than a mother and daughter. Girls are meant to do girly things with their moms. Dads for them, are there to fix everything. A son often feels deserted without his partner around. It's hard on both the father and the son and a distance grows between the two that's no one's fault."

"They're both great strong kids. Things might not have worked out the best for you and Willie, but you two produced two children you can both be proud of."

"We always are," said Cherise, as they pulled up to Malley's.

"How are you going to get home from here?" asked Cherise.

"You never know, some lady might get lucky," laughed Dale. "Whomever that might be, I'm sure she wouldn't even know how lucky she really got."

"You're too kind, Cherise, thanks for the lift," said Dale, as he got out of the car.

"And thanks for dinner too, kind of. Bye now."

Lisa was at the bar. It was her week to work the Friday night shift.

She gave Dale a beer and a menu and went off to deal with other customers. Dale looked over the menu, he had memorized long ago and decided to skip it after an incredible meal at Cherise's!

Lisa came back to him during a lull in her activity. "What brings you in tonight?"

"Just your smiling face. Actually, I just delivered the last giveaway car of Willie's.

"Who was the lucky person this time?"

"It was his daughter Hope." "He left her the XKE Jaguar."

"That would be tough to accept, I'm sure. She was at Willie's launch party, wasn't she? She seemed to be the more emotional one there, as I remember."

"Yeah, they had kind of a special bond between each other."

"If someone was going to give me an XKE, I'd have had a hell of a bond with them, too."

"Hope? what kind of name is that for someone anyway?"

"I like it. It's uplifting and inspiring I think," said Dale.

"Really, I think it's a horrible word. Everyone is always saying well there's always hope. Well, what does hope really get you? Hope is a major disappointment waiting to happen. Hope can end up shattering your dreams into pebbles on the bottom of a cliff. Hope is nothing but the bastard stepchild of wishing. Both are there just to set you up for the pain of disappointment. Wishing and hoping will not get you anything unless you apply effort to them, and if you put out the effort why do you need to hope and wish? I'll take luck any day, over those two."

"Yeah, the easy way out. With luck all you have to do is lay around and wait for it to happen to you. How's that working out for you?

"Hope, she doesn't need to hope or wish for anything. She's already has everything. I pity her."

"Wow, now that comment is going be reflected in your gratuity."

"You know what, you can take your gratuity and go fuck yourself."

"I was just really hoping you were feeling better?" said Dale.

"I wish I was, said Lisa, as they both burst out laughing, realizing they were both wishing and hoping.

Lisa headed down the bar to tend to another customer. She was apologetic when she came back "It was uncalled for. She seems nice and probably deserves everything she has."

"Don't worry about it, and your kind of hot when you get all feisty like that," joked Dale.

"I hate it when we fight. That's what boyfriends are far."

"Not a problem, all in is forgiven." offered Dale.

"You're too easy. It's just been a bad time for me lately. Finally, I've achieved zero financially and I'm sure Shannon has now realized going to college is probably out of the question for now. That bothers me the most."

"Hate to hear all that. Give me one more and I'll let you get back to work. Looks like it's going be a big tip night. Dale finished the last beer she brought him and rose to go. "Here's to be hoping and wishing that luck comes your way."

"You know what Willie used to say?"

"He would say lots of stuff, but what in particular?"

"He would say, "you know what I like about you? "Nothing!" laughed, Lisa.

"Lisa, you love me, and you know it."

"See you next time."

Pepper called into dispatch and told LeAnn to clock him out for the rest of the day.

"Not wanting to miss happy hour?"

"No, I'm actually going home."

"Your wife will go into shock," I'll alert 911.

"I guess I deserve all that," said Pepper.

"Ok, said LeAnn, you're off the clock. "

Pepper held the bucket and reread the sentence. It was true you couldn't go back and make a new beginning, but you can start over and make a new ending. Pepper had never been the physically abusive type with Debbie. His biggest crime really was going AWOL in his marriage. He felt it was time to correct a few things. Although he liked being on the water, he didn't think he would like floating on it for eternity in a pickle bucket. He took out a pen and piece of paper and wrote down the connection for Hope. He then started the outboard, and headed for the mouth of the river. Upon reaching the Mississippi, he put the engine in idle and returned the bucket to the river. He was overcome by the impact it had made on him. He headed for home, to try and save what was left of his marriage.

"What are you doing home already? Did you finally get fired or did the bar burn down?" Pepper let all the comments from his wife, slide off his back. He was sure they were deserved.

"No, I came home early to see you, before you went in for your night shift."

"Well lucky me." Pepper understood his wife had no reason to be excited to see him. He was a big reason she had turned so callus, but he was determined to break through to her.

"It's about something I found out on the river today".

"What, an abandoned cooler of beer a fisherman left behind?"

Where did the woman go, he had married, what had he let happen to a once cheerful young woman, not much more than a girl when they met? The harshness she now exhibited made Pepper resolved that much more to break through to her.

"What I am about to tell you will probably make you think I did stop off for a drink, but I didn't. I pulled a bucket out of the river, inside of it, it said, where the ashes of someone who decided he preferred to float the waters of the world, then stay close to his family after his death."

"Well, why does that create this great empathy for you?"

"It wasn't the bucket so much as what was engraved on it."

It merely said, *"a person can't go back and make a new beginning, but you can start over and make a new ending."*

"That's what I want to do, start our lives over and make a new ending. A different one from the one we are headed for." Debbie was silenced by what she could tell was a sincerity in his voice coming from his heart that she had never heard before, but she was cautious.

"You know Pepper, I've heard this all before."

"Yes, I know you have, but this time will be different."

"And why is that?"

"Because this time I'm actually going to try."

Reed answered his phone when he saw it was Hope on the line.

"What's up Hope?"

"You're not going to believe it but I got a call from dad."

"Oh, I'm sure you did. Did he happen to say where he was calling from?"

"Well of course it wasn't from dad, himself. It was from a game warden who found him up a creek somewhere south of Memphis."

"Up a creek, huh without a paddle? I suppose. What did the game warden say by the way? And how did he get your number?"

"I asked him the same thing and he said the bottom of the bucket had an engraved plaque on it with my name and contact information on it. Dale had that covered by a sheet of paper, so we couldn't see it, knowing it would wash off quickly once dad hit the water.

"Well, why did he call?

"The plaque told him to call my number for hope, and he said he needed all the hope he could get. He said he didn't know if I was a real person or if he was going to get some recorded and spiritual message about hope."

"It would have been a lot less confusing for him if you had been named Shit Head, instead," laughed Reed.

"He really called to tell me, that he was moved by the whole experience, and to tell me he sent dad back on his way, as he had requested on the plaque."

"I have to say, the old man really gets around. Keep me posted if he washes up anywhere fun. We could go see him, NOT!" said Reed, as he hung up the phone.

Lisa's phone rang, but it was a number she didn't recognize. Usually, she didn't answer those or just let them go to voicemail or junk messaging to be glanced at later. For whatever reason, this time she thought "oh hell, I'll live dangerously, what is someone going to do, drain my bank account?"

"Hello, my name is Trey Lawrence. I'm calling to contact Shannon Williams to welcome her to the fall semester here at Missouri State and to give her some general information that may be helpful for her enrollment process."

Lisa was shocked and confused. "I am her mother, but I think we have a problem you may not be aware of," said Lisa.

"What might that be," asked Mr. Lawrence?

"Well, basically we're penniless, and it just gets worse from there."

"Well, now I'm the one who doesn't understand. Are you not aware that Shannon's entire tuition has been paid for, plus funds set aside for books and housing?"

"Is this some kind of fucking joke?" Pretty cruel, as everyone knows I have no money for college."

"I will say it came as a little surprise to us here at the Administration Department also, but I assure you this is no form of a prank. "Is Shannon interested in studies revolving around archeology by chance?"

"No, not at all, why would you ask that? That again makes me suspicious of this. Where are the funds coming from?"

"It is a group we have never dealt with before, but we've verified that the funds are definitely good. It's an organization called "The Fossil Group." The CEO seems to be a person named William Lovd.

"Oh my God, You crazy bastard."

"Excuse me?" said the administrator.

"Oh sorry, not you, forget that. I do know a William Lovd."

"So, you're all good with this?"

"How could I not be? I'll talk to Shannon as soon as she gets in. She will be as thrilled as I am. You will be getting an excellent student, that I can promise you. Thank you so much Mr. Lawrence for calling me, and I hope you can forgive my expression of shock? It's was a total surprise."

"I can see how it would be. We look forward to having Shannon here with us in the fall. You will receive more information concerning all this in the future, and I hope to see you also at orientation."

"Goodbye for now and enjoy your day."

"I'm pretty sure I will."

"OMG, OMG, OMG," was all Lisa could manage to say when she got off the phone. "OMG, OMG, OMG, "Willie, you old fossil." Lisa couldn't wait to call Shannon and tell her the news. It was all true and it was still beyond belief. "Willie. You, old fossil." It was more than she had wished and hoped for.

And Dale, she wondered, how long had he known about all this, without telling her. Wait till I see him, she thought.

Chapter Thirteen

It was a picture-perfect morning the day the tide deposited Willie on the sands of Orange Beach, Alabama. The tide entering at the East Past in Perdido Key, brought him to rest at the beachfront Grande Point Condominium property. A swelling wave left him in a pool of water on the beach.

"Where are these guys at?" asked Joy, the bride to be.

"I'm sure they're right there in front of the preposition," joked Tawney, her maid of honor.

"Fuck you, laughed Joy. You know what I mean." They had been friends for life and always would be.

"They went to the mullet tossing competition at the Flora- Bama lounge. So, I'm sure they are still there, bushwhacked to the wind."

"Great, they'll all come back smelling like fish for the wedding."

"Are you sure about all this." asked Tawney. Joy was silent for a bit.

"Yeah, it's all good. I'm 27 so the clock is ticking. It's the woman's curse, get married and have kids by 30, or risking being a spinster forever."

"You guys are great together. You'll make it work out. Just remember to live in the real world. "Every day is not going be a honeymoon.

Take it from a woman who knows." Tawney's wedding had lasted four years.

"Sometimes I wonder if the whole concept of marriage is realistic. It's asking for an impossible situation to work out. I mean really, what happens when the new car smell wears off?"

"That is what I'm talking about, Joy. You have to have a plan for when that happens. It's few marriages where it doesn't, but that doesn't mean you can't still be great life partners."

"You're right, I've struggled about all this, but I still say, if I were 22 instead of 27, there's no way I would be standing on the sand tomorrow and saying I do, to anyone, even Josh."

"He'd be a tough one to let get away. Which is more than I can say for his pick of a best man, Derek. Joy, that guy is a loser. I can never see him and Josh as being compatible friends. So different. I've told you from the beginning of this 'wedding on the beach thing' that you will be lucky if Derek doesn't manage to fuck it all up somehow."

"How could he really do that? He doesn't have that much of a role to play."

"Trust me, he can be brilliantly stupid. If that guy thinks being the best man and me being the maid of honor gives him some kind of "couples privileges," I'll grab the nearest mullet and slap him senseless."

"We better get over there and rescue them, from flinging fish, or from fishing for fling." They both laughed as they left the condo. The girls met the guys at the bar. Josh seemed in good shape, but it was easy to see Derek was already headed for Lala land.

"Josh, is he going to be ok tomorrow?" asked Joy, when they were apart from the others.

"Oh yeah, he'll be fine. What do you ladies have planned for Joy's last night of singlehood?"

"We're just going to a nice quiet restaurant out at the Wharf, then back early. I don't want my eyes looking like two piss holes in a snowbank tomorrow."

"You do have a way with words."

"I know, that's why you're marrying me."

"Uh, not really."

"What plans do you have?"

"There is a foam suds party at the Hang Out. Derek thought it would be fun to check out."

"Oh great, I'm sure that's what he needs, but then again, maybe at least he won't be smelling like a fish tomorrow."

"He's really not as bad as you think. I've known him a long time, and we were in Iraq together, so we have that."

"Well that explains the, PTSD."

"How about this. Let's meet early in the morning and go for a stroll on the beach, since I'm not supposed to see you tonight?"

"I'm not sure we're even supposed to see each other today, as tradition goes."

"That's too tough, just tonight is bad enough."

"Ok, I'll bring some coffee and we can walk the beach and plan our lives together, or at least hope we get through tomorrow."

"I love you Josh, and I always will." "I love you too Joy, and I always will. See you in the morning."

"How long have you known about this?" asked Lisa

"Known about what?"

"This," said Lisa, as she placed the letter from Missouri State in front of Dale on the bar.

"Oh, you mean that"

"Yeah, that."

"For a little while. There were details I had to work out, per Willie's instructions."

"Dale, do you have any idea how wonderful this makes things for me?"

"Yeah, I bet it's quite a game changer in your life."

"And a shock too," said Lisa.

"These are the things I wish Willie could express for himself, instead of just having put all these things in motion for people. I'm sure he knew you would be thankfully relieved and happy to have a financial burden lifted from you. He told me, you deserved it. He said he never heard you ask for anything for yourself. Your concerns were always for your daughter that meant a lot to Willie."

"I told you before, one of his cars wouldn't have done you any good. So, he picked the perfect one to sell for you."

"Which car would be so perfect for him to sell for my benefit," asked Lisa?

"Willie had a car, that was a little different from the others. He always called it the valedictorian of summer school. It was a high dollar car but a little on the wild side. He always joked it didn't play well with others. Some people thought it was a little uh, somewhat socially unacceptable. Like you," laughed Dale. "One day in the garage, he told me it was time it got a proper education. It was time it went to school. He didn't tell me then, but looking back on it now, I'm sure he was talking about selling it and financing someone's education.

"Upon his death, mixed in with all the packets of instructions was a packet with the details about selling the car and funding your daughter's tuition with it."

"So, you've known about this since Willie died? Why didn't you tell me?"

"I wasn't sure how much the car would sell for, or when, so I didn't want to get your hopes up, until I sold it. I was stunned, and by now you probably have a good idea how much it sold for. 'The valedictorian of summer school ' is off to college, at least the money from the sale of it is."

"Who came up with the name, The Fossil Foundation?"

"That was all Willie. He thought you'd get a kick out of it."

"It's still all unbelievable and now that he's gone, how do you thank a person like that?"

"Yeah, that's quite a gratuity I'd say."

"You got that right. Here, here's one on me."

"I'll take it, said Dale, thanks. And can maybe my gratuity come out of Willie's gift?"

"No", laughed Lisa.

Josh and Joy met early on their wedding day on the beach, as planned. They kissed good morning and began a stroll into the easterly rising sun. They walked barefoot, hand in hand. These two were meant for each other. They darted in and out of the gentle morning surf, scanning for the perfect shells, occasionally stopping to pick up one from among the millions. Joy spotted one she's thought was especially nice and picked it up. She rinsed it in the morning tide to wash away the sand.

"Hey Josh, you think you could find the matching other half for me?" she laughed.

"Joy, that would be easier, then finding a better match for me, than you."

"That might be the nicest thing you have ever said to me."

"Well, I mean it and I love you," said Josh

"And I do you, Josh lets never fight. Josh would only hope that would be true, but he was sure the shit was about to hit the fan.

"Joy, I have to tell you something, he began."

"Hey look there's a bucket," said Joy, as she ran ahead towards it. "Saved by a fucking bucket, thought Josh, "at least for now."

Joy picked up the bucket and the two examined it. This was no ordinary bucket that just happened to wash ashore, tossed overboard like trash.

"Look there's an inscription on the bottom."

"It's like some large message in a bottle thing or something."

"It's a message alright. The message is someone's ashes are inside."

Sure, enough the message said, "these are the final remains of Willie B. Lovd." This is all that's left of me, kindly return me to the sea."

"Who would do something like this," asked Joy. Look at the inscription."

"You can never go back and make a new beginning, but you can start over and make a new ending."

"That's beautiful. It's like an omen, like a wedding wish for us. Can you believe we found this on our Wedding Day? I love it, said Joy. It's perfect, oh and what were you about to tell me? Sorry I ran off."

Oh, I hope she won't, thought Josh, when he told her the news. That bastard, he thought, to himself.

"I may as well come out with it," started Josh, Derek is missing in action."

"Missing in action, exactly what does that mean?"

"He may still show up, it's still early," said Josh.

"What do you mean, he may still show up?"

"What did that asshole get himself into. I knew it. Tawney even warned me about the trouble he could cause. Where is he?"

"Last night at the Hangout, he hooked up with some people and they carried the party to Fort Morgan. I wasn't about to go, but couldn't talk him out of it, so he left with them and as of now, no phone service for him."

"Fort Morgan, are you kidding me! Well, that is the perfect place for him."

"Everyone out there is either waiting for their court date to show up or they are in the witness protection program. Why do you think they put Fort Morgan 25 miles out of town? It's some kind of prison colony I heard."

"It's not that bad. Just because you like to be hidden away, that doesn't necessarily mean you're a bad person."

"Whatever do you plan to do about this? Don't tell me he's carrying my ring around with him?"

"Oh no, I have that."

"Thank God or we'd both have to go checking all the pawn shops in Fort Morgan to find it by now. I've asked you before, but I guess you're sure you're still going to defend him as your best choice for a best man. You have a lot of nicer friends that him, you could have chosen."

"It's early, don't worry, I'll get ahold of him," said Josh.

"You know what? Don't. I don't want him in my wedding or our life after we're married."

"Well, we have to have someone. I can't just ask the bartender in the Flora- Bama lounge you know."

"You know what, I have just the person to be our best man, said Joy, as she marched off the beach with the bucket under her arm."

"I'll see you at 1:00 o'clock to marry you, please don't go to Fort Morgan looking for that loser. We don't need him."

Something had just dawned on Josh that was a harbinger of married life. Sometimes it's best to just not argue with them.

When Joy walked into the condo with the bucket, Tawney instantly asked "what's that?"

"It's not what's that, it's who's that."

"Really, well who's that then?"

"It's your partner in the wedding. It's Josh's new best man? You nailed it. That damn Derek has gone AWOL and I told Josh to keep him away from our wedding if he even shows up."

"I'm for that, but what's the deal with the bucket?"

"OK, here goes," began Joy.

After listening to the whole saga, Tawney announced "it works for me." Do I have to dance, with it or him, he's kind of short?" laughed Tawney.

"Does it really matter? The wedding is really just about Josh and I anyway."

"Willie B. Lovd is as welcome as anyone, and he comes with a great sentiment. I believe he was a wonderful guy."

"It wouldn't take much to top Derek, I'll give you that."

"Ok, then let's scrub him up a little and find him a tie."

"Steal one of Derek's if you have to, he won't be needing it."

Josh was the first to arrive at the beachfront ceremony site they had chosen. He wasn't about to be late. Across the beach came Joy in her beach appropriate wedding gown, followed by Tawney carrying a four-legged stool and a bucket.

"Meet your best man, Willie B. Lovd," announced Joy to Josh, as Tawney placed the bucket on the stool next to Josh. It was all too ridiculous for words, so why utter any, thought Josh. Laughter seemed more appropriate. The person chose to officiate the ceremony also thought it was a bit odd, but after a quick pursual of the Holy Scriptures, could not find any case where it said a pickle bucket wearing a tie could not be a best man at a wedding, so it must be a sanctioned ceremony. Let's get on with it, the Bushwackers are getting warm. "

"Yad da, yad da, yad da, now both of you say I do." "I now pronounce you man and wife, kiss her and let's get off this beach. It's hot as hell already."

That officially ended the ceremony. They all had a wonderful afternoon and evening celebrating. Derek never showed and no one missed him, least of all Tawney.

In the late morning Joy sent an email to the person named Hope on the bottom of the bucket.

"Hope, not sure what your relationship is to a Willie B. Lovd but I wanted to tell you he was the best man at our wedding yesterday. He washed ashore just in time. Our best man bailed on us. What's he doing floating around the world alone anyway? His request was to be thrown back into the sea. We tried but he kept washing back to shore. Tomorrow for our honeymoon we're going deep sea fishing in Destin. We'll take him along and throw him overboard when we're way offshore. I guess you're good with that. Seems sad to me, but he was a great best man. See pictures."

Love Joy, Orange Beach AL.

"Joy, I'm his daughter, and thanks for responding. It's a long story. Best wishes on your marriage, word is there's nothing better than a good one, and nothing worse than a bad one. So far, I haven't taken the risk."

Hope Lovd.

Hope stopped by her mom's house to surprise her with news of dad's latest appearance.

"What brings you over sweetie?" asked Cherise as she let Hope in the front door."

"We missed a wedding."

"What wedding?"

"The wedding dad served in as the best man in Orange Beach AL."

"What?"

"Yes, dad was in a wedding in Orange Beach last week, as the best man.

"Funny, I thought he was stuck in a pickle bucket?"

"Oh, he was and wearing a tie."

Hope showed Cherise the photos of Willie perched on a stool beside the groom, on the beach in Alabama. She told Cherise how it had all happened and told her today he was deep sea fishing off the coast of Destin.

"I'll say this, he is having the time of his life, no pun intended.

He always liked the Gulf Coast area, I guess he decided to go back."

"Remember when we rented the house in Gulf Shores?"

"Remember when Reed lost his beach ball and couldn't get over it?"

"Remember when you got stung by a jellyfish, and everyone wanted to pee on your leg to make the stinging go away?"

"Remember when I tried to make dad eat raw oysters.

"Yeah, I remember he wouldn't do it."

"I remember all the great times we had there. Then we all grew up." laughed Hope.

"Funny pictures. He doesn't even know what happened to

him, nor will he know when he's thrown off the fishing boat tomorrow."

"This all makes me miss him", said Hope. Seems like other people are enjoying him more than we can."

"I really don't know what to tell you Hope, I'm sorry. Call Reed and tell him just to drive him crazy," laughed Cherise.

Chapter Fourteen

"Grab the bucket. Bobby, grab that bucket."
The boys were in trouble, against better advice, they sailed offshore earlier in the day. Even in a calm sea the small sailing skiff they were on, was unsuited for venturing this far from protected shores. Young, and tough as they were, they weren't smart enough to head in at the first sign of the coming storm. Though they were experienced sailors, they were still not able to stay in front of the storm. Thankfully, their lifetime of sailing experience taught to them by their father, who was a charter fishing boat Captain sailing out of Sanibel Island, had allowed them to keep the small craft upright in tossing seas. Then the main sail broke away and rendered them at the mercy of the waves. Eventually the sailboat pitch- poled, throwing them into the water, far from the boat and far from shore. Bobby managed to get to the floating bucket, just before another wave would have tossed it far from his reach. Thank God, thought Dennis, his older brother. They would need all the extra buoyancy they could find to ride this out to make their way to shore. "Mom would really be pissed if I let Bobby drown," thought Dennis.

Just as bad luck had brought them a sudden sea squall, good luck might have they been their savior. The combination of their life jackets and the bucket allowed them to keep their heads at least above the wave tops. The mist caused by the foaming seas in this intense rain was enough to cause a drowning effect, if they couldn't keep the water out of their lungs. The situation was dire, even though they could faintly see the lightened shore. Thankfully the storm was overcoming the approaching evening ebb tide that would try to hamper their efforts of progress towards the shore. At least that was one blessing brought on by the storm. The sailboat was lost.

"Are you ok Bobby?"

Dennis could see his younger brother was starting to shiver from the cold rain, though the water temperature was fairly moderate. "We'll make it, we always do."

Bobby was starting to look uncertain about that. The bucket was incredibly buoyant and showed no signs of leaking. Dennis blessed the sea gods for bringing it to them. Even he was uncertain about their chances without it. Efforts to dog paddle toward shores seemed fatal but there was little else they could do. By now already, he was sure mom was in her worry mode. There was going to be hell to pay if they survived but, it was better than the alternative. Dennis knew now, he should have skipped sailing today instead of school.

Dennis knew no boat would be sent out to search for them. No one knew for sure where they were, or if they were even still out, not to mention it would soon be dark. Their best hope was that the sea would spit them ashore, just as the whale had done for Jonah.

They both wrapped their arms around the bucket and rode out the waves.

Ruth had decided to call her husband Noah.

"Noah, I'm scared. The boys are out in this and there's no sign of them."

"What are they doing out in this, it's a school day?"

"Well, it's best to deal with that later, but their boat is not in the slip."

Knowledgeable that Noah has, he still, knew there was little he could do. There had been a small ship advisory out for 4 hours already.

"You have to do something Noah", pleaded Ruth. Noah had no idea where they may be, but knew they were smart enough to try and make it inward to shore.

All I can do is keep paralleling the shore in an outward pattern from the marina and hope to spot them heading in. He knew the chances of that were slim to none. He left the marina in his boat, all lights on in hopes that if he couldn't see them, maybe they would spot him. There was still some daylight left but the storm had caused the afternoon skies to darken. Weather reports showed that the storm was to blow inland over the coastline at Sanibel soon. That would help. Running his boat somewhat parallel to the waves risked the danger of being broached by a rogue wave, but his boat was large enough to handle that, he hoped. Just in case he kept piloting with his bow slightly turned to sea. He also alerted the Coast Guard, about a possible May Day. Once a bit from the shore, he repeatedly blasted the air horn, in an attempt to draw attention to himself, yet all his efforts seem futile. Prayer seemed the best solution at this time.

"Bobby, Bobby, you hear that?" Bobby seemed groggy but perked up a bit when he finally heard what he knew was a ship's horn, repeatedly blasting. Hearing it and getting to it were two very different things though. Noah had no way of knowing if his efforts were of any avail. He just had to convince himself that he had not missed them on his way out, so he kept continuing a zigzag pattern away from shore. It was really all he could do. His spotlight in the dim afternoon light wasn't fully effective, but it was worth scanning with it. Non- oscillating binoculars also helped, as the pitching waters, rocked his boat.

As the skies darkened towards evening, Dennis saw a scanning search light as it flashed over them. They did all they could to attract its attention, but there was little motion either could create. Shouting would be a waste of time and do nothing but limit what little energy they had left to keep them somewhat afloat. It was back to praying.

Ruth was worrying herself sick at home. Now she knew why she preferred Colorado. She had always been a ski Bunny, not a beach bum. The boys had never seen snow. They loved the sea. Now she just hoped it wouldn't claim them.

"There, there," shouted Noah to himself. He spotted something in the water off his portside. He hit it with his spotlight and laid on the horn in a signal he knew the boys would know. "It was them, damn it, it was them. Where the hell was their sailboat? He quickly motored the boat in their direction until he was alongside. They're frantic flailing of their arms told Noah they were ok. He got them aboard and seated safely. He was about to engage the engine to make way for shore, but they pleaded for him to bring the bucket aboard. He couldn't see the reason for it, but he ran below and grabbed a fish net and snatched up the bucket, bringing it aboard.

"You two are in for a world of shit, but for now I'm glad you're safe." He immediately sent a message to Ruth telling her the boys were safely aboard and they were heading in. "Miracles do happen," she thought when she heard the news.

The boys shivered under the warm blanket all the way to the harbor. They were saved from the sea, without their beloved sailboat, but safe. When they reached their slip, the boys were quick to hop to the dock. They grabbed the line thrown to them by Noah and quickly secured the boat to the dock cleats. Noah lowered the fenders over the side of the boat to protect it in the still tossing water even with the marina's protection behind the stone jetty wall. They had been extremely lucky. Luckier than they would be when they got to the house. They had lost everything they had when the boat went down. All they had to carry ashore was their bucket. It looked a bit rough, and Noah asked, "why they even wanted it?"

"Well, other than the fact that it probably saved our lives, started Dennis, we really want to check it out. It's a little different than just some floating rubbish."

"Suit yourself, but let's get to the house, I'm sure mom will be relieved to see you before she starts the thrashing," laughed Noah.

Dennis and Bobby, both cringed at the thought of that. After a period of hugging and tears of joy and relief from their mother she told them this had all happened at a very opportune time. "Your dad's boat could use about a month's worth of barnacles scrapped off the hull. I'm sure you two won't mind doing that, will you?" asked Ruth. Dennis and Bobby both knew that wasn't really a question. Great, there goes a good portion of the impending summer school break.

"The slippery, clean hull will save your dad some fuel, maybe enough to make up for what he used this afternoon, looking for you two. That didn't pay well, as you boys know, but I still think you were worth being the catch of the day. Now, get yourself cleaned up and ready for supper. You're both staying in tonight, that's for sure."

With that, the boys headed for their rooms. After eating, they were anxious to get to their rooms to check out the bucket, and for now to escape further wrath from their parents.

"Hey Bobby, there's a dead guy in here."

"What! a dead guy. How do you know that?"

"Look at the plaque on the bottom."

Bobby read the inscription. It depicted that the bucket carried the remains of a Willie B. Lovd.

"That is wild, said Bobby, should we open it?" it says he wants to be returned to the sea, if he is found snagged somewhere. Let's show it to dad."

The boys showed the bucket to Noah in the morning and asked him what they should do. "Noah admitted it was an odd find but told the boys he thought it was only right to return the favor that the bucket had obviously done for them. After all what would you do with it except set it in your room, and that doesn't seem to be Mr. Lovd's request. I think the thing to do is to honor his request. Seems like he was in the Navy once, having signed as an Ensign. Let's really send him on his way. I have a friend in the Keys that is taking a charter out tomorrow, close to the territorial fishing waters off Havana. He's in town. I'll get him the bucket and have him drop it off in the strait between Key West and Havana. Ensign Lovd is liable to get caught in the Gulf Stream, and he can visit Europe if he never has before. I also think it's best to send a message to that Hope person, telling her you all sent him on his way as requested. He put her contact's name on the plaque for a reason. You may as well follow through."

With that, the next day Willie was headed for the Gulf Stream. Dennis emailed Hope the next day. He really didn't know how to begin.

"Dear Hope, my name is Dennis Darnell. I just wanted you to know a bucket with your contact information saved the life of my brother Bobby and I. We were caught off the shores of Sanibel Island in Florida and our sailboat capsized. We were thrown into the sea, with limited flotation devices. Miraculously this bucket floated our way. We hugged it until finally we were rescued by our dad, a fishing boat Captain. Is he a relative of yours? We want you to know how grateful we are that he came our way. We are returning him to sea, per his instructions."

"Ok, bye. Where is he from BTW?"

"Dennis, this is Hope, he is my father. It's a strange voyage but this was his wish upon his death. He started out just south of Saint Louis, months ago. I'm really starting to miss him. Glad he came your way when you needed him most. He was always like that for me too. Glad you are both safe. Thanks for responding".

Hope.

CHAPTER FIFTEEN

"Let's take Devlin on holiday for a few days. The other two will be fine if your mum drops by and checks on them a bit. It will be good for him. We can pack some things and just take the lorry to motor over to the Isle of Wight. We can ferry over from Portsmouth and stay on the island for a couple days, then head back. We can camp. It's been warm for a fortnight already."

"The other two will have a row."

"Oh, they will think they have the run of the hut for a few days. It will be holiday a plenty for them. They get about more than Devlin. They will get their time soon."

"I might fancy that myself, said Maggie's husband, Trevor. I'm in que for some holiday at present. I'll put in for a few days next week."

"That would be lovely, I'll see that everything here is spot on to go."

"Right- O, and bring those frilly knickers of yours too."

"Well, this will be a right holiday won't it be then."

"I'll give it my all."

"That's all a lass can ask, as best I recall."

The way from Southampton was quick to Portsmouth. They drove the lorry onto the auto ferry in the crossing to the Isle of Wight. As luck would have it, it was a rare sunny day on the English sea coast, just a bit balmy, but as pleasant as could be hoped for.

Devlin was quiet all the way, seated in the lorry seat between the two. He perked up somewhat on the ferry crossing. Something new for him was always a blessing. Maggie and Trevor always enjoyed seeing him take an interest in something, anything. Autism had stolen him from them. When he was two, they remembered putting a healthy alert boy in the night tram and waking up to find their second son had gone missing in the night and had yet to return to them. It was an utterly shocking transformation in the period of just a night's sleep. Physically he was with them, but socially he had been absent for a long, 20 years already.

At times, Maggie had prayed instead for a child with an obvious affliction that could be dealt with no matter how severe, but autism doesn't grant that luxury. It's a cruel, sick guessing game to try to find a way to help Devlin, when no one seems to know the source of the problem, nor would or could few try to help. Maggie learned early on, that autistic children were considered by most to be beyond hope, locked forever inside, with no way to relate to others, no matter how dear they were treated. It was an affliction that could drive caretakers to the break of insanity, searching for a solution that everyone said didn't exist. Strangers could be hard pressed to know there was anything ever a miss with Devlin. He at times seemed, perfectly normal, and oh how Trevor and Maggie hated to be told he wasn't. He was more than just a shell to them. They knew there was a wonderful person inside who just could not be reached. Sometimes you had to just try and set it all aside just to survive and this is what this time away was all about.

Again, it was another attempt to give Devlin a different perspective on life. He deserved it so badly for all the things he endured over the years. At home he seemed like the perfect child, and when he wasn't, and there were those times, he was blameless. The only thing Maggie was searching for on this holiday was fun and folly and maybe a chance at finding her husband again.

They drove about and found a lovely sight to camp close to the shore area. Trevor liked camping. Devlin of course would sleep where you put him, never a complainer. Maggie would endure it for their pleasure. They set up campsite quickly and Trevor lit the pit. Maggie had to admit, Trevor knew his way around outdoor cooking. His lamb chops and grilled shallots were always heavenly. Though camping was not her idea of comfort, at least this evening would be dry.

"I see the moon," announced Devlin, pointing skyward, as the evening sky darkened. Devlin was basically nonverbal, rarely did he initiate conversation, other than for his basic needs. Words out of his mouth were always a thrill to Maggie and Trevor. A smile was to die for. He usually being expressionless. In comparison to his siblings, he had never asked for anything in his life. Maggie wished he would. She would have given him the world. Autism stole all the interests from Devlin that other children enjoyed. He never played with toys, participated in any games or developed any friendships. His different manners made him stand out from others. It made it difficult for others to relate to him, so he was excluded from everything others enjoyed. If there was a blessing in disguise brought on by autism, it was the fact that Devlin didn't care anyway. He was in a world unto himself. That is a sad blessing to be sure. Mum and dad were all he had. He had a passing camaraderie with his brother and sister, but nothing developed there. Maggie also thought it was sad Devlin's brother Danny never knew what having a real brother was like, again no fault of Devlin's. Both Danny and Devlin's sister, Louise, did their best to always at least acknowledge him, and again seemingly that was enough for Devlin. No less demanding soul existed. Devlin was a hard person to read. At times he would laugh in his sleep. Trevor always vowed he'd give a 1000 pounds to know what he was dreaming of. He was a riddle they were constantly trying to solve, because they loved him so. His answer to every question was always "yes!"

"Did you dance around Trafalgar Square with the Queen Mother last night?"

"Yes!"

"Did you play football with Manchester United yesterday?"

"Yes!"

"Did you see The Beatles in concert at Earl's Court today? "

"Yes!"

"No matter the question, the answer was always yes."

"Did anyone know why?" "No!"

If he spoke at all, it was in mono word sentences, that is if he even felt the need to express himself. Speech was seemingly at times just a necessity. He never shouted and never cried. Again, autism had robbed him of the emotions to do either.

They awoke at sunrise for a trek to the small hamlet for breakfast. "Why must there always be a stone beneath me, when I sleep?" asked Maggie, as she rubbed her aching back.

Devlin thankfully was fairly adept at dressing himself. After years of trying to teach him to tie his laces, Maggie thought, there's more to life, so from then on, slip-ons would do just as well. At times he may have put his shirt on backwards, but at times so did Trevor, she laughed, thinking to herself. And underwear inside out, does it really matter?"

Today Devlin had done well, with only the pockets of his sweats turned out. You learn to decipher what really was important and what really wasn't. It was the big picture that mattered, one of the many things Devlin had taught them.

"Are you ready for breakfast Devlin?" asked Trevor.

"Yes!"

"Is mum ready? Who are we waiting on?" asked Trevor.

"Waiting on the women," said Devlin. It was always a hilarious response Trevor had taught Devlin to say. Whenever Maggie or his sister were lagging, Devlin would say, "Waiting on the women," with the accent strongly on the word WOMEN. It wasn't much more than a habit, but once Devlin learned something he rarely forgot it.

"Now Devlin, said Maggie, you know it takes mum longer to get tidy, but I look lovely don't I"?

"Yes! said Devlin.

"Fashioning your own compliment from Devlin, is too easy game", said Trevor.

"Well, do you think I look lovely."

"Yes! laughed Trevor, mimicking Devlin. Alright let's be off, while they still have the kettle on."

After a delightful meal, they strolled the quaint little village, which as luck would have it, seemed to be having some kind of festival. Trevor wasn't sure what they were celebrating maybe nothing more than an unusually sunny day in South England. There were craftspeople displaying their handy works, and a local farmer's market from which Maggie selected a few items for their next meal. There were vendors of all sorts, with offerings of everything from fish and chips served in newsprint, to sweet vendors and even an ice lolly cart. Maggie and Trevor both hoped the fair was something Devlin was enjoying, but they never knew. That didn't stop them from exposing him to as many activities as they could. Just as they couldn't tell if he was enjoying something they also couldn't tell if he wasn't enjoying himself. Anything to expose him to the life around him, was the goal. They did all they could for him to have a participating form of a lifestyle. It all seemed pleasant. They were knocking off some time until the warmest part of the day arrived when they would head for the shore area and hopefully splash about a bit in the sea.

While heading back they spotted the ice lolly vendor and knew to steer clear of him. Devlin had eating disorders and iced creamed dairy treats were something his body couldn't tolerate, no matter how much he craved them. The wrong food item could affect his physical health and even cause psychotic events in his brain. It had taken Maggie years to determine what he was able to eat and what had to be avoided or suffer the consequence. Much like a person affected by peanuts, certain things were off the menu for him. It really pulled at the tassels of Maggie's heart at times to have to deny him the treats that other children were able to enjoy. He had had a taste of them, and he craved them, but he had to be denied. She discouraged the siblings from eating their sweets in front of him, to lessen his feeling of being left out. On rare occasions when he was offered a treat it made his day. He would gladly forgo opening his gifts for a small serving of cake with a dollop of cream. It was hardly a comparison. He had little interest in the gifts, enjoying unwrapping them more than playing with what was inside. It could all seem so cruel, yet he never complained. Seeming just to except his lot in life until another treat came his way, offered or snatched, if he could. Such was the life of Devlin.

It was a short jaunt to the campsite. They readied themselves for a stroll on the shore. Maggie packed a light lunch along with a few bottles of Shanty and some water for Devlin, all in a basket with a blanket to sit on. She was so happy they had decided to take this holiday, brief though it would be. Devlin seemed placid. They walked the small stone pathway to the beach, single file with Devlin leading the way. He always had had a strong sense of direction, and pattern like behaviors, contributing somewhat to his OCD condition. They were happy to follow. They rolled up their trousers and walked in the water's edge. The Canary Islands it wasn't. The chilly water sent Maggie and Trevor back to the open blanket. They watched as Devlin walked about the beach, always in sight He didn't always need to be handheld, thankfully, because he was no longer even a teenager. At times Maggie dreaded each of his birthdays. He was getting older faster than his situation was improving. His general health mostly seemed fine. Trevor and Maggie realized he would probably outlive them, as most parents wished for their children. The thoughts of what would become of Devlin without them, frightened them. They would always be parents, all the way until the end. It was rare for Trevor and Maggie to spend time alone together. Taking care of Devlin was an all-consuming endeavor, leaving little time for themselves. When times presented itself, it came too late as weariness had taken over. Tomorrow we'll have time for each other, or the tomorrow after that, or after that, or after that. This was nice however, and they savored it, yet with an eye always on Devlin.

Devlin headed down the shoreline, getting farther away, but after a bit he turned to face Maggie and Trevor. The backward glance in their direction filled them with joy, more than the parents of non-autistic children could ever understand. It was a relatively new thing also, considered a great advancement to Maggie and Trevor. Non-autistic children, even as toddlers have a built in the safety zone, that established a barrier from their parents they wouldn't cross. Autistic children did have this, as Maggie learned when Devlin was still a toddler. Devlin would walk away and just keep going until he was gone, which had frightfully happened more than once. It was just another autistic trait to be dealt with. Trevor and Maggie were shocked with joy the first time that Devlin turned to face them when he was separated from them. What might seem trivial to the unenlightened, this was a monumental step away from a grip that autism held. It was as if finally, he was acknowledging them as his parents, and had real concern for not only himself, but also his parents. As if to say, "Hey, here I am, do you see me? I'm fine, right now." It was a small, wonderful thing. At once, they saw Devlin step a bit livelier toward something he saw on the shore. It was enough to put Maggie and Trevor on the go, after him. One could never be sure what he could involve himself with. Devlin was basically fearless, but that didn't exclude him from possible harm. He was a distance away, but they could see he had stopped, at a spot down the beach, bending over something. Without seeming to alarm the others on the shore, they hastened to his side. By the time they reached Devlin, he had picked the object from the ground.

"Whatever do you have there, Devlin, sweetie?"

"Pail, said Devlin, pail."

Sure, enough Devlin was clutching a pail of sorts to himself. It had seemingly no handle with which to tote it about. It looked safe, if not somewhat filthy with sea scum.

"Devlin, let mum have a look." Reluctantly Devlin released the pail to Maggie. He quickly indicated he wanted it back.

"Ok, ok, Devlin, how about mum and you give it a little bath?" With that they walked to the water's edge. Maggie did her best to spruce it up a bit. She knew Devlin wanted to carry it. It was rare for him to become attached to anything, or anyone for that matter, but when he did, it became a strong bond. He had few toys he ever treasured, but when he did, one was enough, and he claimed it above all else. They never interfered or tried to understand, they just accepted, it as being something special to him.

This was the day, Devlin met Willie, and the bond between the two began. Now the four of them headed back to the campsite. Quite the sight for others about, but Maggie and Trevor had long ago steeled themselves from the glances of others, another lesson taught them by Devlin. Trevor, Maggie, followed by Devlin, clutching his newfound friend to his chest, in single file marched up the beach. They had planned to have every meal in the village, but Devlin had no intent of leaving the pail, so Trevor produced another meal from the pit. The forecast was for the weather to turn English tomorrow so they decided they would head home in the morning. They could stop in somewhere on the way back to extend their holiday a bit. After Devlin had falling asleep, Maggie got hold of the pail and gave it a good bit of a soaking. In doing so she noticed the plaque attached on its bottom. Willie B. Lovd. Good Lord, how far had he come, she wondered. Kindly return me to the sea. Maggie knew Devlin would have something to say about that, if he could.

It wasn't long before Willie became a member of the family. Trevor fashioned a handle for the pail, so it was easier for Devlin to tote about, whenever he went, and wherever he went, Willie went. They became the talk of the town. Neighbors opened up to Devlin and asked, "and how is your pal in the pail today." The postman asked Devlin about his man in the can, or his bloke in a poke. It was all such fun to see Devlin and Willie be recognized, instead of dismissed as he usually was by others. Willie was something that belonged only to Devlin, both unique as could be. Trevor joked to Maggie, that he was developing an inferiority complex. Most of his mates asked more about Willie and Devlin now than they did about him. Sunday service was especially grand. An extra seat at the family pew was needed. More than once the vicar made Willie the subject of the sermon material, a parable for life. It wasn't the first time in his life that Willie had been the subject of sermon material. Willie was always welcome to attend. Parishioner's also approached Devlin about his friend, everyone making it something special for Devlin, for having such a worthy mate. The depth of their friendship was known only to Devlin. He never spoke of his friend Willie. Maggie asked an analyst one day, what to make of it. He just smiled and said, "let it be". So she did.

CHAPTER SIXTEEN

"MOM, YOU'RE MORE NERVOUS THAN I AM."

"I might be, I don't want a flock of ex-son- in- laws."

"He's a keeper or I wouldn't be standing here in this white get- up today, would I," asked Hope.

"It seems kind of quick, after all, you just met him."

"It's been about a year mom. How long do you think it took me to figure out he was the one for me.? Don't answer that," laughed Hope.

"I do say, you two will make beautiful grandkids."

"Oh shit, I'm going to be a grandma," cringed Cherise.

"Not soon, as far as I know, so rest easy, you're still just a mom.

"Oh, thank God, said Cherise. I always thought it would be Reed first. It might be fun to have grandkids, I guess. They could come to my house, and I could bake cookies for them."

"You wouldn't do that to your only grandkids would you?"

"Hey, I can cook."

"No, you can't."

"Well, I made something for your reception this evening."

"Oh please, say you didn't

"I thought it would be a nice gesture."

"Yeah, it would be from someone who could cook," laughed Hope.

"On days like this I can't help but think of dad, I miss him more."

"I can see how it would hit you a little harder today, on your wedding day. Some of the ceremony is gone with Willie not being able to walk you down the aisle or have the father-daughter dance."

"We already had that, the night he took me out to eat. I even have kisses for his grandchildren to hold for him. I wish he was here."

"Hope, you have to remember 70% of the earth's surface is water. He could be anywhere. The oceans are huge. He could be stuck up a river somewhere, never to be discovered, sweetie. He might have sunk to the bottom. There are 1000 situations he could have gotten himself mixed up in."

"I won't believe he sank, I can't. That would be too final.

Someone will find him, I'm sure of it."

"Hope, try and set it aside today, it's your wedding. He would want you to be happy today as always"

Reed had come in from California with his girlfriend for the wedding. At the reception following the ceremony everyone was able to catch up on what was new with the family.

Hope and her new husband David, were excited to leave in the morning for their honeymoon in Ambergris Key, off the coast of Belize. David had been there before, and he promised Hope, she would love it.

Now it was setting in with Cherise, with Reed heading back to LA and Hope now married, that she was pretty much alone. Though she hadn't been married in a long time the kids seem like they had been more of a part of her everyday life, than she knew they would be now. She wondered if this was the time to get a cat or two and turn into the crazy cat lady.

Cherise and Dale, sat together during their last drinks of the evening. They watched as the staff started to disassemble the reception room and as guests filtered out to leave. It had been a beautiful wedding and a fun reception. The two of them also rose to go their separate ways.

"It was nice to see you again, Dale. It's been a while. I'm glad you came".

"I'm glad I was invited. We're all scattering a little. Willie was kind of the glue that held us all together," said Dale.

"Yeah, I guess he was, but that doesn't have to make you a stranger, said Cherise, stay in touch."

"I will, and you do the same," said Dale as he headed for the door. Nice man, thought Cherise, nice man.

Willie was now a part of the family. He was no longer just the man in the can. Even Devlin now just called him Willie. The townspeople called him Willie now too. They knew his story, at least as much as they could guess, and that's all they needed. Whether he was still a man in a can or just Willie now, he still belonged to Devlin. There were few things in his life that Devlin could control, but Willie was his alone to control. This created an inseparable bond between the two. A bond only Devlin would understand.

Maggie had dreaded making this contact. It was long overdue, but she felt maybe she was being selfish with Willie's time. He asked to be returned to the sea if he was found. It had been quite a while ago since Devlin found him on the Isle of Wight and instead of returning him to sea, they made him a right member of the family. Yet she felt compelled to contact this person named Hope. So today she would.

"Dear Hope, my name is Michaela Mattington, but I've long ago been reduced to just Maggie. No worries, I've lost things much more important than that in my life. My family and I live in Southampton on the south coast of England. To get to it, we have your Willie. I'm assuming he's a relative or friend as you are the contact we have from the pail. Do forgive us, we have caused Willie to overextend his stay, I'm afraid? When you hear the circumstance, I hope you'll be forgiving. Maggie told Hope how Devlin had found Willie on the shore on the Isle of Wight, when they were on holiday. She explained how Devlin, who was autistic, had drawn an extreme bond to Willie and how rarely he ever did something like that in his life. She told her how it was a blessing to watch Devlin and his newfound friend interact. Maggie told her she wasn't much into transcendental mumbo-jumbo, but the relationship between Devlin and Willie made her re-think her belief. Devlin, who because of autism, never could interact with anyone, but somehow the two became as inseparable as could be. I dearly hope you won't mind if he spends some more time with our family. I couldn't bear to separate Devlin from him."

Hope was overcome with the passion that Willie had brought to the English family.

"Dear Maggie, yes, he is my father, and of course keep him in your family as long as you please. I feel comforted myself that he is with you. I've gotten other emails from many places, and I'm always stunned and happy for the impact my dad has been making on people lives. I bet even he would not have suspected it, and of course he himself will never know. Right now, he is seeing to your needs better than anyone else I could imagine. I know a little about autism. I have an autistic cousin. Send me an email at times, just to say hello".

Love,

Hope Lovd, and with that she clicked off.

Time went on and soon it became apparent Maggie's greatest fear was coming to fruition. Devlin was beginning to express pain, even he could not conceal. Maggie knew this would heighten the struggle to find an answer to help him among many sources. Fortunately, Maggie and Trevor had more funds to try and help Devlin, that sadly many other families didn't. They left no stone unturned. Sometimes resorting to things that others felt were extreme, expensive, or considered by some to be not much more then wishful thinking.

Maggie and Trevor however were not deterred. They would give their last 6 pence if it meant finding a way to make Devlin whole. It was an all-consuming endeavor to try and find a clue to help Devlin. They ran up against many well-meaning doctors, but who were of little help when it came to autism. They also ran up against some who were really nothing but arseholes, who Trevor had to restrain Maggie from throttling at times. Why couldn't anyone help Devlin? They had already spent most of Devlin's lifetime trying to unwrap the mystery of autism and now as his physical health was failing, they merely enhanced their efforts. Trevor's mum even asked once. When is enough, enough?"

"The two of you have done everything possible for the child. When will you just resign yourself to being content that he is as happy as he is? Never, said Trevor, until he tells us himself, he is as healthy and happy as he could possibly be. Often, they were asked if anything they tried for Devlin even helped? Many times, things showed little positive responses. Maggie always responded by saying, "how do we know how Devlin would be now, if we hadn't done all these things for him? Are you asking me if any doctor ever provided a miracle? Well, I don't know, Maggie would respond, maybe one did, and we don't even know it. Maybe it helped in ways we don't even know. I've prayed every day for 20 years. Did I receive a miracle? Maybe I did. Maggie would reply. "How do I know what state Devlin would be in now if I hadn't prayed for him every day for 20 years. Maybe I received a miracle and didn't even realize it. But I would no more stop praying for Devlin than I would stop trying to find help for him." They were in it for a pence and in it for a pound. But sadly, they could see, Devlin's organs were starting to become overwhelmed with infection that he was not going to be unable to defeat, no matter how gallantly he tried. Finally, the hospital recommended he be taken home for hospice, to be with family and friends and with Willie. Maggie and Trevor agreed. They wanted him home with them. Once home, they did their best to keep him comfortable and to try and coax a smile, from him. That had never been easy, but it was a gift from God when it happened. They had no way of knowing whether Devlin even understood the concept of life, let alone the ending concept of death. They felt maybe if he didn't, maybe it was the single gift of autism. The autism that had stolen him from them some 20 years ago would at least let him slip away without his knowing his fate.

And so, he did. Maggie entered his room one morning and Willie was on the floor beside the bed. It was a sure sign to her, that Devlin had passed away, with Willie slipping from his clutches is in the middle of the night. Just as when Devlin laughed in his dream, for reasons unknown to all, Trevor would have given his last pound to have known what Devlin's final thoughts were, or to be there holding his hand when he slipped away. Who's to know? For Devlin, Willie might have been that miracle.

"Dear Hope," began Maggie, you have a lovely name you know, Hope Lovd. We and our family hoped and loved for over 20 years. We hoped to make our son Devlin healthy and that he might come back to us. Sadly, neither happened, but there was always hope and love. I can yet, barely bring myself to realize it, but I must tell you our Devlin has passed away. We are still besides ourselves. Such a waste of a beautiful human being. My Lord were we ever blessed to have had him as long as we had. Devlin taught us more than we ever taught him. He was like a mirror reflecting to us the things that really mattered in life. Trevor, got in a row at the pub, after a few pints, I'm sure, with some arse, who asked him if he wasn't glad to just be done with the whole lot of it. It took the local Constable quite some doing to get Trevor from off him. I sure hope his misses fancy's him all the same, with a few teeth shy of a grin full. I don't know Hope if you're married or not, but this I can tell you. Marriage for a woman is an ever-balancing act between being a wife and a mother. I am fortunate to be married to a bloke like Trevor, because I must confess, I left the scale go off tilt for a long time to the mother's side. We never blamed Devlin, how could we, his situation was just all consuming. It exhausted me mentally and physically and Trevor always came last. Hope, I swear to you at times I wish he would have gone astray a bit. He didn't, but I couldn't have blamed him if he had. I just wasn't there for him. I've heard 80% of marriages that have an autistic child end up in divorce. Praise God, I was one of the lucky 20%, and for that I will be forever beholden to Trevor. He never left our side, though lonely at times, as it must have been for him. Our life is hollow without Devlin, but your father brought us a great sentiment. **"Yes, you can't go back and make a new beginning, but you can start over and make a new ending,"** and that's what Trevor and I are about to see if we can make happen."

"We booked a holiday at a seaside beach resort off the coast of Portugal. It's lovely there. We English go there to dry out. It's time to start to tip the scale back from mother to wife, while there is still time.

It will just be the three of us, Willie is going along, of course. We have a sailing charter booked for a day. We will throw Willie back to the sea. God, we will miss him so. If you ever come from the colonies to visit the motherland, we will be extremely disappointed if you don't knock us up in Southampton."

Always with love, Maggie.

"Come stay a bit. I'll put a kettle on and tell you about our Devlin and your father."

Cherise answered the call from Hope. She could tell she was crying. "What's wrong?" asked her mother.

"Oh mom, I just got an email from England, the boy who had become attached to dad has died. From the email I have gotten from Maggie I could tell Dad really was an amazing part of his life. They are all broken up, as you might expect. They had made dad a part of the family and their town even."

"I'm sorry to hear that. It must have been traumatic for them losing their son."

"Yes, but mom it's more than that. Dad made an impact with Devlin that they will never be able to understand. He became a part of the family, and now to honor Dad's request, they are losing him too. They are returning him to the sea, as he requested. They feel obligated to do it for him, for all he has brought to them. He will be on his way again soon. Mom, I miss him. I feel envious of all the people whose life he is touching in so many ways. I want him home with us."

"Sweetie, I think you are way over personifying this, as maybe many others are. I don't want to be too blunt, but it's just his ashes in a pickle bucket."

"No, it's not. It's the idea of dad. Look how many people's lives he is touching. Mom, maybe he's just soot in a can to you, but he's my soot in a can."

"Honey, maybe your mom is right. After all, as long as he keeps asking to be thrown back into the oceans of the world, one day he may be lost forever. Aren't the memories you have of your father enough?" asked David. I know I never got to meet the man while he was alive, before our marriage. I heard things about him, and he seemed like a great guy who would have made a great father-in-law, yet he's gone, Hope."

"I'm sorry David, but I can't explain it. I'm drawn to him more now than when he was alive."

"Sweetie, if I had the answer for you about how you could best deal with it, I would give it to you in a heartbeat, but I'm lost on this one."

"I know you would David. Just help me by believing I'm not losing my mind."

"Ok, as long as you don't lose your body," laughed David.

"He'll show up again somewhere, I just know it."

"Maybe but it could be a long time. Now get in bed, before I lose my mind."

But it wasn't a long time. Hope saw a strange email pop up.

"Dear Hope, this is Doctor Adrian Lori. I wanted to let you know we have a Willie B. Lovd here and we are holding him hostage pursuant to a payment of a $5000 ransom. Please respond ASAP or we cannot be responsible for his well- being much longer."

Hope responded.

"You are obviously in possession of the finely grained remains of my father, so it should be quite clear to you, especially if you are a doctor as you say that you are, that for all practical purposes he is emphatically dead. Please elaborate as to what kind of torture technique you may apply to him to try and bilk $5000 from me? That would be interesting to hear. Don't tell me you have ways of making him talk."

Hope Lovd.

The boys pleaded with Dr. Lori to be allowed to travel along with the supply ship to the mouth of the river to retrieve items for the village. She couldn't resist, they had few distractions to enjoy.

"OK but do what the skipper tells you and don't make waves or trouble." It was a 50-mile trip to the supply depot on the coast, but it could still be treacherous. She trusts the skipper to look out for them. It was a much- needed trip to collect food supplies and medicine for the village and hopefully mail from the states. Adrian always looked forward to hearing from her fiancé back in civilization. She had promised him, this would only be a one year long sabbatical, but it was starting to seem like a decade for the both of them.

The day trip to the coast was uneventful, although a treat and an adventure for the village boys. The political unrest and guerilla warfare in Angola was at a truce, and had been for some time, so there was little cause for concern. Falling overboard and becoming lunch for whatever might lurk in the river was a greater threat. The skipper had been making this supply run for months and rarely ever had a problem. This trip would be no different.

The boys helped toss the lines to the dock hands at the supply depot. Once the boat was secure, the skipper went to the office to handle the paperwork necessary to retrieve the items for the village. Other than the usual delay brought on by nothing more than the laziness of the officials, all went well. The boys got off the boat and went exploring in the harbor among the many empty slips. The port was mainly for the use of local fishermen, as it had access to the open waters of the mid- Atlantic. It was a sight to see for the village boys from inner Angola. Then they saw It. In the teeming stagnant waters of the harbor, filled with nothing but fish guts, swarmed on by gulls, was a bucket. A bucket they could make a plaything out of especially since their lives were filled with so few. Worthless to others, a treasure for them. A possession. It was well below the walkway of the pier as the tide was out. They could see it was missing a handle, so they were considering how to retrieve it from four feet below. The two larger boys decided to dangle McGill over the side by grabbing onto his feet. They lowered him headfirst toward the bucket floating in the stinky waters of the harbor.

"Don't drop me," pleaded McGill.

"We won't drop you, until after you get the bucket," they laughed. McGill, wrapped his arm around the bucket and the two larger boys pulled him up, dropping him on the pier. The three then raced back to the boat with the prize. They stowed it below, so the skipper wouldn't see it. They feared he would just consider it waste and toss it overboard. Shortly thereafter the skipper approached the boat, followed by dock hands to assist with loading the supplies aboard. The boys helped when they could. When all was loaded, they headed back upriver towards the village. They stopped halfway at dark to spend the night aboard at a local marina. They headed back to the village when the sun rose in the morning.

Back at the village after a few days of kicking the bucket around, and growing frustrated that neither their spears or arrows could penetrate it, they lost interest in it. Chasing animals in the wild was greater fun for them. As they couldn't read anything let alone English, they were never aware that it was Willie who was safe inside. One of the day nurses, found the stray bucket, next to the cook site where the boys had abandoned it and brought it to Adrian to see what she could make of it.

"What, do you think it is?" they questioned Doctor Adrian, or Andy as she was known to many. After Adrian had examined the bucket on all sides she said,

"It looks like a combination message in a bottle-time capsule." Andy noticed the contact notation on the plaque attached to the bottom of the bucket.

"I'm going to see if I can have a little fun with this," she said mysteriously.

To the other girls that was interpreted as a means by her to try and raise a donation for their cause. Just one of the many duties Doctor Adrian was also blessed having to struggle with on a nearly daily so they could continue their work here in the remote village.

"Dear Hope Lovd, I do hope, you are the type who has a sense of humor. My name is Adrian Lori. I'm on a sabbatical in charge of a free clinic in a village in the interior of Angola. The ransom note was in jest, but I do hope you would consider a contribution to our work here. We exist primarily on the generosity of others, of course all donations are voluntary, but also tax deductible. I promise not to let any harm come to your father. This is quite the voyage he is on, and we will return him to sea per his request. If we didn't need the money as badly here ourselves, I might pay you to hear the story behind your father in a bucket, but it's not in our budget. There is an airstrip further into the bush. I'll have the pilot jettison Willie once he has reached open waters. Again, I hope you took my mild- mannered kidding in stride. It's amazing what one must do to amuse themselves while stationed in a place so remote. To be sure this is not a scam, we receive funds only that have been deposited in our account at the Capital city of Luanda. Other than needing a bath, your father seems to be in good shape."

Doctor Adrian Lori, Doctors Without Borders. Angola.

"Mom, it's Hope."

"Oh hi, how is everything in your love life?"

"It's all good, I think I'm going to keep him."

"Well, that's good to know, let me know if he comes back on the market. You owe me for something, I'm sure." laughed Cherise.

"That might be a little strenuous."

"Oh hell, if he dies, he dies. What's up?"

"I just wanted to tell you the native kids in Angola have

stopped kicking dad around and have given up on their spears and arrows trying to penetrate his humble abode."

"Well, that's good to hear, I guess."

"And he's back on his way. The clinic has access to a bush pilot, I guess you would call him, who has dropped dad over the side once he reached the open waters of the Mid- South Atlantic."

"Wow, I'm not a trivia expert, but we're talking an endless body of water, as far as I recall."

"Yes, it is, I'm afraid, he's really out there this time."

"Hope, we talked about this. You need to brace yourself for the fact that you may not hear from anyone about Willie for a long time, or maybe forever, I'm sorry to say."

"I know, it's still sad to me, to think of him so alone out there."

"Hope, that's his life, sorry, I mean the path he chose."

"Call you later."

"Do you have company mom? Sensing an urgency from Cherise to end the conversation.

"Oh, Dale just dropped over for a bit."

"Hey happy for you, he's a nice guy. Please don't try to cook for him. He might be your last chance. Don't risk running him off."

"Oh, it's nothing like that, said Cherise."

"Yeah, thought Hope, sure it's not.

Hope e-mailed Reed and asked him what he thought about the Doctors Without Borders, organization?

"I think it's a noble cause, why do you ask?" said Reed.

"Well, dad was a hostage at one of their clinics in Angola for a few weeks."

"I'm sure he was. It's getting weirder, Hope. Don't tell me they were able to revive him!"

"It's a long story."

"I'm sure it is," said Reed. Is there a reality show in this anywhere? Sounds like pretty soon, he could de-throne Duck Dynasty."

"Maybe, laughed Hope. BTW I think mom has a beau."

"Really. who would that be?"

"Dale Howard, dad's old friend. They're getting kind of chummy I think."

"Good for her, as long as she doesn't try to cook for him, she may have a chance."

"I told her the same thing," laughed Hope.

"How the hell did we ever keep from starving to death?" asked Reed.

"The school lunch program was a big help," said Hope.

"Did you check a map of the world lately? He is now in the midst of or heading toward the greatest expansion of water on the planet. I hope he packed a lunch."

"Sounds like you're starting to give a shit?" said Hope.

"A little maybe. It's getting intense to say the least, and I sure don't wish him any harm. Talk more later, Bye."

Reed was right. Willie was in for a long float trip. Ocean currents took him South and around the Cape of Good Hope toward the South Indian Ocean. Willie was on his way east. The HMAS Frigate, the

Canberra was headed South. The HMAS Canberra and its crew had just completed a five-month deployment in the extreme north Indian Ocean, providing escort security for merchant ships of every flag. Thirty percent of all of the world's cargo ships went through the gulf at the Sea of Odin, into the straits of Hormuz, and they all needed the security of a safe passage through this pass to supply the needs of the world with every imagined commodity, something terrorists and all forms of modern-day pirates we're also aware of. They would attack any unprotected vessel they could. Countries from all over the world assisted in providing this protection. Some more than others, but so be it. Their's was not to question why, their's was but to do or die, as the saying goes. The HMAS Canberra had played its role and was headed for its berth at West Fleet on Garden Island not far from Perth, the western capital of Australia. It had been an uneventful 5 months, probably because of the ship presence in the straits. The HMAS Canberra was one of the smaller displacements of Frigates but plenty aggressive to do its job. Commander Olson liked to say, "it's not the size of the dog in fight, it's the size of the fight in the dog." Commander Olson was known to say lots of things. Boring many to tears. All aboard were waiting to get to their home port, where family, friends and loved ones were waiting with open arms. It was to be smooth sailing all the way to docking, with picture perfect weather. Calming seas all the way.

The line rang as Dr. Lori was coming from a vaccinating session of native children. Her assistant answered and said it was for her.
"This is Doctor Lori. how can I help?"
"Well, it seems like you've already helped a lot."
"Oh really, how so?" asked Andrian.

"First, let me tell you I'm calling from the regional office here in Luanda." Andrian of course knew this was the administration base for all the Doctors Without Borders, serving in Angola.

"It seems like you were able to squeeze a donation out of a stateside person a time back. I hope, it didn't take too much arm twisting, or making too many promises we can't keep, but a Ms. Hope Lovd has seen fit to place a donation with us in your behalf." Andrian was shocked, as she had put it aside. So many pledges of donations often fizzled out, and as she recalled Ms. Lovd had not even committed to a donation. She remembers well now. Andrian was thrilled as their funds were about depleted.

"Actually, in jest, I tried to blackmail her for $5000, it's a long story." She seemed nice in the end. Are you telling me she already sent $5000?" No, said the administrator, she didn't send $5000. Andrian was crest fallen, but anything would help. She didn't send the $5000, she sent $10,000. I'm sure you know how far $10,000 will go towards our efforts here in Angola. Great work down there. We can't have enough benefactors like Ms. Lovd." With that he ended the call. Andrian immediately went to her computer and pulled up Hope's email address.

"Dear Hope, I can't begin to tell you how much good we can do with a donation like the one you so graciously sent. The needs here are great and some days I feel it's all futile to go on, then someone like you sends a ray of well, hope. "I remember the inscription that was on the bottom of your dad's bucket."

"We can't go back and make a new beginning, but we can start over and make a new ending."

"That is now posted on the walls of our humble facility here. It's true we can't go back and make a new beginning for all these kids, but with donations like yours, we can go back and start a new ending for them."

"Thanks, Doctor Adrian Lori. Your dad was sent to us to restore all our efforts, thanks for sharing him with us."

"Should we alert the Commodore?"
"It looks like so much junk to me, why bother?"
"Hey, I'm bored, let's see what he thinks."
"Well, what does it look like to you," barked Commodore Olson.
"Sir, it looks like a bucket."
"Any chance it's some form of an IUD."
"I'll have the explosive ordnance people put eyes on it. You don't want to be bringing some wild ass explosive device on board do you ABLE SEAMAN Squalls?"
"No Sir, I don't."
"You're damn right you don't, stand your watch."
"If EOD says it's safe, we'll hoist it aboard, or launch a RIB to pick it up."
"Yes Sir."

The Commodore was sure it was just some jettisoned trash, but being just a few days sail from port, might as well break some of the monotony, on the way to their berth at Garden Island. In a bit, the Commodore got on the Squawk box and asked EOD what it looked like?

"Sir, it looks like a bucket."
"God damn, I know, it looks like a bucket. I want to know what the fuck is inside it."
"Sir, I'd say it's safe to bring aboard. It has a plaque on the bottom signed by an ENSIGN Willie Lovd, USN.

"Well damn right then. Bring that sailor aboard. This better not be some damn joke, or the HMAS Canberra is going be the cleanest ship in Her Majesty's Service before it reaches West Fleet. You got that?"

"I said you got that?"

"Yes Sir, we got that."

"Well bring it aboard, I'll meet you at the port side gunwale."

"Eye, Eye Sir, will do." By the time Commodore Olsen had made his way from the control tower to midship, the seaman had already brought the bucket aboard, to display it for the Commodore.

"Well, what is it?"

"It looks like a bucket."

"God Damn, if one more of you limey squids tells me it's a bucket, I'll have you walking the plank."

"Sir, ships haven't had a plank to walk in over 100 years."

"Well, I'll request one from central command. Why and when the hell did they ever stop that practice."

"Sir, I suppose before you were born, Sir."

"God damn, I always said I was born too late"

"You think I was born too late, Squalls?"

"Yes Sir, I do Sir."

"OK enough of this shit, let's look this thing over. It looks like a bucket to me," said the Commodore.

"I'll get the plank ready, Sir"

"Smartass, I'll get you a bucket ready to scrub the deck with."

Everyone under Commodore Olson's command, knew his bark was worse than his bite, but it was his ship, so they always played along. It was a source of amusement for them, something that was often lacking when you could turn four corners in the middle of the ocean and all you saw was ocean. No one played the role better than

ABLE SEAMAN Benjamin Squalls. He was the Commodore's chosen personal assistant. Others thought the Commodore chose him only because of his last name. The job came with some benefits and ABLE SEAMAN Squalls, milked them for all they were worth. Benjamin Squalls missed his calling. He was meant for the theater. He alone could deliver his "yes sirs," as if even he thought they were respectful. It was all a means to an end, for Benjamin Squalls.

"Sir, it's signed here by an Ensign William Lovd, USN."

"Get on your square- headed girlfriend and see what you can find out about what kind of sailor he was. The US Navy can manage to fuck up a lot, but at least they keep good records about it. We want to know all about him, don't we?" ABLE SEAMAN Squalls.

"Yes, Sir, "we do Sir, yes Sir."

"Then get to it."

"Yes Sir, I will Sir."

Benjamin's Squalls went to the ships information command center and began his research into the service career of Willie B. Lovd. It didn't show much but what he found he would report to Commodore Olson in the morning. Before he did so he sent an email to the contact person.

"Hope, this is Benjamin Squalls, I'm serving on the Frigate the HMAS Canberra in the south Indian Ocean at present. We retrieved something from the sea that has your name on it. Who's the guy in the bucket? I'm supposed to report to my commanding officer, Commodore Olson in the morning. Not sure what time it is where you are but would like some intel on the bucket."

Signed Able Seaman, Benjamin Squalls.

Hope saw the email pop up on her screen. She hadn't heard from Willie in almost six months. She assumed he must have gotten entangled in some mangroves on a faraway coast somewhere. God knows what all could impair his progress. She remembered Reed saying, "he may never be heard from again," which was always a possibility, yet she chose not to believe it.

"Dear Benjamin, yes, he is my father. He served in US Navy, but I know very little about his service life. My mother did keep a picture of him in his sailor's uniform for a long time. I do know he served in the Vietnam era and remember hearing he was discharged in San Diego. Sorry, that's all I know. He's been on quite the venture I'll say that."

Hope Lovd.

This should all be enough to brief the Commodore with, thought Benjamin. He would do so at 0800.

ABLE SEMAN Squalls found Commodore Olsen on the bridge at 0800. Commodore Olson passed control of the ship to his next in command and went to speak with Squalls.

"Well, ABLE SEAMAN Squalls, what do we know about USN ENSIGN Willie Lovd?"

"Sir, records show he served time on a US carrier in the Gulf of Tonkin at the start of the Vietnam War. It mentioned he served with distinction, not much more than that. He served his term honorably and was discharge in San Diego, CA. There is no mention of individual achievements and no record of a Purple Heart."

"That all sounds like he served his country admirably, and damn it Squalls, not everyone has to earn a Purple Heart to serve their country well. There's no reason for all to come home with some horrible reminder of their service to their country. Am I right, Squalls?"

"Yes Sir, you are Sir."

"Sir, if I might ask, what are we to do with Ensign William B. Lovd now?"

"Far as I know he came equipped with his own marching orders and we're about to carry them out with honors. The sailor requested to be returned to the sea, and so he shall be."

"Yes Sir."

"Assemble about 100 sailors not assigned to essential tasks to stand ready on the portside gunwale at 0700 tomorrow, in full dress whites. We're going to send Ensign William B. Lovd, USN on his way, with distinction."

"Yes Sir."

"And if I hear any grumblings a cloud will fall over my beautiful face."

"Now you wouldn't want to see that would you, ABLE SEAMAN Squalls?"

"No Sir, I wouldn't."

"And you do you believe it's a beautiful face don't you, ABLE SEAMAN Squalls?

"Yes Sir, I do Sir." Actually, it wasn't.

Commodore Olson thought it would be a good reason for the men to get their dress whites out of stowaway as in a few days they would be reaching home port, where they would all be standing shipside in their finest attire to greet all those waiting for them. It would also break some monotony of the trip's remaining two-day sail to port. A little lesson in military decorum wouldn't hurt them either.

"Hell, ABLE SEAMAN Squalls, make it 0600 instead."

"Yes Sir." Shit there goes two hours extra time in the rack.

At 0600 the ship was lined with sailors in their dress whites. They snapped to attention when the Commodore trailed by ABLE SEAMAN Squalls approached.

"At ease," he barked, and they all assumed the parade rest position.

"Sailors, this morning we are going to pay tribute to a fellow man of the sea, a William B. LOVD, USN. He happened into our lives, and we are going to honor his request and return him to the sea. He must truly have loved the sea as he decided to float upon it even in death, until the ocean claimed him. He served his country honorable. We are all kindred spirits, even if he served with our greatest Ally." With that he again barked the order for all to come to attention. The entire line of sailors snapped again to a crisp attention. All saluted as the bugle blew the final taps for ENSIGN William B. Lovd.

Following that, Willie was catapulted from the deck via a ready-made sling. He landed far from the wake of the ship. He was in the open waters of the South Indian Ocean.

"You can all resume your duties. We dock in two days at Fleet West. That is all." When Benjamin was released from duty for the day, he sent a note to Hope.

"Dear Hope, to let you know we returned your dad to the sea, with full military honors, I might add. It was an idea of our Commodore. We sure hope this was your wish for us to do so, but the Commodore saw the inscription on the bottom of the bucket, seeing it was your dads' request to do so, and no one knows more about following orders or giving them, than our Commodore. Our ship HMAS Canberra is less than two days from our Port of call. We are all looking forward to stepping foot on solid ground after five months at sea."

"Best of luck," ABLE SEAMAN Benjamin Squalls.

Hope closed her laptop. She really wasn't sure if it was her wish for everyone who encountered Willie to return him to the sea, even if it was his request for them to do so. The interactions her dad, or his remains, was having with so many people, made him seem more human than ever to her. They were all presenting situations to her, not of her dad's doing, but how he still impacted all their lives. She began to feel she was missing out and was beginning to have thoughts about bringing him home, before maybe he might one day sink beneath the waves to be lost forever to everyone. He had been gone over two years now. "Oh dad, enough is enough, now how about us?"

The HMAS Canberra reached her berth in West Fleet, way before Willie washed up at Meelup Regency Park near Dunsborough, about 175 miles north of Perth. The ship stayed in port long enough to resupply and long enough for all on board to get some much-deserved R&R, after which it had set out with All Souls on board except for one. ABLE SEAMAN Benjamin Squalls had jumped ship, or at least had not returned by the mandated departure time. He was now AWOL. Benjamin left with the few things in his footlocker, and he helped himself to one parting gift as a keepsake from his time on the HMAS Canberra.

"That bloody son of a bitch," yelled Commodore Olson as he opened his uniform locker. Everything was present and accounted for except for his full-dress Commodore uniform with its chest full of citations and awards. He knew exactly who had it. ABLE SEAMAN Squalls had just promoted himself to Commodore.

"Don't be bringing your rubbish in here with you. You know bloody well this is a reputable establishment."

"Oh, and what makes it so?"

"The fact that I said it, makes it so."

"It's a good thing you do, as no one else would say so."

"Well, it's been respectable enough to have been here for the last 200 years now hasn't it, mate?" and I see you spend more time here than I wish you did."

"Oh, only because I've always appreciated the finer things in life, is all," laughed. Anson, as he ordered his usual Foster.

"Here's for you, as always but you got to tell me, what's with the rubbish bucket?"

"Can't be sure, said Anson, I found it awash, bouncing ashore. I'm hoping it's a bit of the sea booty sent just for me".

"Something tells me, to doubt that for sure," Anson and the pub keeper began looking the bucket over. I think what you have here is a floating dead man's chest with the dead man still inside, as going by the wordage on the bottom side.

"That's a rare find for sure, not worth a pint of Guinness, but a rare find nonetheless," laughed the pub keeper, Darby.

"Says here to contact some Sheila. Name is Hope." Probably be sending me a few quid to do so."

"Oh, I'm sure of that, I'll wager", laughed Darby, but till it shows up how about settling last week's drinks before you get too deep into this week's tally."

"How about if I just promise to split the bounty with you, instead?" laughed Anson.

"How about, no bloody way," laughed Darby.

"You know you've been quite an arse of late."

"Yeah, and I intend to stay that way, as you keep taking advantage of the finer things in life as you say."

"Are you going to call the Sheila? asked Darby.

"I will when I get at it. I'm going to the Outback for a few days to shoot a few roos. Thought I might take Willie boy here along and see how the Kevlar holds up."

"That would be like you, shooting at the Sheila's dearly departed one. Your quite one of the Queens finest subjects, I'll grant you that."

"That's why I hang in your respectable establishment, nothing but the finest," laughed Anson.

"Every daughter has the right to disobey her father at least once." Such an odd thing for her dad to have said the night they went out for dinner. Why that night? wondered Hope, and Willie had seemed grateful she had never picked up on the option, so why offer it, wondered Hope."

Willie had been gone over two years by now, yet thoughts of him were almost daily. Hope felt something was missing in her life with him gone, yet his wish or so he said was to be continually returned to the sea. The ones he had encountered had always honored his request. She had begun wishing he was home a long while back already. It troubled her, and tonight she spoke to her husband David about it, really for the first time. She had often been tempted before. David could tell she was distraught.

"Sweetie, I think you're way over personifying this thing. Maybe it's best to just let it go. We all have loved ones we have grieved over, and miss, but we have come to grips with it. Is it tougher for you, because your dad chose not to really have a final resting place?"

"Maybe somewhat, said Hope. It just seems like he is still exploring a lot of life events."

"This is when I think you are over personifying things. Honey, your dad died over two years ago. He hasn't experienced anything since then, I can assure you."

"Well look at the impact he has made on so many people's lives, David".

"Again, Hope, how could he? It's the people who have found a bucket floating in the seas of the world, who have read all these things into their lives. What could your dad have done for them? He obviously wasn't in a position to contribute to these people's lives."

"No, you're wrong, he has made an impact on many of the lives he came in contact with."

"Listen to yourself, Hope. I hate to see you so pained by this, but how could he have played a role in the lives of others. Sweetie, he is no longer with us. He has passed away."

"Well, you're wrong David. He changed people's lives for the better, saved some and brought comfort and inspiration to others. He's played a role."

"Hope, I'm at a loss as to what to tell you, I can barely remember the time or two I even met your father, and those times were before I ever met you. I wish I had an answer that would make sense to you, but I just don't. Sometimes I wish he would have just sunk to the bottom of the sea never to be heard of again, just so you could have the closure you deserve, but as luck would have it, it hasn't happened at least not yet."

"David, I know you meant well but, that was a cruel thing to say."

"OK, I give up. So, what are you going do about it?"

"I'll tell you what I'm going to do. I'm going to get him the next time I hear from him."

"You know that is not his wish. He asked for everyone to send him merrily on his way. He may not want that, and for someone, who pictures him still having wishes and desires of his own, aren't you maybe, violating his last requests?"

"No, I don't think I am. I think he wants me to come and get him."

"Really, what makes you think he wants his last request not to be honored?"

"I know now why he said it."

"Said what?" asked David.

"A daughter has the right to disobey her father at least once. It was a message. He wants me to come get him."

"Hope I say, if you want to bring him home, just do it, if that's what you want."

"Well, it's not just for me, one day we might have kids?"

"You know there might be is a chance of that, if you just shut up and get in bed," joked David.

"Just think of the bedtime stories we can tell them about the adventures of their grandpa. You can't make that kind of stuff up."

"Yeah, and I can imagine the therapy bills it will take to get them over the nightmares those stories will create."

"Oh, they'll love it."

"You know, I agree, of course right now I will agree to anything as long as you just come to bed."

"It's a deal, but it does make me wonder where dad is though."

"Oh brother, I'm sure he's just bobbing along fine somewhere, now turn out the lights, will you?"

In the morning Hope called Cherise to see if she was home today.

"Sure", said Cherise, I have pretty much the whole day open, what's up?"

"I just wanted to stop by and go over something with you."

"How does lunchtime sound to you, I'll make us a little lunch."

Damn, Hope, said to herself, I should have known better than to schedule this around a mealtime, but said, "that would be fine, but told Cherise she didn't need to make a big fuss out of a meal.

"Oh, it's no problem for me."

"Well, it's a problem for me having to eat it," thought Hope.

"Jesus when will that woman learn to cook" wondered Hope, I'll see you about noonish."

"Great," said Cherise, I'll fire up the stove."

"Great, said Hope, I'll see you then."

Hope rang the bell at Cherise's but entered unanswered. She made her way to the kitchen, which looked like a war zone, just from her mom attempting to make a light lunch. Order in, mom just give up and order in.

"Hey Hope, how's everything? You look fine, of course how would I remember what you look like. You never come to see me anymore now that you're married."

"I know, I've already abandoned you and spend all my spare time trying to find you a suite at one of dad's facilities," laughed Hope.

"If you do, at least pick one with a view."

"Of what, the parking lot? "

Hope walked through the kitchen to the door leading to the garage. She could never resist at least a glance at the Jaguar Willie had given her. David and her were house hunting, and she of the two, was most adamant about a proper garage space so she could bring the XKE home with her. It meant more to her, than it did to David, who like Reed's idea of a car, was one you plug in at night, like your phone. The kind of cars that would make her dad roll over in his bucket right now. Hope more than the others had recognized Willie's cars for what they were. Pure art, that you could drive.

Cherise had what slightly resembled something edible set out on the counter when Hope returned from the garage. Whoopi, thought Hope, lunch is served. It always amazed her, that her mom never seemed to notice how people would disseminate her offering into little pieces on their plates to try and make them disappear. She often wondered if her mom ever found remains of some food in her house plants. Cherise always asked why the kids thought she should get a dog. She figured the kids, thought the companionship would be good for her. Actually, the kids were hoping to slip their food to the dog under the table. They always suggested a large dog, a large hungry dog.

"You didn't have to go all this trouble to make lunch. "

"Oh no bother, I love to cook."

"I can see that. It shows," said Hope, keeping as much sarcasm out of her voice as possible.

"So, to what do I owe the pleasure of your company today? "

"Mom, I've had a long talk with David, and there's something I want to let you know. Something I've already decided to do anyway."

"Well, there's very little anymore that you need my blessing for so, forge ahead. "

"I've decided to bring dad home."

"Wow, really where is he?"

"That is a part of the problem. I haven't heard from him since he was tossed overboard in the Indian Ocean."

"How he loved the sea," laughed Cherise.

"I'm serious mom. I'm going to get him and bring him home, from wherever he is."

"I'm sure it's not unusual to ask why? I mean after all most daughters don't have a father whose remains are floating around the world in a pickle bucket, but I guess I still have to ask, why now?"

"Mom, you sound a little like David, but I've felt this way for a while. I wasn't crazy about this decision of dads from the beginning. I've thought about it. Maybe it was an attempt of his to not be forgotten. If he were 6 feet under, I am pretty sure I wouldn't have been receiving emails from him for the past two years."

"Well, you're right there. I'm afraid the reception would not have been all that good."

"And I think he wants me to bring him home," continued Hope.

"That goes a little contrary to his request to be released to the sea, by everyone who has found him?"

"That is kind of what I mean, he wants me to disobey him."

"Remember that night he took me out to dinner?"

"Oh yeah, that sounds wonderful even to this day. "

"Well, that night he said something to me, that caught me off guard, and I just let it wash over me. He said every daughter has a right to disobey her father at least once."

"So, you're saying your disobedience would be breaking his final request of always being returned to the sea, and to be brought back home instead?"

"Mom, you got it. He wants to be brought back home, and to do it I have to disobey his final requests. He might already be wondering why I've waited so long. What really convinces me that he wants me to bring him home is the fact that he put my contact info on the bottom of the bucket in the first place. Why did he do that?"

"Hope, I understand your feelings but, I'm pretty sure Willie hasn't been wondering anything for the past two years. No wondering, just wandering. Don't take that the wrong way. Go get him if you want. You do have to come to grips one day with the fact that Willie won't know if he's in St. Louis or Singapore."

"Yes, but I'll know where he will be. Home with us."

"Well go get him then."

"I plan to but, this has all created a new worry. What if I never hear from him again. What if I'm too late to honor what his final request really was. All I can do is wait and hope that someone who recognizes what they happened upon will contact me."

"Hope, remember a lot of people have."

"That's true but we have no way of knowing how many people may have encountered dad and never responded to me or had a means to do so. Internet service in Bora Bora, may be limited, or God knows where." Enough of that. How are things with you, mom?

"I'm fine, staying busy." I get together with Dale sometimes. He's really a nice man."

"How nice? asked Hope

"It's nothing like that, we're just good friends. "

"Yeah, so were David and I, then we got married."

"It's nothing like that, seriously."

"Yeah, I bet, thought Hope. Just don't cook for him. Have you heard from Reed lately or has he abandoned you too?"

"He calls about as often as you visit. He's 2000 miles away so it's a little tougher for him to just pop over and have lunch with me like you can."

"Hum, 2000 miles away. That's a thought, mused Hope to herself. David and I have a few houses to look at today we are considering buying. All with garages, so I can bring "Why Not" home with me, before you use it for a laundry table."

"I would never do that."

"I'm just kidding mom. I really appreciate you letting me keep it here for this long."

"Not a problem, let me know how the house hunting goes."

"Will do, see you next time mom, and thanks for lunch, really." Not really. With that, Hope let herself out, beginning the wishing process for a word from Willie's whereabouts.

Hope emailed Reed and told him her plans to go get dad if he ever stopped somewhere again.

"Really, what are you going do with him once you bring him home? I guess you can sit him on your mantel like everyone else does."

"I'll just feel better if he's home. One day I can tell his grandkids all about him."

"I'm sure that will impress them, and if not, they can always dump him out and make sandcastles with him."

"Very funny Reed, I don't know why I bother to tell you."

"I'm just kidding. Go get him next time he calls. He's had enough fun to last a lifetime. Is that the appropriate analogy? Really, I hope you hear from him again, and if you're travels take you far, be safe."

"Thanks, I expect it to be quite a trip. It's doubtful he will wash up in front of the Arch, laughed Hope. Check back with you later, BTW, how things going with your girlfriend?" "It's all good," typed Reed as he signed off.

"Fosters, Guinness?"

"Fosters always, as you should well know, Darby."

"How was the walkabout in the Outback? "

"Not bad, 6 roos and a glancing blow at a veggie bucket."

"I'm not sure about the legality of all that? "

"All in self-defense, well maybe not the first one, but the rest of them were pissed after that. A bloke has the right to defend himself, as I hear it, and there's plenty more where they came from. They're nothing but hopping varmints."

"You contact the Sheila from the bucket yet?" asked Darby.

"Other than the Foster's, that's why I'm here. I need you to start up your gizmo. You know I don't have a computer. I'm not going to fall for that fad. They'll be a thing of the past one day, they will."

"Hate to tell you this, mate, but they've been carrying on steady for the last 25 years or so. "

"The hell with that, I'm still going wait and see if they fizzle out."

"Oh, you go with that. I'll be free in a bit, and I'll fire up the relic and see if we can get some smoke signals to come out of it."

"After my Fosters or two, we can ring her up."

"Ok, Darby, let's have at it, said Anson, after his Fosters or two or three."

"Right then, I think the drunks are settled in for a bit."

The two went to Darby's computer in the back office. Darby turned it on. He knew Anson would be clueless on how to do so."

"Can you at least type," asked Darby.

"This may knock you for a loop but in Primary school I could type 60 words a minute."

"So, I heard, too bad you had 59 errors."

"Sit here and start your hunt and peck method and send this lass your thoughts. You have some, don't you?"

"Such an arse aren't we," said Anson as he sat before the keyboard, and began his message to Hope.

Darby stood over his shoulder, waiting for him to mess something up.

"Dear Hope, I think I have someone in a bucket that belongs to you. My name is Anson."

"You are so smooth Anson," said Darby.

"Least it has your name on the bottom of it, to ring you up with, "Who's in it anyway?" It says to chuck him back in the sea once we met him. I found him on the shore at Meelop Regency Park near Dunsborough, West Australia. South of Perth. You can look up on a map where we are. Is it someone you know, a William B. Lovd?"

"You, dumb arse, she's just going to Google it. Nobody looks at the map anymore."

"I do," said Anson.

"Yeah, cause you're a nobody, laughed Darby. Just get on with it, I got drunks to attend to."

"I'll say he has, been a bit of the conversation around the pub here, where I spend a lot of time."

"Ok, said Darby. I don't think you have to tell her you're the local drunk, either."

"Bugger off might you, I'm trying to type here."

"I've taken him to the Outback with me."

"Don't tell her you shot at him."

"I ain't going to tell her that. You think I'm an idiot?"

"You want me to answer that?"

"So, I guess we've had our fun with him. It says to throw him back in the sea. So, I guess we'll do what he wants. Bet there's a long story behind that."

"Now what do I do, just say goodbye, or how do I hang up?" Should I give her a way to get back to us?"

"Remember when you asked if I thought you were an idiot? "Well, you are, she knows how to contact you, when you hit send. So do it. Anson hit the send button and just sat there, wondering what next. Get up, you're done. So how do you like using the Internet to talk to someone?" asked Darby.

"Seemed like a lot of trouble. If I want to talk to my neighbor Dell, I just step out on the porch and fire off a round or two and he steps right out of his house."

"And so does the rest of the hamlet, I suppose."

"Well, I didn't call for them, I just called for Dell. The rest should tend to their own business."

"You're an idiot. Come out front. I'll get you a Fosters."

Hope had an off- the- grid day with David. When she got back online, she saw the message from Anson was hours old. She panicked. By now they may have already sent him on his way, lost again for who knows how long and forever maybe. She scrambled to get her screen open and immediately pecked in a return message to the person named Anson.

"Dear Anson, this is Hope, I missed the message you sent a few hours ago. Yes, he is my father, and yes, it is a very long story, and for him it has been a very long journey. He left Saint Louis over two years ago. If you don't know where St. Louis is you can look it up on a map. Please. I'm hoping you haven't thrown him back into the sea already. Please don't, please keep him safe for me. I'm coming to get him. I'll find you wherever you are."

Hope Lovd.

Darby saw the message on his back-office computer and raced to the front of the pub.

"Where is Anson, where is he?"

"He was here a bit ago and left with his prized possession under his arm."

"Where is he going?"

"He said he was going on a walkabout down by the shore."

"Oh shit," thought Darby. We've got to stop him. "Heather, get your arse back here and tend to the drunks. I have to get after him. Darby stepped outside and onto his bike and headed for the shore at Meelup Regency Park. He knew to head for the elevated cliff area.

And there he was.

"Don't throw it Anson," he waved his hand and shouted frantically as Anson was winding up to throw. "Stop, stop." At last Anson heard the shouting and saw Darby racing towards him. "Don't chuck it, stop," yelled Darby as Anson backed away from the cliff's edge, with Willie still by his side.

"You got a message from the Sheila. She said she's coming to get the bucket, and to keep an eye on it until she arrives. Let's get back and I'll email her for you. She's just had a stroke of luck, she has."

"Dear Hope, this is Darby, the pub owner, Anson's friend." That's a stretch thought Darby. "Anson means well, sometimes he actually does what he's told. I caught up to him in the midst of him as he was about to toss your dad back in the sea, headed for Tasmania, no doubt. We have him safe and sound as you asked. We will keep him close, long as you need us to. We feel he is special to you. I'll send the address of the pub. It's easy to find, and even in an area you might enjoy visiting. I assume you'll be connecting into Perth from Sydney. Just let us know when you'll be knocking us up. Till then, we got him. Anson says hello."

Signed, Darby."

"Ah, did you see there," asked Anson.

"See, what?" asked Darby.

"She said if we want to know where this St. Louis place was we could look it up on a map. Now, how about that?"

"She could just probably tell you were an idiot, from 10,000 miles away," laughed Darby.

"Dear Darby, I can't say how grateful I am to you both. Expect me next week. I'll get in touch when I reach Australia.

Love, Hope Lovd

"David, David, I found him. He's in a pub in Australia."

"Sounds like him." said David.

"Oh, I am so thrilled. They are keeping him for me. Make plans for a few days alone next week. I'm booking the flight today. I'll call you when I get there."

"Just be safe, and hurry back, I'll miss you when you're gone. Where do we keep the skillet, by the way?"

"Mom, mom," Hope squealed into the phone.

"Hope what's wrong?" she could tell she was crying.

"Oh my, absolutely nothing. Dads in Australia and some nice people are keeping him for me until I get there. I can't believe it. They were about to throw him back into the sea. I had missed the email. I got back to them just in time or he would have been on his way again. Mom, I'm so excited and nervous all at once."

"I can tell that, when are you going?"

"Next week on as early a flight as I can get."

"Mom, can you believe it. I'll be bringing daddy home, home to us."

"Good for you sweetie, good for you."

"Delta Rewards, We're Ready When You Are. Where Are We Going?"

"I need a flight to Sydney, Australia with a connecting flight to Perth."

"When would you like to travel, and how many people in your party?"

"Next week, if possible, one ticket to, but two tickets for the return flight, with a return flight a day after arriving in Perth."

"Are you traveling for business or pleasure?"

"I'm traveling for the business of pleasure," said Hope.

"There is a flight out the end of next week."

"That will work for me, any time of day is fine. I'll just have one carry-on bag."

"Ok, you're set to go. Enjoy your trip."

Hope was beside herself with anticipation. She slept, so little that she called off work for the days prior to her departure. The time couldn't go by fast enough for her.

"Sweetie, you know you're not going to actually meet your dad?" said David.

"Of course, I know that, but I will be meeting all that he represents, and I'm bringing him home to stay."

It was a long flight to Australia, yet it had taken Willie over two years to get here so she didn't let herself complain. After a short layover in Sydney, she boarded a plane for Perth. Excited that she was, she couldn't help but take in the dialect of the Australian language. In Perth, she rented a car from the drive to Dunsborough. The car was right-handed drive. Dads XKE would have been right at home here she thought. She couldn't help but draw the connection to picking up Willie in a country where people drove on the opposite side of the road. Thankfully for her safety, he had switched the Jaguar back to left hand drive for her use in the US.

After two years she was but hours away from her dream of re-uniting with at least her daddy's remains. It was all so surreal. To come 10,000 miles, to fulfill a journey she thought she would never be able to fulfill, yet today was the day. She could no longer express the feeling even to herself. She was now in a state numbness, as if not knowing what to expect. The MapQuest feature on her phone was leading her straight to Darby's pub, not far from the Meelup Regency Park area, which she could tell was a semi- beach resort area. Nice place to wash up, dad. She saw the pub map quest had sent her to. She parked in a spot close by and shut off the engine. She couldn't get herself to step out of the car. She dialed the pub's number Darby had given her to tell her she was here. A voice with a heavy Aussie accent answered, with some form of slang greeting that was foreign to her, as well it might be being she was half a world away from home. She asked, "if Darby was available?"

Now with welcoming joy, the voice said, "it's you Hope, isn't it? This is Darby."

"Well, hello, I'm glad it's you, I'm definitely on foreign soil here, I'm parked out front."

"Well come in. There's someone we'd all like you to meet."

"I'm nervous Darby. I'm not sure what my feelings will be?"

"Oh, be off with that. We've all been looking forward to your visit. Anson's here too. Do you need me to have him come out and tote you in? laughed Darby. Just get yourself in. I've threatened all the blokes to be on their best behavior. No worries, it'll all be grand."

Hope got out of the car and headed for the entrance of the quaint old pub. Someone opened the door for her before she had a chance to lift the latch. Instead of the silence she expected upon entering everyone broke out with cheers and applause. She couldn't have felt more welcome. Hope wasn't sure if Australia had the happy hour custom, but the place was wall to wall patrons, and all smiles were headed her way. Everyone wanted to be the first to buy her a drink. She glanced around the low, dark oaken beamed ceiling, no doubt hundreds of years old with stone and timbers from a long time passed. Then on the end of the bar she spotted the bucket. The room parted for her as she made her way straight to it. She couldn't believe her eyes. It had been better than two years since Dale had tossed Willie into the river, the day of the bon-voyage gathering.

She wrapped her arms around the bucket and began to cry. The pub grew silent as they all respected her time with her father. It seemed almost impossible for Hope to comprehend all that Willie had been a part of.

First with the conservation Agent Pepper. Then she smiled as she thought of him as the best man for Justin and Joy's wedding in Orange Beach. Then the two boys in Florida who swore to her that Willie had saved their lives in a storm. She shed a tear thinking of all the time Willie had served as a saving grace for Devlin, the autistic boy in England, of Maggie and Trevor, his parents. She laughed remembering how he had been taken for ransom by Doctor Adrian in Angola. I'm sure she thought he would have enjoyed the reception be got on the HMAS Canberra. Hope could only imagine places Willie may have been where people hadn't bothered to, or couldn't connect with her. She couldn't get herself to let go of the bucket. She was oblivious to all things around her. They let her have all the time she needed. Willie had introduced her to a world full of people, and now, all these newfound friends here in Australia. She sat Willie back on the bar and turned again to a round of cheers and applause from people she also didn't know, just as she never really knew all the people Willie had introduced her to on his voyage.

"Ms. Hope, said one gentlemanly patron, join us in a game of 301." Hope hadn't thrown darts in years, but she enjoyed herself doing it here, also overcome with their skill at their game. Thankfully she thought, she was staying the night at a bed and breakfast within walking distance. The offers of drinks were overwhelming her. All waiting to hear the story of Willie. Compacting her daddy into an afternoon's conversation was quite a challenge but she could tell these people had taken an interest in Willie, so she delivered as best she could. It was a wonderful afternoon surrounded by wonderful people. Again, people she would never have met if it wasn't for her dad. Hope wasn't sure if it was the closure or the booze, but a calmness came over her that she hadn't felt in a long time. A sort of stillness that she could take comfort in.

The afternoon had to end. She thanked everyone profusely from Darby and Anson on down. She was actually going to miss these kind people she had just met but a few hours ago. She wondered if it was the same for people whose lives Willie came into, then one day, they had to set him free. She could feel and share their sadness. He would never be back in their lives again, but he was going to be back in Hope's again. Getting out of the door took an hour of heartfelt goodbyes. Carrying Willie with her, was as natural an act to her as could be.

The innkeeper at her bed and breakfast was a little in question of it, but let it pass without comment. Hope entered her suite and sat Willie on the nightstand beside her bed. She wasn't about to let him out of her sight. She slept peacefully for the first time all week. She rose refreshed in the morning to begin her trip back home with Willie. Hope returned the rental car in Perth and boarded her flight to Sydney. She took her seat in the first-class cabin, with Willie fastened in the seat beside her. It had taken some x-raying and some explaining but both were now nestled in first class seating.

Before takeoff the flight attendant asked if all was well, and she couldn't help but ask Hope about the special passenger sitting next to her. Hope explained that it was the remains of her father, who had been on a pretty rough voyage, for a few years and deserved a comfortable ride back home.

"He must be special to deserve a first-class ticket of his own. "
"Oh, he does, and much more."
"Well, he must really be loved."
Hope smiled and said, "he is, he was, and he always, will be loved."

THE END

EULOGY

WILLIE WAS GIVEN A PROPER WELCOME HOME party with all in attendance. Vera, Dale and even Reed made the trip in from California. Lisa couldn't be kept away. She brought her daughter Shannon along to meet Willie.

He was removed from his bucket and given a more fitting container where he could rest in peace. The bucket that had carried him halfway around the world for two years was kept and would become part of the family legacy for generations to come. He was given a place of honor on the mantle of Hope and David's new home. Sitting like a guardian Angel over everyone's good fortune. Some days Hope would treat him to a ride in the red XKE, that now resided with her in her own garage.

Pepper, the Conservation Agent and his wife Debbie went on to a long happy marriage and celebrated their 30-year anniversary the same year as Pepper's 20th year of sobriety.

Joy and Josh continued to enjoy trips to the Alabama Gulf Coast, never forgetting their special best man. Later in life they bought their own beachfront property. Joy was the one who chose the Fort Morgan area. Joy in her later years came to appreciate the Fort Morgan area's serenity and tranquility over the hustle and bustle of Gulf Shores and Orange Beach. Derek was never heard from.

Dennis and Bobby joined the Coast Guard and became rescue jumpers, both receiving many accolades for rescuing others from the clutches of the sea, as Willie had rescued them.

Trevor and Maggie happily restored their marriage and were rewarded with a late in life surprise. Maggie became pregnant and had a healthy baby boy. In memory of their beloved Devlin, they considered naming the miracle baby Devlin also, but decided in a way it would take something away from their memory of Devlin. They settled on the next closest thing and named him Donovan. Donovan grew healthy and strong with no affliction of the curse of autism that had captured Devlin and never freed him. At times they fantasized that he was Devlin reincarnated, so they could all enjoy each other In a more gracious environment.

Doctor Adrian Lori, finished her tenure in Angola with the Doctors Without Borders program and opened a clinic in the inner city of Baltimore, providing a high percentage of pro bono care, to those who could not afford proper treatments otherwise. Behind her desk hung a sign that read "You can't go back and make a new beginning, but you can start over and make a new ending." The message she had first seen on the bottom of Willie's bucket.

The self-promoted Commodore Benjamin Squalls strode ashore on a beach in Tasmania. He contacted his father in South Africa and requested funds from his trust funds his father had denied him until he felt he became a man of the sea. With the trust money Benjamin bought an apple orchard, developed a new strain of disease resistant Fuji apples so commonly grown in Tasmania, becoming very wealthy in his own right.

Doctor Lillenberg took Willie's advice, and stopped practicing medicine, as Willie jokingly referred to his business. He moved to Jupiter Island Florida with the 1967 GTO in tow and spent the rest of his days practicing only his golf swing

Megan Sheepley, the bank teller didn't move up to own the bank as Willie had predicted for her, but she became the senior bank president. She enjoyed outings with Marilyn, the 1955 T- bird, Willie Bartholomew had given her.

Shannon, Lisa's daughter graduated summa cum laude at her class in college. She never missed a class.

Lisa would stay at Malley's as a bartender her entire working life. She became a fixture there to all the patrons as the smartest-ass bartender they would ever be served a drink by, and they all loved every bit of the exchange. Lisa never made a million dollars, but she made a million friends.

Vera and her husband virtually wore out the Mustang traveling the highways of America together. Like Willie said, "these cars are meant to be driven and drive it they did."

Hope eventually had the two grand babies Willie had suggested for her at that long ago dinner out together, and as promised she delivered the kisses to them that she had held for them, since Willie gave them to her.

One day Reed packed up his personal belongings at his cubicle, stood up and announced, I quit! He bought an upscale driving range, traveling to work every day in a red convertible restored MGB, a stick shift.

Dale and Cherise did marry eventually. It was a one-year marriage. Dale would not have to endure the indignity of a long-suffering horrible disease. A split second in a head on collision spared him of that. He was always a nice man.

Cherise found herself alone again. To occupy her time, she decided to take cooking classes. She received only one passing grade, and that was for attendance.

No one would ever know all the lives that had been touched by the voyage of Willie B. Lovd, not even Willie.

COVER DESIGN
By Savanna Hope Steffens
sedonahopedesign.com